AMERICAN
GUNNER 2

CIVIL LIBERTIES

EDDY CLARK   D. ANDREA WHITFIELD

BLACK
ODYSSEY
MEDIA

WWW.BLACKODYSSEY.NET

Published by
BLACK ODYSSEY MEDIA

www.blackodyssey.net
Email: info@blackodyssey.net

This book is a work of fiction. Any references to events, real people, or real places are used fictitiously. Other names, characters, places, and events are products of the author's imagination, and any resemblance to actual events or places or persons, living or dead, is entirely coincidental.

AMERICAN GUNNER 2: CIVIL LIBERTIES. Copyright © 2024 by Eddy Clark

Library of Congress Control Number: 2023919245

First Trade Paperback Printing: June 2024
ISBN: 978-1-957950-22-8
ISBN: 978-1-957950-23-5 (e-book)

Cover Design by Ashlee Nassar of Designs With Sass
To the extent that the image or images on the cover of this book depict a person or persons, such person or persons are merely models and are not intended to portray any character in the book.

10 9 8 7 6 5 4 3 2 1

Manufactured in the United States of America

Distributed by Kensington Publishing Corp.

Dear Reader,

I want to thank you immensely for supporting Black Odyssey Media authors, and our ongoing efforts to spotlight more minority storytellers. The scariest and most challenging task for many writers is getting the story, or characters, out of our heads and onto the page. Having admitted that, with every manuscript that Kreceda and I acquire, we believe that it took talent, discipline, and remarkable courage to construct that story, flesh out those characters, and prepare it for the world. Debut or seasoned, our authors are the real heroes and heroines in *OUR* story. And for them, we are eternally grateful.

    Whether you are new to Eddy Clark, D. Andrea Whitfield, or Black Odyssey Media, we hope that you are here to stay. We also welcome your feedback and kindly ask that you leave a review. For upcoming releases, announcements, submission guidelines, etc., please be sure to visit our website at www.blackodyssey.net or scan the QR code below. We can also be found on social media using @iamblackodyssey. Until next time, take care and enjoy the journey!

Joyfully,

Shawanda Williams

Shawanda "N'Tyse" Williams
Founder/Publisher

PREFACE

~Previously in American Gunner

It'd been six months, and Raphael had taken the money that was once Alex's and flipped it in a myriad of ways. He cleaned up her under-the-table businesses and moved everything into legit ventures that passed the government's smell test. Shayne left everything to Kaion in the event of her death, and those funds sat in an interest-bearing trust for Kaion until he turned twenty-one. In the meantime, the lawyer worked it out where he was able to receive two grand a month, which was damn good for a child under eighteen with no job. It gave Kaion a sense of independence, which Raphael felt was needed more than anything in this world. Raphael and the attorney were able to teach him how to save the money and invest it. So far, he'd been good with it. He'd always been a stellar kid, and he'd made strides since being with Essie and Raphael.

Essie and Raphael had even tied the knot. It was a small ceremony, with only the pastor, Kaion as Raphael's best man, Rhys as their witness, and them. Although Essie missed her sister and would have wanted her to be there, it was perfect for them with their family. She was more excited to be Mrs. Raphael Waters than she was concerned about who wasn't there. As long as it was them and Kaion, the day was complete. They were living comfortably in the Meridian-Kessler area of Indianapolis. Raphael owned a security firm and a few cocktail-hour lounges while Essie focused her time on selling her original art pieces to the buppies and companies. Kaion was a star basketball player and a straight-A student. They were comfortable and happy.

Raphael walked into the house, removing his parka and snow boots, followed by Kaion, who did the same. The play-boxed each other as they strolled through the house, following a succulent smell to the kitchen. Raphael stopped in the doorway and held onto the top of the door frame as Kaion rushed into the kitchen and playfully tickled Essie from behind.

"Kai!" she shouted and giggled. "Stop scaring me like that."

"You like it, woman." Raphael laughed at their interaction.

Essie turned and playfully popped Kaion with the dishtowel. "I told you about coming into my kitchen without washing your hands first, and you let him get away with it. I should pop you, too."

Throwing his hands up, Raphael motioned with his head for Kaion to head up the stairs. "Go shower up and change before dinner, kiddo."

"A'ight. I'll head up so Essie can soothe your bruised ego," Kaion joked, referencing his win in football as he dashed up the stairs.

"You got lucky!"

"And you're getting old!" Kaion shouted back.

Essie laughed as Raphael turned to her. "Oh, so you are laughing at me too?" He walked to her and pulled her into his arms.

Pursing her lips, she said, "Turnabout is fair play. You laughed when he about scared me to death."

"I am getting old, though. These steps are getting a little slower," Raphael admitted jokingly.

"As long as you still know how to move in the bedroom."

Raphael kissed her. "Depends. Are you going to soothe my bruised ego?"

Cupping his chin in her hands, she bit her lip. "I'll do you one better and lick your war wounds, too."

"Shit, fuck this dinner then."

"You need sustenance."

Raphael licked his lips. "You give me all the sustenance I need."

Essie's hands flew to her mouth as she struggled to hold in the howling laughter that erupted from her. "So nasty, Mr. Waters."

"You like it, Mrs. Waters."

"I do."

The sound of the doorbell startled them out of their kiss. It was unusual for them to have unannounced guests. In fact, the only visitors they have ever had were their next-door neighbors or one of Kaion's friends. All of those interactions were planned.

With a scrunched face, Raphael made his way to the front door. Although Essie didn't go into the foyer with him, she moved to the living room so she could hear what was being said.

Rather than announce he was at the door, Raphael pulled out his cellphone and quietly activated his doorbell camera. He saw that it was Agent Rhys Lander and pressed the speaker activation on the app.

"Rhys, what brings you by on the impromptu visit?" Raphael inquired, his tone all business.

"I'd rather come and inside and speak about it, if that's all right with you."

After a few brief moments, Raphael opened the door and stepped outside. "Essie and Kaion are inside, so if you have some bad news, I'd rather you prep me first so I can prepare them."

"Understood," Rhys said. "Both are serious. Can we talk in private?"

Exhaling, Raphael agreed and opened the door. When they walked inside, Essie looked panicked. Raphael walked to her and kissed her lips. "It's all good. Rhys and I are going to my office. You and Kai stay up here."

Essie looked at Rhys. "Next time, call."

Rhys held his hands up. "My apologies, Essie. Will do."

Raphael led Rhys downstairs to his office then closed and locked the door, activating his noise scrambler so that no one could hear their conversation. Raphael motioned for Rhys to sit in the chair in front of his desk, and Raphael sat at his desk.

"I would say good to see you, but showing up like this, I know it ain't. So, hit me with it. What's good?"

Rhys leaned forward. "I wanted to check on you all since Alex's passing and I have an update about her death," Rhys stated with a pause to give Raphael a moment to respond. Instead, Raphael moved his hand in a circular motion indicating for him to continue. "As you know the initial reports stated she hung herself in her cell. My inside people said the Zos teamed up with the DeMingos, though. You know how it goes in the cage."

"Damn. The enemy of my enemy is my friend," Raphael murmured, more to himself than to Rhys.

That news wasn't a surprise. Alex had crossed the Zos and the DeMingos in a major way. On the outside, she was protected, but not on the inside. Hearing her death was the result of being murdered caused a lump to form in Raphael's throat, and he swallowed to clear himself of emotion. He'd been responsible for locking Alex away and still harbored a lot of ill feelings for her, but a small piece of him still held some regard for Alex. Perhaps it was based on the friendship he thought he had with her, or maybe it was because of his feelings for Kaion. Either way, hearing the details of her demise was a hard pill for him to swallow.

"Thanks for delivering it to me personally. I think it's best if we keep that news to ourselves and not inform Kaion or Essie. The less bones we dig up the less we have to bury.

Rhys nodded. "Sure thing. Fair enough."

"Also, thanks for allowing me to bury Alex by her aunt. She would have wanted that."

Rhys tilted his head in gratitude. "It was the least we could do for Kaion. He deserved peace after the losses he suffered."

After a brief pause to brace himself, Raphael swiped his hand across his face. "What's issue number two?"

Rhys sat back. "In good news, Dage's companies and accounts were seized, and Jabal was killed when he tried to escape custody."

Raphael fanned his hand, interrupting him. "All of that is old news."

"Welp, I didn't know you knew, but I should have figured you'd find out. It was my way of prepping you for the bad news. Abaku popped on the map in Africa. He's come out of hiding and is back to his old tricks with new buyers."

"And what's that got to do with me and Essie? He's not looking for her, is he?"

"Not that we know of. The investigation is just focused on the deal and locking him up for good."

Raphael eyed him. "So, if we are not under a direct threat, what does that have to do with us?"

Rhys leaned forward. "You're the only person outside of law enforcement who was able to penetrate so closely to the underground association. Hell, you were closer. I had to come to you directly with this because it's an ask, but not really. The CIA is cashing in on the favor for Kaion."

He removed a slip of paper and slid it to Raphael. "Of course, with compensation." He tapped the paper. "We need your assistance locating and bringing down Abaku once and for all."

"First of all—" Raphael leaned in closer to whisper his words. "That shit you did to Shayne was *your* call. I just wanted her out of the way."

"And she is permanently out of the way. You don't get to determine how. Just be grateful for what it is. Still, whether you liked the terms or not, the government is ready to settle up this debt. Hence, it's an ask, but not really."

Raphael understood. It was time for him to repay his debt. He didn't understand why Abaku, though. Although Abaku was the big fish, he'd never had direct connection or contact with him.

"If Abaku isn't my threat, then why him?"

Rhys sat back and eyed Raphael closely. "I have a little intel for you that no one knew until as of late. Abaku and Dage were in this together, not as an employer to an employee, but as partners. Dage was the cover man for all the underground operations. He didn't run it. It was their way of always keeping the real culprit covered."

"*Abaku*," Raphael seethed.

"Exactly," Rhys said and leaned in close. "And the greatest piece of intel is that Abaku's half-brother was Dage." Raphael's eyes bulged. "Essie didn't know. Neither did Sienna, we believe."

Anger coursed through Raphael's veins as he looked Rhys directly in the eyes. "I'm in."

PROLOGUE

Abaku sat in his underground bunker office contemplating his next move. He was pissed at the Americans for taking his brother's life and nearly toppling his plans and finances. He'd urged Dage to hide out with him, but his greed left him bodied. If only he'd left, they could have relocated and started anew. Who he truly blamed was that bastard Raphael and that traitorous Essie, with her treacherous ass. If it was the last thing he did, he would eliminate everyone involved with his brother's death. This time he would emerge victorious. He would see to it.

As he leaned back, taking a toke of his cigar, he heard footsteps coming down the hall toward him. Before the person entered the room, Abaku said, "Thank you for making sure our sources were able to secure the rest of Dage's assets."

She sat in front of him and crossed her legs. "It is no problem. I told you I could never repay you for saving me." Her voice choked as she rubbed her flattened tummy. "I only wish you could have saved a piece of Dage."

"Sienna." He looked up at her. "You are a piece of Dage." He leaned forward, staring directly at her. "But I'll make sure that everyone involved in the death of Dage and baby Da'Jenna will pay."

A darkened glaze came over Sienna's eyes as she leaned forward to meet Abaku's gaze. "*We...we* will make them pay, especially Essie and Raphael."

He raised his glass of bourbon and tilted it toward her. "Especially."

CHAPTER 1

The silk sheet slid across Sienna as her smooth, mocha-brown legs stretched out across the bed. Freeing herself, she eased on her back and lifted saddened eyes to the ceiling. Most days she was able to shut the events of the last year out of her mind, but today, that would not be possible. She swallowed the thick lump that formed in her throat before casting her eyes to the bedside table, only to find that her water glass was empty. Empty just like her heart and soul. Closing her eyes, she forced back the gamut of emotions that coursed through her mind, but still a stubborn tear escaped and slid down the side of her face, teetering at her defined jawbone as if it were debating whether or not to fall onto her shoulder.

"What bothers you this morning, Sienna?" Abaku asked, startling her.

She gasped as she inadvertently met his eyes in a sidelong glance. "I thought you were asleep." She hurriedly wiped the tear from her face.

Abaku propped on one elbow and eyed her profile. His hands were massive, and she felt the thickness of his forefinger as it slid down the side of her face. "I am always hyper aware of my surroundings. I felt your turmoil in my slumber." Using his forefinger, he gripped her chin and gently turned her face to his so that they were eye to eye. "And you did not answer my question. What is wrong?"

Taking a deep breath, Sienna swallowed back her emotion. "It's just…it's Dage's birthday today. Or would have been his birthday."

Realization, then shock, then sadness, and last anger flashed in Abaku's eyes at Sienna's words. Today would have been his brother's birthday had it not been for the treachery of Essie and the hands of Raphael. The memories of his brother's death sullied the remembrance of his born day. It always would until the day that both Essie and Raphael met their maker. Then and only then could Abaku celebrate his brother's life.

Sienna raised a hand to Abaku's cheek. "I'm sorry. That's why I didn't want to burden you. I know how difficult it is for you."

Sienna's soft eyes pulled him in. He was ready to get up and go burn down the entire US just to get to Raphael, but something about the way Sienna soothed him calmed his burgeoning fury. Hell, she'd been the reprieve he needed last night when his thoughts had begun to wander back to his deceased brother. It was how they wound up in bed together. He wished he could lie and say it was the first time, but it had been one of several. It seemed they always found each other during times of turmoil, and their comfort of choice was sexual trysts. He hadn't wanted to taint his brother's memory by sleeping with his widow but having to flee their home in Benin to Nigeria, all they had was each other. Eventually, Abaku's needs outweighed loyalty to a ghost, and he figured if anyone was going to have Sienna, it should be him. He was his brother's keeper, after all.

Lifting her hand to his lips, he kissed the back of it. "My only concern is for you. I want to make this right for us, for you. We've hidden out long enough. All of the money is in place. I can get a team together. It's time for us to finally leave these meager means in Nigeria and head to Dubai. I think it is time to devise a plan to get rid of Essie and Raphael."

Sienna's heart pained a bit at the sound of Essie's name. She had no qualms about making Raphael pay, and she wanted revenge on her sister for what she had done. The only thing that gave her pause was the very thing that egged her forward in the plan; Essie was her sister. The loyalty that was embedded for her only sibling pulled at her heartstrings. Oh, how she loathed that shit. She wanted to rip out every connection her heart felt for Essie, the same as Dage was ripped from her arms and her unborn child ripped from her womb.

"I know. I know. But can we not discuss this today?"

The impatience brooding in Abaku was evident. "If not today, when? You have been avoiding this like the plague. Don't you want to avenge my brother—your husband's—death?"

"Yes, of course, I do—"

"And what about baby Da'Jenna? Is her life not worthy of revenge?"

Saddened eyes turned cold as flames of anger flickered in Sienna. "How dare you?" She sat up, coming to her knees. "You know I'd do anything for my child!"

"Your child and Dage's!" Abaku said, meeting her heated gaze. "They took your family away and started their own. While you lay here husband-less and childless, Essie is in the US living it up as a wife and a makeshift mother." He gripped her face in his hands, a crazed look in his eyes. "She took life from you and lives that life in the states. *Your life!*"

The harsh reality of Abaku's words, compiled with the grief she felt for Dage and Da'Jenna, destroyed Sienna, and she crumpled onto the bed a mess of tears. Abaku laid down next to her, pulling her into his arms as she wailed. He coddled her, knowing that no additional words were needed. He'd finally broken through the barrier wall of her love for her sister. He hadn't wanted to push her buttons in that manner, but he was desperate to move forward with his plans, not only to avenge his brother's death, but to get back to his money schemes. While Sienna was stuck in her "woe is me phase," he had money lying on the table that needed to be made. And while he cared for her, he was growing intolerant of her incessant pity parties. He had love for her because of his brother— and her sex was otherworldly. No wonder his brother wifed her up. However, she would not come between him and his payback or his paycheck. *Especially not his paycheck.* She needed to get on board, because now that he had access to Dage's financial assets, he had no problem throwing her overboard.

Once her cries were little more than whimpers, Abaku lifted her face and kissed her cheeks, then her lips. Sienna melted into his arms as he moved from her lips to her neck. "I didn't mean to upset you, my sweet Sienna. But we have to make moves. I don't want to make them without you." He trailed his kisses down her collarbone to her breasts. "Help me. Help me devise a plan to take back what was stolen from us."

Sienna was lost between hurt and lust as Abaku's lips encased her thick nipples and his tongue encircled them, delivering slow and soft licks. When her eyes rolled back, a devilish smile spread across Abaku's face as he eased down her body, tracing kisses between her breasts and down her stomach to the crease at her thighs. Sienna's stomach muscles clenched from the pleasure. She had not meant to fall into a sexual relationship with Abaku, but too many lonely nights were disastrous for her aching heart and throbbing yoni. He'd been the mental release and the stimulation she needed to assuage her mind and body, even if it was only temporary. In a strange way, she loved him because of his connection to Dage, which allowed her to feel close to him, but she'd never fall *in* love with Abaku because her heart would forever beat for Dage.

"Ahh!" The moans slipped through her lips as Abaku's tongue found its way to her sweet succulence.

Her legs gaped further apart as he lapped at her ripening bud and moistening folds. As the pleasure mounted, her hips fell into a rhythmic sway with his mouth. Abaku would never admit it to Sienna, but he was addicted to her sugary honey. It was a feast fit for a king—or a prince, rather. And feast on it, he did. Gripping handfuls of her full buttocks, he held her body close to him, feverishly dipping his tongue inside and scooping her savory essence. When his lips closed around her bud, he lightly suckled on it the way she loved.

"Ahh, Abaku," she moaned, gripping his head in place and tilting her pelvis to meet his mouth.

Abaku released his mouth from around her sex. "Tell me you're with me. We'll devise this plan together."

Panting, Sienna gazed down at him. Lust filled her as she bit her lip. "Please, don't stop."

Grinning, Abaku captured her bud again, causing her to shout out his name in pleasure. She was almost there, he could tell. She withered beneath him as he held her in place. He was determined to suck her into submission. He lifted again.

"Tell me, Sienna." She pushed her hips toward his lips, and Abaku shook his head, keeping her body in place with his massive arms. "No, tell me."

"Yes, God, yes, Abaku. We'll plan it," she said in a rushed tone because she needed him to finish what he'd started.

With a smirk, Abaku went in for his kill shot. Her sex wet his mouth deliciously as her sensual screams and moans serenaded them in a perfect backdrop. Her sweetness on his lips was enough to harden him to full salute, and it was time for her to perch on the prince's throne. Lifting up, he revealed his hardened tool, priming it with a few slow strokes, then slid across the bed, lying down on his back.

Once Sienna had released, the reality of what she'd agreed to struck her. She felt so ashamed. Tears welled in her eyes because she felt guilty for her betrayal, both to Dage and Essie. However, what was done was done. Abaku had no remorse for seducing her into an agreement on that day—of all days. Yet another reason she'd never be in love with Abaku. He lacked compassion on the lowest of levels. It worked out for her protection, but it opened the door for him to stomp on her heart. She was about to lie beside him when she felt a strong hand grasp her arm.

Pulling Sienna atop of him, he whispered, "You rode my face, now it's time for you to ride me." With a pop to the ass, he pulled his arms behind his head and waited for her to mount him.

Although Sienna was drained and still saddened, thoughts of Dage filtering through her mind, she lifted her leg and straddled Abaku. Abaku was old school, and in that way, he was different from Dage. She knew all too well that she mustn't disobey his request. She refused to be met with a backhand for insubordination. Besides, she made that bed for herself the moment she allowed herself to get caught up in a sexual rendezvous with Abaku. He'd claimed her now, which meant he could have her any time he wanted. Her only obligation was to oblige. Sometimes, she obliged out of need, sometimes out of want, but sometimes, just like now, it was out of obedience. The last thing she wanted to do was have sex with him on her deceased husband's birthday, but she instead of voicing that, she mounted him, closed her eyes, and allowed thoughts of Dage to invade her mind as she rode him to his satisfaction.

CHAPTER 2

B y the time Rhys left, Essie had dinner ready, and Raphael was grateful for the momentary reprieve. Essie was a traditional woman in the sense that once dinner was prepared, everyone sat down to eat immediately, together, as a family. To ensure there was no time for a quick intervention, Raphael called Kaion down to eat. It was an underhanded move because he knew that neither of them would dare discuss business, especially *Rhys* business, in front of Kaion. Essie cast a hard glare at Raphael as they heard Kaion's feet pounding down the stairwell.

Raphael gazed back at Essie. "What?" he asked nonchalantly.

Essie cast her pointer finger at him with a hard scoff. "You know what. Just don't make any plans to sidestep this conversation after dinner. You can't avoid me forever, nor this conversation."

Just then, Kaion entered the kitchen, rubbing his belly. He wrapped his arms around Essie's neck from behind and drew her back to him for a kiss on the cheek. "What's for dinner, Essie?"

"Your favorite." She turned to the side and delivered a return kiss to his cheek. "Stewed chicken, yellow rice, and broccoli and cheese casserole."

"That's what I'm talking about!" Kaion clapped his hands excitedly as he took his place at the dining table in front of his plate.

Raphael watched Essie closely as she brought the serving dishes to the table, and each of them filled their plates with their desired helping of food. By the time Kaion and he had packed their plates, Essie had poured each of them a glass of sweet tea before she sat and made her own plate. They held hands as Raphael said a prayer to bless their meal, and they began to dig in.

Kaion filled the dinner with tales about school, sports, and his budding relationship with a young girl named Shantrice, none the wiser to the drama. While Essie gave him motherly advice and warnings in regard to Shantrice, Raphael's mind swam with how to explain to Essie what Rhys wanted and, moreover, what he'd agreed to in angry haste. No doubt she'd be ready to murder him. No wonder every morsel of his dinner filled his belly with greater deliciousness than ever before. He felt as though he were partaking in his last meal. He was Judas and Jesus wrapped in one.

By the time they'd finished dinner, Raphael couldn't come up with any reason to give Essie that would make her understand his decision, so he faithfully bided his time. At least he had a few more minutes to spare while Kaion cleaned the kitchen and washed the dishes, but once he bounded back upstairs, it'd be his day of reckoning.

The sound of a cell phone ringing startled Raphael from his thoughts. It was Kaion's. Vaguely, he heard Kaion laugh and say something, then place the person on hold. "Raph, this is Shantrice. Her best friend, Elle, and Elle's boyfriend, Travis, are going to the movies. It starts in like forty-five minutes. They want to know if I can go. If I can go, then Shantrice will go with them."

Before Raphael could answer, Essie spoke up. "Yes, you can go to the movies with your friends. But no funny business and come straight home afterward."

Kaion paused and glanced at Raphael. He respected Essie as a guardian, and he definitely listened to her, but he knew that Raphael wore the pants in the house. He wanted to be sure it was approved by both of them. Raphael took one glance at Essie and her pursed lips and agreed. Typically, Essie would be the one arguing against impromptu outings. She was a fierce protector. However, he knew exactly why she'd readily agreed and knew better than to push his luck. He wore the pants, but his wife hemmed them. And that was a fact.

"Great! Thanks, you guys," Kaion said and told his friends he'd be on his way. When he hung up, he took one look at the dishes in the sink and groaned. "Can I please clean up when I get back? I don't have much time."

Essie patted his back. "Go get dressed and go meet your friends. Raphael will take care of the kitchen and dishes tonight," she said, eyeing Raph with a stony expression.

Kaion smiled and hugged Essie. "Thank you," he said and walked toward the exit of the kitchen. He stopped by Raphael's side and patted his arm. "I don't know what you did to get doghouse duties, but thanks," he whispered and made a mad dash before Raphael could say a word.

Raphael slid a hand down his face and eased up to Essie. "Essie—"

She held up her finger as she placed the last container of leftovers in the refrigerator. "When Kaion leaves."

With that, Essie sauntered out of the kitchen into the family room and turned the television on. Raphael decided to join her. Perhaps a moment to chill out would ease the tensions between them. Ten minutes later, Kaion came down looking fresh and date-night ready. He hugged Essie again, dapped up Raphael, and then left the house to have fun with his friends.

As soon as they heard the car pull out of the driveway, Raphael turned to Essie. "I guess I'll tackle this kitchen first—"

Essie stood with him. "Kitchen last, this conversation first." She left the family room and headed down to the basement to his office, and Raphael followed behind her.

The moment the door was shut, Essie started throwing out questions like bullets from a gun. "Why was Rhys here? What is going on? Are we in trouble? Has something happened?"

Raphael eased up to her and gently held her upper arms before bending down and kissing her forehead. "Baby, calm down. I can only answer one question at a time."

She shook her head. "I know it isn't good. You're already trying to sweet-talk me."

Damn, she knows me so well. Outstretching his hand, he offered Essie a seat. She sat down, and he slid his desk chair around so that they were side-by-side.

Slipping her hand into his, Raphael gazed up at Essie. "Do you know a man by the name of Abaku?"

Her answer wasn't immediate. She had to think. Falling back slightly in the chair, her eyes rolled upward as she considered the name. It sounded familiar enough, but she couldn't quite place a face with it. She toiled for a few more minutes before her face lit up with recognition.

"I believe he worked with that crooked Jabal. If that's who you're referring to." Hunching her shoulders, she leaned forward. "I'm not sure, though. That crowd was unsavory, and I stayed away from them. Hell, I didn't even know Dage was in bed with them. Why? What does he have to do with anything?"

"He was the true person behind the scam that I got trapped in."

Essie's blank stare told the story that she was not connecting the dots. "Abaku didn't work with Jabal. Jabal worked *for* him."

Realization spread over Essie as her mouth formed an "o" shape in understanding. Still, she shook her head with a look of confusion. "And? So what? You never had any direct dealings with him. What does it matter to us?"

"Rhys confided some new information that we didn't know before." Raphael sat back, taking a deep breath before he continued. "Dage was Abaku's half brother."

Essie was stunned, and she swallowed the thick lump that formulated in her throat. "I didn't…I swear…I didn't…I didn't know," she stammered.

Raphael placed his hand on Essie's cheek and caressed it with his thumb. "I know. Rhys already knew you didn't know."

As if lit on fire, Essie sat erect. "Wait. If Abaku was the one in charge and he's Dage's half brother, that means…" Her voice trailed off before she moistened her lips and continued. "We're not in any danger, right?"

"Not an immediate threat—"

"Then why come here and bring that news to our doorstep?" she snapped, searing into Raphael. Her words were like molten lava.

Cutting to the chase, Raphael said, "Rhys wants me to help bring down Abaku."

Essie gasped, covering her mouth before she bit out. "I knew he was up to no good. You told him no, didn't you?"

"I did." He slid his hand over his short wavy hair. "At first, I did."

"What do you mean—at first?" Essie put her hand up, ceasing any further comments.

"I don't have a choice in the matter. The government is cashing in on my debt. They made sure I got custody of Kai. They want Abaku."

"Then tell Rhys to get him for himself. They don't need you for that. You were only a bodyguard for your former employer. How could you be of any assistance?"

"They were impressed by the way I was able to infiltrate my way into Benin and get close to Jabal and Dage. Not to mention, you forget Rhys witnessed my gunplay firsthand. I'm thinking they want someone who they feel could get the job done. Not some suits. Besides, I do have a personal reason to bring Abaku to justice for myself. I'm sure they are counting on that as my ammunition."

"If he isn't after us, then why rock the boat? Your involvement will only rain a shitstorm down on our heads. We're happy and comfortable. And what about Kai? He's been through so much already. We all have." She turned to face him with fear-laden eyes. "No, Raphael. It's too risky. Rhys will just have to find someone else or do it on his own."

Raphael leaned forward in his seat, bringing his elbows to his knees and resting his face in the palms of his hands. He took a deep breath before he returned his gaze back to Essie. "Baby, I don't think he'll take no for an answer."

"Then give me the damn phone, and I'll tell him!" She banged her hand against the desk. "Who the hell does he think he is? He will not come in here and rip my family apart. I won't allow it."

"Essie—"

She jumped up with her arm flailing in the air. "No, Raphael! No." She paced back and forth then she stopped suddenly. "What aren't you telling me?"

Shaking his head, Raphael stood with apologetic eyes trained on her. "I already agreed."

"You what?"

Before Raphael could react, Essie ran up on him and beat him in his chest, shouting "No! No! No!" Her punches stung a bit but were really futile. He let her get them off on him because he knew his decision had hurt her. He'd decided to go into the lion's den without even consulting her, and he felt terrible for it. Once her steam had run out, he held her hands and brought her into a tight embrace. Her yells turned into cries as she buried her face in his chest and wailed out her anguish.

"Raphael, I'm scared." Her true feelings finally emerged. "I can take a lot of things. Have been through a lot, but we narrowly escaped the last incident with our lives. This was supposed to be our new beginning. A chance at normalcy." Raphael lifted her face to his, and fear and despair stared back at him. "If Abaku comes for us, then we will fight. We'll do what we have to do. But why do you have to go into the fire? It's one thing to defend yourself from the enemy. It's another to go knocking at the devil's door. If you knock, he'll damn sure answer. And Kaion needs you. *I* need you."

Essie fell back into Raphael's arms as he stood holding her and trying to soothe her as best he could. She was right. He'd kept his nose clean by only stepping into the ring when the fight was brought to his doorstep. This situation was another unknown. He'd been blessed the last time, but no matter how good he was, he couldn't be sure he'd have the same fate this time around. For now, he'd heard nothing of the Russians, or even Abaku, for that matter. Perhaps it was better to leave well enough alone.

"Let me run you a bath, baby. You need to relax," Raphael offered.

Essie only nodded in agreement. She'd run out of fight. She didn't know whether or not she'd gotten through to Raphael, but she couldn't stomach any more of the conversation for that night. She spun on her heels and walked slowly toward their master bedroom, heading for the bathroom. Raphael followed behind her. As he walked, he took in their family photo, the dining table that still needed cleaning from their family feast, and the trophy Kaion received from basketball. Everything in the house reminded him of the family life they'd fought so hard to build. Normal. He couldn't take them through the drama.

When Essie eased into the bubble bath, Raphael crouched down beside the tub and held her hand before kissing it. "I won't do it. I'll call Rhys in the morning and let him know that I'm pulling out."

A wave of relief rushed over Essie, and without thinking, she propelled forward, thrusting her arms around his neck and hugging him tightly. She pulled back in realization and giggled. "I'm so sorry, baby."

Raphael glanced down at his soaked shirt and shrugged. "Haven't you realized there's nothing you can do that will make me upset with you?" Their smiles met each other, and he cupped her face in his hands. "I love you, Essie."

"I love you, too."

———

"That movie was so good," Elle cooed, lagging on Shantrice. "Wasn't it?"

"Yes, girl." They giggled.

"That's enough outta you two. Y'all just liked the movie because Idris Elba was in it," Travis scolded, rolling his eyes.

Elle shrugged. "Well, you said no chick flicks."

"I should've said no sexy men *and* chick flicks. He don't look better than me and my boy." Travis draped his arm around Kaion. "Ain't that right, Kai?"

"That's right!" He laughed.

Shantrice turned to Kaion and pulled him to her about his jacket. "You are right about that, Mr. Gatts." The flirtatiousness in her voice was evident around her sing-songy tone.

Kaion slipped his arms around her waist. "Is that right, Ms. Bennett?" She nodded, and they lightly kissed on the lips.

"Aww, shit," Travis belted. "Bae, do we need to go and let those two have a moment?"

Kaion and Shantrice turned and laughed at their friends, who were teasing them and making silly kissy faces. "Actually, I better be getting home. Y'all know my people don't play."

Travis pushed him in the chest lightly as they arrived at their cars in the parking lot. "Come on, man. We were going to head out to Huge Impact to grab those wings and cheese fries."

Kaion shook his head. "I ate before I came, remember?"

Travis shook his head. "Then have a coke and enjoy your company." He walked up close to him and whispered, "Besides, if you don't come, I gotta foot the bill for three people, and I don't get paid until next Friday."

Kaion laughed, then slapped fives with him. Shantrice pouted as she turned from side to side. "I really want you to come hang out with us. Just for a little bit longer. Please."

Her cute, pouty, and flirty gaze shot an arrow right through Kaion's heart. Shantrice was sinking her claws into him. He loved everything about her, from her kinky coils to her cinnamon skin tone, her killer curves in those painted-on jeans, and even her stiletto nails. If she were a sin, he was her devil's advocate.

"Yeah, I'll hang out with you for a lil' bit."

Shantrice bounced up and down, clapping her hands. "Thank you, bae."

He held up his finger. "Just let me call Raph right quick." He slipped his cell phone out of his pocket.

Shantrice kissed his cheek and then scurried to the side to talk to Elle and Travis. When Raphael answered, he'd told him it was cool to hang out but advised him to be home before midnight and to call him when he was on the way. When Kaion hung up, he slipped his phone back into his pocket, and an eerie feeling came over him. He looked behind him and saw two men sitting in an all-black Chevy Tahoe staring at him. When the men caught him looking at them, they rolled up their windows, started the SUV, and slowly began to pull away.

"So what's up? You coming or not?" Travis asked, hitting Kaion on the shoulder.

Kaion jumped, startled. "You scared the shit outta me."

"Shit, my bad, bro." Travis looked past Kaion. "What were you looking at?"

Kaion looked back over his shoulder, and the SUV was gone. He shook his head. "I don't know." He turned back to face Travis. "It was probably nothing."

Shrugging it off, Travis eyed him with questions dancing in his eyes. "So you coming?" he asked again slowly.

"Oh, yeah. I am." He shook his head to clear out the uneasy thoughts, then tapped Travis on the arm. "Listen. How about I just ride with y'all, and we can come back for my car when we leave? I just gotta be home before midnight."

Travis slapped hands with Kaion and brought him in for a one-armed hug. "Bet, bro. We'll swing by before eleven so you can make it home on time." He turned to the ladies with his arms outstretched. "Look who's coming to hang out," he said excitedly as he ran toward the girls.

Kaion turned around and looked back over his shoulder again. The SUV was still gone, but he couldn't shake that feeling. Discarding it for the moment, he turned back and joined his friends as they all eased inside Travis's Nissan Altima and drove off to the restaurant.

CHAPTER 3

Raphael pulled up to the public park, located a parking spot, and waited for Rhys to show up. His mind raced over what he had to do and thoughts of the previous night. After Essie's bath last night, they had lain in bed together talking about their future and what that picture looked like. Essie was quick to remind him of the beauty of their new normal. He couldn't deny anything that she'd spoken. While Essie grew up in a loving home, he had not. It was the first time ever that he had a true family and all that it entailed. He'd finally grasped what it was like to live the so-called American Dream, and nothing short of a direct ambush could snatch him away from the cozy lifestyle. For once, he was comfortable. The ability to breathe easy while residing in a home on a tree-lined street with picket fences, with a stay-at-home wife, their adopted son who was a beast on the basketball courts and a whip in the classroom, and be financially sound the legit way wasn't lost on him. He had a life that was so far removed from when he was a kid that he couldn't even dream it up. Thinking over his past, there was no way he could jeopardize his future… *their future*…for the government, who couldn't give two damns about him or his family. Nah. They got paid to be involved in these missions. His days of beatdowns and bullets were done.

Once he'd made sure that Kaion had made it in the house safe and sound, he eased back into the bedroom with his wife and coaxed her into a little midnight snack, with her on his menu. As they'd made love, Essie reminded him, yet again, as to why his place was with his family and his new and current lifestyle, not chasing criminals around other countries. If Abaku or the Russians had been a threat to them, he'd for sure know that trouble would have graced his doorstep by now. The fact it hadn't meant that the only people looking for trouble were the government, and it would not come at his expense, and especially not Essie or Kaion's. They'd been through enough to last two lifetimes. Raphael would ensure that once was enough.

The sound of a car pulling into the parking lot jarred Raphael out of his reverie. It wasn't loud. However, Raphael had ears that could hear feathers rustle and eyes that could spot a federal-issued vehicle out of a hundred car lineup in gridlock. When the black Chevy Impala with black tint eased into a parking space, he automatically knew it was Rhys.

"Here goes nothing." He rubbed his hands together before pulling the handle of his driver's side door to open and exit his truck.

Placing one of his size thirteen Jordan shoes on the pavement, he peered out to see Rhys exit his car and stand with his arms folded across his chest, leaning against the truck of his car. Raphael shook his head as he grabbed his basketball out of the passenger seat. Rhys had him fucked him if he thought he was about to have this conversation without pretenses. Nope. He wasn't about to get labeled an undercover or worse get an informant tag placed on his head. They were a short yet long way away from his tree-lined neighborhood, and the hood of South Bend still had his name ringing in the streets even though he'd been out of them for over a year. Though it was a morning just before the usual crowds gathered and no one was around, Raphael was cautious. He didn't trust the hood any more than he trusted Rhys.

Gingerly walking onto the blacktop, Raphael opened one of the closed gates and began dribbling the ball. He made a couple of buckets when he saw Rhys approach him. Not bothering to acknowledge him, he tossed the rock up once more, and when it swooshed through the net, Rhys caught it and walked toward him.

"Raphael Waters."

"Rhys Landers."

They stood face-to-face, and Rhys held a smirk on his face. He shrugged and then turned to take a shot. He missed.

"Not as good as my trigger finger," Rhys joked as he refocused on Raphael.

Raphael lifted an eyebrow to his analogy, then grabbed the basketball and began shooting free throws again. "I won't hold you long. I called you here because I've had a change of heart."

With a grunt, Rhys folded his arms. "I figured as much." He scratched the side of his head. "Let me ask you this. Did you have a change of heart, or did Essie change your heart?"

Raphael stopped bouncing the ball and slightly turned to face Rhys dropping a stern glare at him. "First of all, leave my wife's name out of your mouth. Second, it does not matter why I changed my mind. It only matters that I did." He bounced the ball hard one time before grasping it underneath his arm. "I'm out. You and your federal boys can take care of this one."

"You must've forgotten that if we didn't pull the strings we did for you, you wouldn't even have Essie to call a wife. Hell, Kaion, either." He flicked the tip of his nose.

Raphael's nose flared. He was trying his best to hold his peace, but Rhys was trying his best to disrupt it. One thing he didn't play about was his family. Rhys was pushing the right buttons with the wrong muthafucka.

"And I appreciate all you did for me—for us. But that don't make me indebted to you. Real talk, you were looking to take down Dage and nail Alex to the cross. I did that. Not you or your government." He pointed at himself. "So any so-called debts you feel I owe, I already paid in full." He walked up to Rhys so that they were directly eye to eye. "So don't come here threatening me like you did me a muthafucking favor. Our business is square. Been square." Raphael put his index finger in chest. "What you asking of me now is on a clean slate. I plan to keep it that way. Clean and clear."

"Maybe, but the fact still remains that you forget one other thing that we—scratch that—*I* did for you."

"And what's that?" Raphael asked menacingly.

"Cleared the way so you could *afford* to support your family," Rhys seethed.

"And what is that supposed to mean?"

"Oh, I think you know exactly what that means, Raph. You're a smart fellow."

Raphael dropped the basketball to the court, not caring that it rolled off the blacktop into the dirt before landing against the enclosed fence. The scowl on his face showcased that Rhys had, in fact, found the red button to Raphael's burgeoning temper and stomped on it without regard to the possible detonation. Rhys stepped back just in time before Raphael pummeled him.

"Tsk. Tsk. Tsk. You might want to think about that. I'm a federal agent." Rhys wagged his finger at a huffing Raphael. "Besides, don't think that I would meet you and someone in my agency not know where I was headed. Anything happens to me, it's a shitstorm arriving on your doorstep."

"You son of a—"

Raphael's rant was interrupted by Rhys's hand claps. "That's the Raph I know. Use that rage. That aggression will get the mission accomplished faster than any government agency. That's why you're the chosen one, Raph. You possess a certain *je ne sais quoi*—that means—"

"A quality that can't easily be described," Raphael usurped his language arts lesson. "I know what the fuck it means."

Rhys snapped his fingers. "And that right there is exactly it. You're a chameleon. You're of the streets, but you have the ability to move and think as if you're not born and bred in the hood. Still enough aggression to get special operations completed swiftly and efficiently. The X-factor."

"How many times and ways do I have to tell you 'no' before you understand?"

Shrugging, Rhys admitted, "Oh, I understand, Raph. It's acceptance that's my downfall." Standing back on his legs with his fingertips on his waist, he said, "And it's your downfall, too. I'm prepared to accept your final answer so long as you are prepared to accept the consequences."

This time Raphael's head turned in curiosity. He should've known that Rhys's willingness to assist when he was in Benin fighting for his and Essie's life was a setup for future assistance. He'd always known you couldn't trust the government, but they'd allowed themselves to trust Rhys. He'd even been a witness at his wedding. Now he was here acting as if he hadn't stood by his side when he squeaked out his "I dos." It was a slap in the face to know that, on some level, he'd allowed himself to befriend Rhys instead of treating him like the pig he knew he was. He'd never make that mistake again. From this moment forward, Rhys was nothing more than a pawn for the government to him.

As Rhys stood there with an air of cockiness oozing off him like bad-smelling cologne, Raphael wanted to knock his block off and take the chances at fed time rather than get entangled in the Mission Impossible challenge that Rhys had laid at his footsteps. He'd happily accept the two hots and a cot and years of boxing other inmates than this suicide mission. At least he could see his family and one day make it back to them, even if he was old and gray. This shit was not built for the longevity of life. He'd be of no use to his family if he wasn't breathing. Before he risked it all, he needed to know what other consequences lay in store for him.

"Fuck you mean?" Raphael bit out, so angry spittle flew out of his mouth.

Fanning his arms outward, he explained, "Losing your income, possibly getting tied to Alex's old drug, arms, and murder rings. Let's not forget you were as deeply involved as she was. There's not much work on my part to make that stick. Now it's one thing for you to risk prison time. It's another to leave Essie and Kaion out here to defend themselves. And by defend, I don't just mean financially. Tell me. Do you think Abaku would not hesitate to come after your family if he knew that they didn't have you nor the means to defend themselves? You murdered his brother, sister-in-law, and their unborn child while you and Essie live the good life with the son of the woman who you helped to ruin his empire. Revenge does not get any sweeter than that." He began to walk away and then snapped his fingers. "Oh, before I forget, the agency will have no more ties to your family. You can't call on me to bail you out because I won't. No one will. Try walking down that prison sentence with that on your mind, Raph."

His words steeled Raphael. *This muthafucka.* As much as he hated to admit it, the truth of the matter was Rhys was right. His actions were dead-ass wrong, but his words held truth and depth to them. Even if Rhys was being an asshole of enormous proportions, he had issued a warning that Raphael had to heed.

Rhys had taken a few steps before Raphael called out to him. "Hold up." He strolled over to meet up with Rhys. "The fuck do you want from me, man? You know the bullshit we went through on account of Alex, personally. You were there." He pointed into his chest. "I saved your fucking life."

"And I saved yours!" Rhys shouted back. "I'm trying to do that again."

Those words stung Raphael to his core. "Speak on it."

Rhys nodded his head in the direction of trees that were visibly out of the line of vision. Raphael followed him. "I'm not supposed to tell you this unless you agree, but seeing as though you are just as stubborn as you are certified, I'll tell you. We know for certain that Abaku is primed and ready to get back into his illegal dealings. We have not been able to nail his ass to the cross, and the department wants this shit handled. So I'm recruiting you because this is a special assignment."

"Above-your-pay-grade shit?"

"Off-the-grid shit." Rhys took a deep breath after a small gasp escaped Raphael. "Operation OMECA, the official mercenaries elite classified association, is a level-12 classified group that was organized to restore balance. We are called in when no peaceful resolution is in sight, nor can the agency itself haul in or convict suspects. The fact that Abaku has evaded us all these years puts him at the top of the list. The team is fairly new, but we need someone who—"

"Has a certain je ne sais quoi," Raphael finished.

Rhys tilted his head to him. "Exactly."

"So that bullshit about them being a threat to me—"

"It was bullshit to get you to come on board, but honestly, I can't confirm or deny that a threat on you and your family isn't imminent. It's Abaku, after all."

"Listen, I get that you need someone like me on the team, but you know I have a family to protect here. This mission is a death trap."

"Correction." Rhys held up a finger. "I don't need someone *like* you. I need you."

That slip-up confirmed to Raphael that Rhys was the one behind this recruitment. As he'd so eloquently reminded him, he'd saved his life. Rhys knew firsthand the strategies, ploys, and gunplay that Raphael could put down, so the reason why he wanted him came as no surprise. Still, that didn't mean he was eager to jump back into the game. He feared no one or nothing, but he did exercise caution because he had more than himself to think about. If it were him, he'd already be on the mission. However, he was stuck at a crossroads. If he didn't assist, his family would be left wide open, and if he did, he'd walk into the belly of the beast. Rather than concede to either option, Raphael thought of a happy medium.

"Listen, I can't jump into this, but what if I could still help in a way that didn't put me in direct danger? Offer my services as a liaison of OMECA."

"I'm listening," Rhys grunted out, stroking his chin in contemplation.

"What if I play decoy? Lure Abaku out. I'm sure he still wants to exact revenge on me, if for no other reason than the death of his brother. What if I lure him to you guys? It's the perfect setup. Catch him in a criminal act."

Raphael watched as Rhys considered what he'd offered. With his arms folded across his chest, he shifted his weight from one foot to the other as contemplation displayed on his face. He couldn't read his thoughts as he waited in silence for Rhys to respond. Scrubbing his nonexistent beard with his hand, Rhys slightly shook his head in doubt.

"I don't think that would work, Raph." Raphael went to speak, and Rhys placed a hand on the front of his shoulder and patted, urging him to hear him out. "That not only puts your family at direct risk, that puts the ball in his court. He has the power to call the shots. That leaves you vulnerable to be caught off guard. Not to mention the manpower that type of coverage will demand. We're a small team."

"Then let the CIA handle it!"

"CIA is out," Rhys boomed in return, his anger returning. He huffed and lowered his voice. "Why do you think OMECA was created? Don't be stupid, Raph. You don't call goons for debates, and you don't create special ops for arrests."

Turning away, Raphael walked a few paces to consider what Rhys had said. As much as he wanted to argue his case, he knew Rhys was right. He just didn't want to admit it. Admitting it on some level meant he accepted it. Accepting it made him want to do something about it—something he'd already promised Essie he wouldn't do. He understood what was at stake, but he couldn't go through with it. Essie and Kaion were the only two good things he'd had in his life besides his Pops and Rah. His life was good now. Balanced. He didn't even have that with Pops or Rah. Though he loved him, his Pops was nothing more than a drunkard whom he had to take care when it should have been the other way around, and Rah introduced him to this same life that, years later, he was still trying to escape. Nope. This time he would choose goodness. Change had to start somewhere. It would start with his decision to let the chips Rhys held fall wherever they fell. This time he was choosing the legit path for his family.

He turned back to Rhys. "Then I got nothing for you." He bent down, retrieved his basketball, and began to walk toward Rhys, then stopped when they were side-by-side. Rhys faced one direction; Raphael faced the other. "Listen, I get it. But you have to find another guinea pig for this one. My loyalty belongs to my family. I can't risk that." He took a step and then stopped and stepped back, leaning in Rhys's ear. "And if you even think about fucking with my money, Abaku will be the least of your worries. Don't stop by or call me again."

With that, he left Rhys standing there, gazing off at him, as entered his truck. Raphael threw up deuces to Rhys as he wheeled out of the parking lot and onto the street.

The smirk on Rhys's face faded when Raphael was out of sight. He whipped his cell phone out of his pocket and punched a number, then placed the phone to his ear as it dialed.

Leaning back with his other hand in the pocket of his casual tan slacks, he cleared his throat when the line connected. "You were right. It was a no-go. Put down the play." Rhys pressed the END button on his cell, slipped the phone back into his pants' pocket, and glided back to his Chevy Impala.

CHAPTER 4

Sienna sat at the dinner table, diverting her eyes and nodding her head at the chattering happening around her. She had no use for conversation, not because she didn't want to talk, but because there was no one there she wanted to talk to. Ever since Abaku had moved them to Dubai to realign his organization and reconnect with his family, Sienna had felt like the oddball out. This portion of the family wasn't even the Dage side, so that made her feel even more like an outcast—and a tad bit treacherous for hooking up with her deceased husband's half brother. Hell, the least he could have done was move them around his father's side; that way, she would be accustomed to a few family members. But that was Abaku, selfish and self-serving as always. Everyone was always cordial, but the questioning stares and snooty glances had not been missed. Abaku carried on, none the wiser, and she felt as if she'd explode every time she had to endure a gathering, which seemed more often than not. Not to mention that Abaku acted as if she were nonexistent now that he had people he was familiar with in his corner.

He was nothing like his half brother. Where Dage was tender with her, Abaku was brash. Dage had been suave, while Abaku was pompous. Dage had been concerned where Abaku was nonchalant. Dage had placed her on a pedestal while Abaku placed himself on one. She'd thought it wise to connect with Abaku to stay close to someone who was a reminder of Dage, and because she needed someone to take care of her. She hadn't been self-sufficient under Dage, and it hadn't mattered. She'd known that she was a kept woman and that Dage would always make sure that she was. Abaku was a different story. She felt in her bones that the moment he got what he wanted, and she was of no use to him, he'd toss her away like yesterday's garbage.

In fact, she was almost to the point she wouldn't mind if he did want to part ways. To be honest, she was about ready to part ways now. The only hiccup, either way, was that no one in her family knew she was alive. Everyone thought she was dead. As angry as she was with her sister, she missed her and longed to simply hear her voice. Anger had consumed her to the point of insanity after losing Dage and baby Da'Jenna. She was ready to give both Raphael and Essie a dirt nap and let them join her beloved husband and daughter. As time passed, she couldn't help the feeling of love that crept back into her heart. She still loathed Raphael with a passion. It was his fault that she'd lost her family, her sister included, but she had begun to realize just how much she needed Essie. She had no clue how that would even work out. Even if Essie could forgive her for lying, Sienna couldn't forgive Raphael. She'd never do that. There in lay the problem: Essie would never accept Sienna back into her life without she and Raphael being able to bury the hatchet. Now how could she do that when she wanted to bury the hatchet in his back? Yet, she held faith that her sister would eventually forgive her, the same way that she had forgiven Essie. Of course, she'd be pissed about her contribution to conspire with Abaku regarding his ill-fated plan with Raphael, but just like she had, Essie would eventually forgive her. She was her sister, after all, and she knew her best.

"Sienna, you are extremely quiet. Is there a problem?" Abaku's aunt Ayo asked out of the blue.

Sienna's eyes snapped up in her direction, and that's when she noticed all eyes were on her. She quickly assessed the expressions from one person to the next, with her final assessment landing on Abaku, who held a straight-faced expression.

Picking up her wine glass, she drank a sip before lowering it slightly. "Umm. No. Everything is fine. A little tired, I guess, is all."

Abaku's cousin leaned over and nudged Sienna softly with a cackle. "Stop letting my cousin keep you up at all hours of the night, honey."

"What?" Sienna asked, shocked by her abruptness and forward comment.

For a moment, the air seemed to be sucked out of the room. Sienna had come off far more abrasive than she'd intended, but the last person she wanted teasing about her sex life and relationship was Abaku's cousin, whose name she couldn't even remember, or any of his family members, to be exact. Sienna's tight face turned everyone's mood sour as their cold gazes turned to her.

Abaku's cousin glanced around the table before ending back on Sienna. She let out a chortle and then gently tapped Sienna on her hand, which rested on the table. "So funny." She wagged her finger at Sienna. "I'm kidding."

The tension lifted as everyone except Sienna burst into teary-eyed laughter. Sienna eased up, taking a deep breath and sipping more of her wine. Everyone began making quirky jabs at Abaku about Sienna's reaction, and he laughed boisterously. She didn't miss that when his eyes fell on her, his face held a grimace. His nose flared, and his jaw clenched as she lowered her head. She knew that he was displeased, and she wouldn't hear the end of this embarrassing moment.

Excusing herself, she went to the ladies' room and splashed water on her face. *I have to get away from him*, she mused as she gathered her bearings. Staring at herself in the mirror, she patted her hair to tame the few loose strands that were flying away then pulled out her compact and powdered her nose and cheeks. Satisfied with her appearance, she smoothed out her midi dress before spinning on her heels and opening the door. As soon as she cracked the door open, she jumped back, startled to find Abaku standing at the threshold. A lump formed in her throat, and she took two steps backward as he brushed inside, closing the door behind him.

For the briefest of moments, Abaku stared at her expressionless. "Everything all right?"

Nervousness spread through Sienna's core as she observed Abaku's stern features. Still, she mustered the strength to answer him. "Yes, of course. Just needed a bathroom break."

"Probably from all that wine you're consuming."

Sweeping her bang across her forehead with her fingers, she agreed. "Yes, it is flowing right through me like a river," she said with a chuckle.

He gave the same chuckle, then pulled her to him about her elbow. "Then maybe you should stop drinking." His hard, no-nonsense gaze met hers. Sienna was stunned speechless. Leaning his lips to her ear, he said, "You know I need their money to get back into the swing of things. Don't fuck this up with your stupid little antics. You need this as much as I do. So stop acting like a fucking cunt." His spittle slapped her ear as he spoke.

He pushed her back and leaned forward, his eyes studying hers with bent brows. Fanning two fingers back and forth between them, he asked, "You and me, we're on the same page, right?"

Though her core shook, she exhaled and licked her lips to calm the tremble. "Yes, of course."

He nodded. "Good. Then act like it."

With that, he exited the bathroom. With Abaku gone, Sienna finally released the breath she'd been holding since she saw him at the door. She resented ever getting into bed with Abaku. He was so menacing and demeaning. It put the fear of God into Sienna, and she hoped for an escape. Not wanting to be any ruder than she had, Sienna took only a second to recover from his scathing reprimand before she headed out to rejoin the dinner party as the dutiful sidekick.

———

After Abaku's guests left, Sienna busied herself in the kitchen, tidying up and making sure the dishes were clean. As she closed the cupboard, she couldn't help but long for her own home in her home country. Nothing about where they were felt homey or familiar to her. Not even Abaku. When they were on equal playing fields, she had been able to psych herself up to believe they were on a mission they both equally wanted. Now, being pulled away from everything and everyone she knew and being thrust into this unwanted lifestyle with him, she couldn't bring herself to settle into it. She knew they would probably be in a better place with each other if she weren't so tied into her sister, her homesickness, and wishing that Abaku were any semblance of Dage, but she couldn't. Abaku lost a brother, but she lost everything, and he didn't help the situation, because he didn't care how she felt. He just wanted her to be a good little accomplice and sex toy while going along with his revenge mission. Oh, how she needed an escape. She desperately needed her sister.

"You want to tell me what your real issue was tonight?" Abaku's voice infiltrated her thoughts, and she turned to see him standing behind her, leaning on the kitchen island.

"Nothing." She shrugged, wiping around the sink with the dish towel.

He stood coming close to her. "You've been acting very strange. And that shit tonight was unacceptable. My family has the means to provide, and my stupid aunt is being stingy with the coins since she knew a target was on my back, so you know what your participation means." He spun her around so they were face-to-face. "We have to pretend to be a settled, doting couple so that she can give me this fucking money. That money is the key to my operation and the key to exact revenge on Raphael and Essie. We have a plan."

"I know we do—"

"Then fucking stick to it!" He turned away to grab the beer he'd been drinking. "My aunt has expressed that my transfer will be secured in another week or so..." He lifted his hand and pointed at her. "Don't fuck this up."

"I'm not. I've just been thinking—"

"Well, that's original."

Sienna's lips pursed at his snide remark, but she held her tongue. "We both want revenge on Raphael. He's the one that is responsible for me losing Da'Jenna, he killed Dage, and he stole my sister away from me. It's him. Our focus should be on him."

"Ahh, I see." He tapped his temple with his forefinger, then wagged it at her. "Your reservations are about your sister."

"Well, yes," she admitted. "I know she was wrong to choose Raphael, but she's my sister, Abaku. We can go through with our plan and leave Essie out of it. Losing Raphael will be punishment enough."

Slamming his beer bottle on the island, he yelled, "She still had a hand in killing my brother and fucking up my organization!" Taking a beat, he huffed and shook his head at Sienna. "Have you forgotten that by choosing Raphael, she also chose him over you? Her actions helped him take away from us!" He beat his chest.

"I know. I know," Sienna pleaded with her hands up, begging for him to see her point of view. "I understand that, but—"

"But what, Sienna?" he boomed.

"*She's my goddamned sister!*" The words belted out with furor. "What the fuck would you do if it was Dage or any one of your other precious family members?" She casually tossed her hand out as she posed the question to him.

Dage rounded the island before Sienna had a chance to react. Before she could brace herself, his arm flew up, and she was met with a backhand slap to her face. Her head snapped back, and she stumbled on the tiled flooring, just catching the island to brace herself so she didn't tumble to the floor.

"Abaku!" The words came out weakly as her face flamed and fresh tears stung her cheeks.

Still slouched over the island, trying to gather her senses, Abaku eased up close to her and pointed a stern finger in her face. "First of all, my brother and my *precious* family are loyal. They would have remained loyal, unlike your bitch of a sister. As far as I am concerned, her hands are just as bloodied as Raphael's, and we will leave no room for witnesses. They both go, and you just better stick to the plan." He snatched her by the chin and gripped her fear-stricken face. "Are we clear?"

"Perfectly," she agreed through mushed lips.

Abaku roughly released her and stepped back. "Good. Now clean yourself up and this kitchen." He slid items off the island onto the floor and shook his head. "Such a disgrace you are beginning to be. What would my brother think of you?"

With that, he walked out of the kitchen and left Sienna there to sulk in the aftermath. Sienna rose up from the island and dabbed her tears with paper napkins from the dinner table. Without another word, she did as she was instructed. One thing she knew for certain was she had to find a way to get on Abaku's good side, and hopefully, her good graces would convince him to leave her sister out of his plans. If not, she'd have to sacrifice and contact her. She would not allow her sister to be set up for the slaughter. For now, she had to play the willing participant, or she might just meet Dage and Da'Jenna again herself.

CHAPTER 5

Essie sat at her vanity, finger curling the last few strands of her curly locks. Her mind had been scattered all day, but she'd made it her mission to get her act together before tonight. Although she was still in somewhat of a funk, the excitement of tonight had begun to seep in as she got dressed. Kaion's basketball team was in the semi-finals, and a victory tonight would guarantee their spot in the finals. It was a huge night for him, and she had to put her best foot forward so she could cheer him on from the stands. Adding her favorite berry-flavored lip gloss for the finishing touch, she rubbed her lips together and then popped them.

"You almost ready?" Raphael's voice floated from behind her.

Fluffing her hair, she turned, slapped her hands on her knees, and nodded. "Yes, I am."

Raphael tugged up the sleeve of his shirt to glance at the time on his watch. "Good. We really need to head out now so we're not late." Dropping his hand, he glided over Essie and leaned down, delivering a soft kiss to her forehead. "Are you all right?"

Essie absorbed the kiss, allowing the sugary sensations from Raphael's tender lips to travel through her body. Inhaling, she closed her eyes momentarily before she reopened them and stood. "Yes, it's just—"

"Sienna's birthday."

A gasp escaped Essie as her hands lifted to cover her heart. "You remembered?"

Raphael encased her face between the palms of his hands and nodded. Then he brought both of his hands to hers, clasped them, and brought them to his lips before tenderly kissing the backs of each hand. "Of course I do. I remember everything you shared with me. It's the reason I have not bothered you today. I figured you needed a minute. I knew you'd come to me when you were ready to talk."

Essie fell into Raphael's arms, and he embraced her tightly. He was such a good man and an even better husband and father. She never had to feel alone, because he was always there for her in whatever capacity she needed, and it seemed he always knew exactly how to be there for her. She loved that man with her entire being, and as she melded into him, she couldn't do anything but thank God almighty for how truly blessed she was to have him.

"Thank you, babe."

"You ain't ever gotta thank me. Not only is it my duty to be there for you, it's my honor. You're my queen, baby. I got you for life."

Essie pulled back, flirtation dancing in her eyes. She eased her hands down his chest to his stomach until it rested on the growing bulge in his jeans. "So you don't want me to *thank* you?" Seduction oozed from her lips as she said the words in a sing-song fashion.

A mischievous grin flashed on Raphael's face. "You can always thank me that way. In fact, when we get home tonight, feel free to thank me all night long."

Essie giggled and began walking toward the door. "As my man wishes," she said, licking her lips seductively.

Raphael shivered and tapped her on the ass, to her pleasure. "Let's hurry up and get out of here before we miss this game and Kaion disowns us." He walked behind her and shook his head. "Damn ass hittin' in them jeans," he added, taking in her sexy body in fitted, distressed jeans, a buttoned-up blouse, and bleu-bottomed heels.

As they made their way to the car, he couldn't help but admire his wife. He lived to put a smile on her face. He'd known that she'd be down today about her sister, so he decided the best course of action was to be there when she needed him rather than force her to release her emotions on him. He was happy that he'd chosen the right move with her.

In fact, he was happy he'd chosen the right move on everything. It'd been two weeks since he met Rhys in the park, and he hadn't heard a word from him. Everything on the home and work front was copacetic. Rhys had wanted to pull him into the government's debacle, and he'd almost fallen for the okie-doke under the guise of protecting his family. Essie had been his saving grace; otherwise, instead of driving his beautiful wife to see his son play in their last semi-final game, he'd be on foreign soil, fighting for his life while they were worried to death. At the light, Essie caressed his hand that lay draped over the middle console, and he glanced over at her with a sly smirk and winked.

Her eyes batted, and she bit her lip. Yep, these moments were definitely worth him giving Rhys his ass to kiss. He wasn't ungrateful for the things he'd done. He just was done with that lifestyle.

When they pulled up to the high school, the parking lot was packed, as expected. It seemed like all of Indiana had shown up to bear witness to this game. If they won, it would be the first time in twenty years the school made it to the finals. So this sweet victory was long awaited and well overdue. Raphael finally found a parking space, and he and Essie exited his truck and headed into the gym. They were grateful Kaion had gotten their tickets earlier, because the ticket counter line was wrapped around the outside. Once they entered, they made their way to the home-court side of the stands to try to get a good seat. As they made their way to the top of the stands, Raphael's preferred location, Essie and a woman collided and bumped shoulders.

"I'm sorry—"

"Watch where the fuck you going!" the woman spouted.

Her harsh tone caused Raphael to turn around to investigate who was speaking to Essie in such a manner. As soon as he saw who was speaking to Essie, Raphael saw red.

"Wow. You didn't have to speak me like that," Essie said, tossing her hand on her hip.

Raphael jogged back down the steps, inserting himself between Essie and none other than his old on-again-off-again fling, Tatiana. His face and body language were menacing as he glowered at her.

"We gotta problem?" Raphael boomed.

Tatiana sucked her teeth. "Nah, ain't no problem. She just needs to learn to watch her step. That's all." A toss of her Brazilian weave accompanied her scathing words.

Raphael waved his hand back and forth showcasing his disapproval. "Cut that out. She apologized. Act like a lady and be gracious and accepting."

Rolling her eyes, Tatiana crossed her arms. "Look who thinks he's hot shit just because he found an African connection. Fuck you and this uppity bitch," she spewed with a finger point.

Raphael advanced on her before he knew it, but he found his restraint when Essie touched his arm. Scoffing, he sneered at Tatiana, "Let that be the last time you disrespect my wife."

"Yeah, whatever your *wife*."

"Yeah, one of those things you could never be to me and probably not for the next nigga either."

She went to say something, and Raphael cut her off again. "Watch your tone. You know how I get down. Don't let the time apart make you forget."

Tatiana held her hands up in surrender and bowed her head. "You got it. You and Mrs. Africa can go ahead."

Ignoring her comment, Raphael turned and allowed Essie to walk ahead of him to ensure that she and Tatiana were separated. Glimpsing back over his shoulder, he gave Tatiana one final warning glare before she spun on her heels and kept moving down the steps to a group of other women. *Birds.* He wondered how he ever let himself get tied down to the likes of Tatiana as they found a nice seat and sat down. *Had she been that bad years ago?* Probably, and he hadn't noticed. One thing was for sure, once he tasted sweeter fruit, he couldn't fathom how he'd settled, and he knew for damn sure he wasn't going back. Essie and Tatiana were the difference between royalty and ratchet.

When they were seated, Essie turned to him. "The ex-girlfriend Tatiana, huh?"

Raphael sat with his leg propped on the empty seat in front of him, elbow on the armrest, with his fingers cupping his mouth. He exhaled slowly. "No, ex-jump-off. Don't give her that much credit."

"She sure seems a bit touched for her only a jump-off, as you say."

"Most jump-offs are." Raphael finally glanced over at her and took her hand into his. "Don't let her spoil the night for us. She's jealous of you. Besides, we're here for Kai. I don't even know why she's here at a high school game."

Essie turned to face the court, deciding to let it go. "She probably knows someone who is playing, just like we do. Her presence may be an unpleasant one, but it does not mean it isn't warranted. At least for someone."

Raphael smiled and brought her hand to his lips for a kiss. "That is one of the many reasons I love you. You always see the good in others and in any situation. You're pure gold."

"Aw, babe." She squeezed his hand in hers. "I love you more."

They focused their attention on the pregame festivities and enjoyed the show. When the game was about to start, they called out each team's starting lineup. Since Kaion's team had home-court advantage, their starting lineup was called out last, and when they called his name as starting forward, Raphael and Essie jumped to their feet along with other spectators, mostly young females and the school, who all let out a roaring cheer for him. After Kaion slapped fives with his other teammates, he pointed into the stands, and Raphael pointed right back at him. Then he blew a kiss to Essie, who caught it and made a heart symbol with her hands. Kaion called it his "good luck" routine. Everyone admired the gesture so much. The local newspaper even included it in the write-up they'd done about the basketball team and its star players.

Essie didn't miss the googly eyes that he and Shantrice made at each other either. She made a mental note to bring it to Raphael's attention. She would like for Kaion to invite her over for dinner to formally introduce her. She didn't mind him dating. However, this relationship seemed to be heading in a far more serious direction, and she wanted to meet her to know the young lady's intentions as well as set up some ground rules. The last thing she and Raphael needed were crazy Tatiana-type chicks around Kaion—or to be grandparents before he could get into college. But tonight, she'd let him live. It was his night. Heck, it was their night with him.

Once the game began, the atmosphere and noise turned up. The cheers and jeers from both sides of the gym were so thunderous you couldn't hear the plays, barely heard the whistles, and it sounded like they would break the sound barrier. You'd think it was the NBA Finals with the Lakers and the Celtics, the way the crowd carried on. The game was so tight it went into double overtime. In the end, Kaion's school came out victorious with a score of 112-110. Once the team won, the cheer squad released streamers and confetti all over the gym, and the students, parents, and fans stormed the court to celebrate with the team. Essie and Raphael found Kaion smack in the middle with his teammates.

As soon as Kaion spotted Essie, he lifted her up into a bear hug and spun her around. "We did it, Essie! We won! We're going to the state championship."

"Yes, you are!" She smushed his face between the palms of her hands. "I'm so proud of you, Kai!"

"Thank you," he boomed with a wide-mouth smile.

When he turned to greet Raphael, Raphael brought him into his chest with a one-armed embrace. "My boy! Congrats, Kai. Y'all did that shit." He tousled his hair once they broke their embrace.

"We did. Thank you, Raph. Man, I can't believe it." He laughed, knocking confetti from his face.

"I can. You guys worked hard," Raphael reassured him, squeezing his shoulder.

Just then, other teammates came up to Kai, slapping fives with him and giving him daps. Raphael and Essie shrank back into the crowd of onlookers to give him time with his teammates and classmates. Shantrice made her way over to Kaion, and he wrapped his arms around her and pulled her close for an embrace. When their lips met for a sweet kiss, Raphael looked over at Essie.

"Mm-hm, you're late to that party. I saw that earlier. It's time for that talk."

Raphael nodded. "Indeed. But I'll let him live tonight. If I'd just won my conference game, I'd want a little sugar love, too."

He and Essie cackled at his joke before Essie added, "Hell, you want that anyway. So does Kai. He may be young, but he's still a young *man*. The one thing you all have in common is that you'll never turn down some *sugar love*."

Raphael turned to face her and lifted her chin by his forefinger. "But I only want sugar love from you."

Essie playfully tapped him. "Really? I thought Tatiana still might have a chance."

Raphael let out a roaring laugh. "There you go with that good bullshit."

Just then, Kaion interrupted them to explain that the coach wanted to meet up with them. He also introduced Shantrice briefly before she went off to catch up with her friends. Kaion explained to them that some of the teammates wanted to meet up and go out to eat afterward. Realizing how special tonight was and the importance of cherishing this win with his teammates, Raphael and Essie gave their approval.

Since Kaion had driven and they didn't have to worry about transporting him to any after-game festivities, Essie and Raphael decided to break out while all the students and fans were still crowded around talking so they could beat traffic. As they made their way to the exit, someone bumped into Essie with a hard shove, knocking her back into Raphael. If it hadn't been for Raphael's quick hands, Essie would have eaten the ground with her ass.

"Oops, my bad." The woman shrugged.

When Essie turned around, she was facing a group of women, with Tatiana smack in the center, and they all snickered at Essie.

Essie gazed at Raphael, who was steaming mad. She shook it off. "No worries. It's not your fault. You have big feet and broad shoulders. I'm sure it's always a hassle."

The insult came out so unexpectedly that a couple of the women in the crew with Tatiana laughed before they could stop themselves.

"Bitch," Tatiana said, stretching the word out, showing her intent to retaliate.

Raphael stepped in front of Essie. "This left hook ain't been used in a minute, but I guarantee it still works. I don't fight women, but I damn sure defend this one." He pointed at Essie. "Step to her if you feel testy."

He glanced around to all the women with his final gaze landing on Tatiana. "That goes for all of you."

Tatiana's glare burned through Raphael for the briefest of moments. Then she lifted off the side of the building she'd been leaning against and, as if on cue, her friends parted a pathway like the Red Sea. She plastered a smile on her face and sauntered up to him, each stiletto heel clicking against the pavement as she walked. She stopped in front of him and clicked her lips together.

"Raphael, we all know you ain't about that life anymore. You've been…" She paused and glanced over at Essie before tossing her hair and refocusing on Raphael. "Domesticated." She giggled, then patted his chest and dragged her stiletto nail down the front of his chest. "But I do know how you can get, and off the strength of who we *were* to each other, we'll behave," she said, pursing her lips in a seductive curl.

Raphael gripped her hand and removed it from him. "*Were* is the operative word."

A smirk crossed Tatiana's face as she nodded. "You are exactly right. *Were*," she said, turning serious before she deadpanned on Essie. "My apologies, *Essie*, is it?" she asked, knowing she knew her name. "Take care of my *ex*-man for me." Spinning on her heels, she did a finger wave at them and then motioned for her friends to follow her as she led the path with an extra twist in her hips, making her bodacious backside jiggle harder in her painted-on jeans.

Raphael turned to Essie. "I'm sorry about that, baby. Are you all right?"

Essie huffed with a roll of her eyes. "I'm okay. I'm just not going to ruin the day for Kaion. Otherwise, I'd *bliksem* her ass."

Raphael couldn't help the chuckle that escaped him. Yeah, she had definitely reached her breaking point with Tatiana. Any time she used African slang, she was at her wit's end. "Come on, Ali. I don't need you knocking anyone out. You are too pretty for all that. My left hook got that all under control," he said, making a fighter's fist with his left hand.

"Pretty or not, my right hook is power-packed."

He wrapped his arm around her neck and led her to the truck. "As long as I never find out, I'm all good," he joked as they both shared their first true laugh after the incident with Tatiana and her friends.

CHAPTER 6

Once they were in the truck, Essie flipped the visor down to reapply her lip gloss and added, "You're not the one who has to worry about my right hook."

Slipping his hand on her thigh, he winked at her. "The only hook we need to be worried about is the one between my thighs. He's the only hook that matters now, baby."

Essie burst into teary-eyed laughter and smacked her lips. "Damn it. You know just how to turn me on. Be careful, or Captain Hook might have to make a freeway appearance."

A groan escaped Raphael, and he pulled in his bottom lip. He loved it when he brought the freak out of his wife. Essie was fire in the sheets, and when she spoke like that, Raphael could barely contain himself. If they weren't careful, he'd be pulled over in a parking lot, letting her ride the wave in the back seat of their SUV.

Essie leaned into Raphael, and their lips met for a sensual kiss. When Essie pulled back, Raphael peeked down at his massive hard-on and shook his head. "Let me hurry up and get to this damn house."

As Raphael drove, they flirted with each other, heightening their anticipation for when they arrived home. About five minutes away from their house, Raphael noticed a black sedan, and while Essie continued to joke and sing to the slow jams playing through the speaker, Raphael got quiet and paid attention to the sedan that seemed to be trailing them. When he turned on their street, and the sedan turned with them a few yards back, Raphael kept driving past their house.

"Babe, you passed the house. What are you doing?"

Raphael eyed the rearview and gripped the wheel. "I think that car is trailing us."

Essie slowly peeked into the side view mirror and sat back. "You think?"

Raphael nodded slowly. When he got to the stop sign, he made a right. Instead of following them, the car continued straight. Raphael relaxed and then headed back to their house.

"See, Rhys has you paranoid."

Raphael let a nervous chortle. "Yeah, I guess." He didn't tell her that he still had a knot in the center of his stomach, but he shook it off.

By the time they pulled into their garage, Raphael felt better and was excited to finish the evening off with his beautiful wife. Giggling like teenagers, they entered the house, groping and kissing all over each other. Raphael's eyes caught a shadow in the corner, and immediately spun around, pushing Essie behind him.

The swing of a fist came out of nowhere. Raphael narrowly missed as he caught the assailant with a powerful left hook which sent them reeling backward. Before they could fall, he grabbed the person and brought a knee to their forehead.

"Ahh!" Essie screamed, rushing so fast to turn on the light that she ran out of her shoes.

When she clicked the light on, another assailant grabbed her by the arms from behind and lifted her up as she kicked and screamed. Raphael was still tussling with the first assailant, but hearing Essie's screams caused him to whirl around. Panic and aggression rose inside of him. He picked up the first assailant and body slammed him over the kitchen counter, sending the toaster, blender, and knife block crashing to the floor. The first assailant slumped to the floor, out cold. Swiftly, he slid across the floor and grabbed a butcher knife as he and the second assailant did a standoff, circling each other as he held a screaming, flailing Essie hostage.

"Let her go, muthafucka!"

The man's sinister laugh rumbled through the quiet house as he flicked a switchblade out and stuck it to Essie's neck. "Come any closer, and I will gut her like a fish," he roared in a thick African accent.

"Raph!" Essie cried out.

"Stay calm, baby. I got you," Raphael directed, never moving his focus off the man. "Who sent you?"

"You know who." The man laughed.

Though Essie was hysterical, she knew she had to think quickly to help Raphael to save her life. She wailed out and leaned her head forward.

"Shut up, bitch!" the assailant ordered as he and Raphael continued to do-si-do around each other.

With all the force she could muster, Essie threw her head back, head-butting the assailant in the nose and mouth.

"Ahh, fuck!" he yelled out, instinctively releasing her to grab his face.

She slipped out of his grasp, and when her knees hit the tilted kitchen floor, she threw her head back once more, slamming her skull into his groin. The unknown man shrieked in pain, dropped his switchblade, and gripped his genitals. Essie scrambled away, and Raphael wasted no time. He dashed forward, bringing the butcher knife underneath the man's throat, and used his left hand to jam it through, killing him instantly. His body dropped on the kitchen floor, and his cold eyes stared back at them.

Without a moment's hesitation, Raphael ran to Essie and gripped her in his arms, kissing her all about the forehead and the top of her head as she wailed and cried.

"Are you hurt?" he asked frantically.

"No, no," she cried, wiping her tears with the back of her hand. "Oh my God, Raph! Who are these men? Who sent them? What is going on?"

Anger ignited in Raphael, and he said, "That's a good question. I'm about to find out," he spewed through gritted teeth before stalking over to the man on the counter, who was groaning in pain and unable to move.

"Raphael, no!" Essie screamed out but could only watch in horror as Raphael continued forward with nothing but evil intentions for the intruder.

Raphael picked up another knife on the floor and then patted the man down. He pulled a switchblade and a 9mm from him. Slapping the man's face and sticking the knife to his neck, he asked, "Answer me or end up like your boy."

The man groaned in agony, unable to answer him.

"Who the fuck sent you?"

The assailant let out a small chuckle, and Raphael took the switchblade and sliced a gash in the man's arm, causing blood to pour out as he screamed in pain.

"Think this is funny?" He pulled the hammer back on the gun and aimed it at his head. "Keep playing with me."

Just then, Raphael's cellphone rang. "You might wanna… wanna…answer that," the assailant huffed.

Essie rushed over to Raphael and lifted his cellphone out of his front pocket. Staring at the name, her hands shook. "It's Kai."

Raphael's eyes furrowed. "Answer it!"

Essie's hands shook so fiercely it was hard for her to press the button, but she did and placed it on speakerphone. "Kai!" she screamed.

"Essie! Raph!" he yelled. "It's a man in a sedan. He keeps following me. I have Shantrice in the car, and I don't know what to do. It's creeping me out. I'm really nervous, Raph."

With the gun still aimed at the intruder, Raphael stared at the phone. "Kai, keep driving. Whatever you do, don't stop driving. Do you hear me?"

"Yes, sir."

"I mean it. Keep going!" Raphael boomed, making sure Kaion knew it was serious. "Where are you?"

Raphael paused, giving Kaion time to explain exactly where he was located. "Okay, I got you. Stay on the phone with me. I'll be down there in ten minutes. Don't worry. I'll find you. Just keep giving me directions to where you're at, and I'm on my way."

"Yes, sir."

Raphael looked at Essie; her mothering skills had kicked in, because she no longer shook with fear. Instead, the same concern and anger reflected in her eyes. "Kai, don't hang up, but I'ma have to put you on hold for just a moment, okay? I promise I'll be right back."

"Okay, Raph. I'm holding on."

Essie muted the phone and nodded for Raphael to do what he had to do. A shrill sound rang out as Raphael put a bullet into the dome of the intruder lying on the kitchen counter. His half-headed body slumped and slid down to the floor across from his partner-in-crime.

He gave Essie the gun. "You remember how to use this?"

"Yes."

"Good. Stay here in this kitchen. If anybody comes through that door, don't even hesitate. Put a bullet in their head." Reaching behind her, he pulled her cellphone out of her back pocket. "Call Rhys."

With that, he unmuted his phone. "Kai, you still here?"

"Yes, sir," he answered through shaking breaths.

"You still driving, right?"

"Yes, sir. Can you hurry? They are speeding up now."

"I'm on my way."

CHAPTER 7

Raphael listened to Kaion describe where he was driving as he bent the street corners on damn near two wheels to get to him. This had to be Abaku's doing. As Raphael reflected over the intruders in his home, he remembered that one had an African accent. He didn't even have to bother to ask, because deep down, he knew. He'd only wanted confirmation. However, confirmation went out of the window when they attacked his family. He was aiming for everyone involved to take a dirt nap. He'd tried to be, as Tatiana had said, *domesticated*—but the attempted hit that went down couldn't be glossed over. Nah. Muthafuckas wanted to feel the wrath of Raphael, and now they'd awakened the sleeping bear. Raphael was about to roar like a muthafucker, too.

He knew what he'd promised Essie, but they couldn't afford hits like that. Kaion would soon be off in college, and he and Essie couldn't be around each other twenty-four-seven. If he'd come home to her dead body or received a phone call about Kaion's demise, there would be no limit to the amount of carnage that he'd leave behind. Now, it was time to eliminate the threat because it'd just come barking at his doorsteps.

"South or north?" Raphael asked Kaion as he arrived to the street that Kaion was driving on and trying to maneuver to the right direction.

"North," Kaion confirmed.

"Kai, I'm scared," Shantrice said. "Who are these people? Why are they following us?"

Kaion reached over and patted Shantrice's knee. "I don't know, but I won't let anything happen to you. I swear. My father is on his way. He's going to help us. Don't worry."

The word slammed into Raphael's chest like a load of bricks. *Father*. It was the first time he'd ever referred to him as such. Of course, he was fatherly to him, and Raphael viewed Kaion as his son, as if he'd planted the seeds in Alex himself. However, they'd always maintained a boundary of sorts. Although Raphael felt that way about Kaion, he never pressured him to view him as a father. A father figure, yes. But not a father. Raphael would never put that kind of expectation on Kaion, no matter how he felt for him.

That simple word caused him to press a little harder on the gas and catch up to the sedan that was tailing his son. Although he loved Kaion, knowing that Kaion viewed him as his father bubbled up in his core and exploded in his heart. His love for Kaion hit the stratosphere, and now the people in that car didn't stand a chance. He caught up to the car and brushed right up on their tail.

"I'm right behind the car. Keep your car steady. Okay, Kai?"

"Okay," Kaion said.

Raphael pulled up closely to the sedan following Kaion and slightly bumped them. That only caused them to press harder on the gas and lightly bump Kaion's car.

"Ahhhhhh!" Shantrice screamed.

"It's okay. I got it. I got it!" Kaion yelled out. "Dad, what do I do?"

Raphael could have kicked himself. That fool could have caused Kaion to spin out of control. He thought fast. At the next approaching light, Raphael was going to pull to the side of the car and tell Kaion to make a quick hard right so he could clip him off his tail.

"Tell Shantrice to quiet down," Raphael directed and then he heard Kaion relay the message to Shantrice. "Now at this next light, make a quick hard right. Don't throw on your blinker, just turn sharply and try to keep the car steady. I'll tell you when to go."

"Yes, sir."

Raphael counted down the seconds and then shouted, "Turn!"

Kaion made a sharp right turn and that caused the sedan behind him to slam on brakes. The pause was just the right amount of time Raphael needed to swing to the side of the sedan and make the turn with them. As they turned, Raphael jerked his wheel and slammed into the side of the sedan and pulled back. This made the sedan swerve, running off the road, sideswiping a pole, then coming to screeching halt with its wheels spinning. Kaion slammed on brakes and pulled over to the side. Raphael stopped right beside the car and jumped out, snatching his gun from under the seat and striding over to the car with caution.

Kaion jumped out of his car. "Dad!"

"Get back in the car, Kai!" Raphael bellowed as the driver climbed out of the car holding his right arm, with a gun in his left.

Seeing the weapons startled Kaion, and he physically jumped before climbing back into the car and slamming the door. Onlookers began to gather as Raphael and the unknown man pointed guns at each other.

"You ain't gonna shoot me in public," the unknown man said.

"Neither are you," Raphael shot back.

The man laughed and wiped blood from his lip. "Let's just call this a night. Shall we?"

"Who the fuck sent you?"

"Wouldn't you like to know?"

Raphael pointed the gun at his head and aimed, ready to pull the trigger. People began to scream and run away from the scene.

Raphael and the man stared each other down as the man pointed the gun at Raphael.

"You must not mind dying tonight?" the man asked.

"The only sure thing I got in this life is death. So fuck you, nigga."

A smile crept on the man's face. "Fuck you, too."

The sound of sirens halted their exchange, and in one swift motion, the man turned the burner to his chin and pulled the trigger, ending his life right in front of Raphael and whatever lingering spectators were on the street. His leaking head fell back against the car and his body slumped over, falling onto the car door.

"Dad!" Kaion jumped out of the car, crying.

Raphael ran up to him and hugged him close, burrowing his face in chest to keep him from seeing the dead body. "It's okay, son. I'm all right. Are you guys good?"

"Yes. I heard a gunshot, and I got scared. I didn't know if it was you," Kaion sobbed into his chest. "Did you—"

"No, he shot himself." Raphael bent to look inside Kaion's car. "Are you okay, Shantrice?"

She jumped, lifting her tear-stained face from her trembling hands and nodded. "Yes, sir."

"It's over now." Raphael patted the car and looked at Kaion. "We've gotta go. Get in the car and drive straight to the house. We have to talk to Shantrice. Don't argue—just go and do like I said."

Kaion immediately turned, got in his car, and pulled away, heading to the house. As the sirens got closer, Raphael made a mad dash to his truck and jumped inside. He pulled off and trailed behind Kaion all the way back to his residence.

As soon as Essie heard cars pull into her driveway, she jumped up, gun aimed and ready. The shrill ring of her cellphone startled her, and she brought her hand to her chest from the anxious thump of her leaping heart. Looking back on the sofa, she saw "Babe"— Raphael's nickname—scroll across the screen, snatched it up, and answered it.

"Babe?" she called out.

"Yes, don't shoot. It's me, Kaion, and Shantrice."

At the sound of that, Essie placed the gun on the sofa and released a sigh of relief that she didn't realize that she'd been holding. When the door opened and she saw the two terrified teenagers enter the house through the front door, a floodgate of tears opened. She sprinted to Kaion and gripped him in her arms tightly. He held her back with equal vigor as they both poured tears of fear onto each other.

Essie pulled back, cupping his face. "Are you okay? No one hurt you, did they?"

"We're okay. Nothing happened. Dad saved us," he cried.

By then, Raphael had stepped into the house. Essie hugged Kaion again and threw a glance over at Raphael. In response to her unspoken question, he nodded his agreement with Kaion. Essie then turned to Shantrice and hugged her, and the young girl fell into her arms weeping and wailing.

"It's okay, sweetheart," Essie reassured her as she coddled her in her arms.

Essie motioned her head to the kitchen, and Raphael made quick work of going to the garage and grabbing a tarp to put over the entryways of the kitchen to keep the dead bodies out of the line of sight from the teens. Essie ushered them inside to the family room so Raphael could handle it.

"Essie, what is going on?" Kaion asked. "A man killed himself. We heard a gunshot. I thought…I thought—"

Essie leaned over and patted Kaion's knee as he bowed his head, trying to thwart his tears, but it was no use. Essie understood what he meant. He thought Raphael had been shot. Seeing him go through this gutted Essie. He'd been through so much in his seventeen years of living. It was too much for one child to bear.

"It's okay, Kai. Nothing happened to Raph." Her gaze found Shantrice, who was quiet and trembling. The toll of tonight had obviously crashed down on her. She patted her knee as well. "Sweetheart, I am Essie. I'm Raphael's wife. Can you tell me your name?" It was her attempt to bring a sense of normalcy to the young girl.

"Shan…Shantrice," she barely whispered.

"It's nice to see you again, Shantrice."

"Same." The one word came out as shakily as her name.

"Listen, you guys. I know this is very bad. Raphael will be in here in just a moment to explain everything. Can I trust you guys to sit tight for a minute? You're safe here."

They both nodded their agreement, and Essie went in search of Raphael. He'd just finished blocking off the kitchen and held four bottled waters in his hands. He handed Essie three of them then twisted the cap on one and drank a long swig.

"Those are for you and the kids," he said. "Did you talk to Rhys?"

"He didn't answer or call back," Essie informed him. "Raphael, what the fuck is going on? And what are we going to tell this young lady?"

Raphael was stuck. What the hell could he tell her? Damn sure not the truth. To be honest, he believed he knew what the truth was, but he couldn't be sure. Even if he was correct in his assumption, he damn sure couldn't tell some teenage girl at Kaion's school that they were in the middle of an international crime syndicate revenge plot. To add to his distress, Rhys hadn't contacted him. He had been just as serious as Raphael in regard to the "no contact" clause that had been handed down. Unfortunately,

Raphael knew he needed Rhys. There was no way he could explain to the local authorities about two dead men in his home and one on the street without Rhys's assistance.

Thinking quickly Raphael surmised, "We'll tell her that it was just some old street people from the old club. Kids will believe in some gang shit before they believe what's really going on. I don't want to scare the girl to death, and we don't need her talking to anyone about this."

Essie agreed. "You're right. Let's go talk to her."

They entered the family room, and Essie gave them the waters, which they both demolished within seconds of receiving them. That's when Raphael and she sat down, and Raphael began his elaborate story. Though she still seemed scared out of her mind, and rightfully so, she seemed to calm with understanding.

"We have cop friends who will take care of this. I assure you that you're in no trouble, but I do need for you to keep this to yourself. Don't even tell your best friends, and definitely not your parents. If you need to talk about it, talk to Kaion. Can you please do that for me? I want to keep you as safe as possible."

At the word "safe," Shantrice's eyes bulged, and Raphael knew she wouldn't utter a word to anyone else out of fear. "Yes…yes, sir."

"Okay, good. I'm so sorry this happened to you. Kaion and I will make sure you're taken care of. I promise," Raphael said to Shantrice. "And I'm sorry to invite you over under such circumstances."

Kaion reached over and brought Shantrice into his arms. "It's okay, Shan. I got you. I'm never letting nothing happen to you." He kissed the top of her head, and she melted into his arms.

"I was so scared, Kai." She held him tightly. "But I know you've got me. I got you, too. I promise you and your parents I won't say anything."

Essie and Raphael gave each other looks of uncertain relief. The last thing they wanted to do was pull Kaion into this mess, and on top of that, another innocent child. They wouldn't be able to break their bond now, no matter what happened. They were tied to each other for life. It hurt that it had to be under such dire circumstances and not natural love.

"Shantrice, please feel free to go to this hall bathroom right here and freshen up. Is there a friend you can call to pick you up?" Essie asked.

She nodded. "My friend Ella can come get me. I'll just tell her that me and Kaion got into an argument. I'll spend the night at her house to give myself some time to calm down before I head home to my parents."

Essie and Raphael smiled. She was a bit more street savvy and cunning than they'd given her credit. Perhaps she was a better fit for Kaion than they imagined.

"Good. Please do that, and you all stay in the living room," Raphael instructed.

Once Shantrice returned from the bathroom looking somewhat refreshed, she called her friend and put the plan in motion. They all sat in the family room and waited for Ella to show up. When she did, Shantrice and Kaion put on an Academy Award-worthy performance as they pretended to disagree, and Shantrice stormed out the front door to Ella's car.

"How was that?" Kaion asked as he reentered the house.

"Perfect, son." Raphael placed both hands on his shoulders. "Go up to your room and stay there. Essie and I have some business to handle."

"But I want to help. I want to know what's really going on, because I know you lied to Shantrice."

His assessment threw him for a moment. "How do you know that?"

Kaion cast his eyes downward. "You have a tell."

"What did I tell you about talking to a man?" Raphael's words came out razor sharp, and Kaion's eyes shot to his. "That's right. Eye to eye."

"You have a tell," Kaion repeated. "When you're fibbing, you scratch your ear. It's how I know whether or not you're going to give me what I ask for. You never tell me no, but rather you'll think about it. When you're being serious that you'll consider it, you don't scratch your ear. When you're feeding me BS, you scratch your ear. Tonight when you were explaining what happened to Shantrice, you scratched your ear."

Raphael was taken aback and turned to Essie. She shrugged, displaying her shock as well. She'd never noticed it, but Kaion had. Raphael was thrown at the young man's sharpness. Although he shouldn't have been. He was a product of his mother and led under him. What else did he expect?

Raphael chuckled and pointed at him. "That's a real good observation. Keep that skill." He sighed and brought him in for a hug. "I understand you want to help, but I'm the man of the house. I'll handle it. I promise you that I will be honest with you about everything once I know fully what's going on. Right now, I need you to do what I ask and to keep what's going on between me, you, and Essie. Not even Shantrice. It's for her own good." He pulled back and stared him directly in the eyes. "Understood?"

Kaion agreed. "I understand. I got you." With that, he bounded upstairs.

Raphael turned to Essie. "He's a helluva kid."

"He takes after his dad." Essie walked up and hugged him. "I hate that moment came behind this, but at least he trusts you in that role, especially now. What are we going to do about those men in the kitchen?"

Raphael grabbed her hand and they walked to the kitchen. Raphael pulled out his cellphone and called a number he hadn't wanted to call in a long time. Nick from the old club was also a cleaner, and he needed someone to come in and take care of this. He dialed the burner number and gave the coded information. Within half an hour, Nick and three members of his crew were knocking on his door.

"Long time," Nick said when Raphael answered.

"Yeah, I never planned to see you."

They entered and Raphael dropped the stack of bills in Nick's gloved hands. Nick counted it and nodded to his workers, then looked at Raphael. "Give us thirty minutes, and we'll be out of your hair." He patted Raphael's shoulder. "I do miss you, man."

Raphael nodded. "Same."

The men cleaned up the mess and were out in exactly thirty minutes, as Nick promised. Once they were gone, Raphael pulled out his cellphone and dialed a number.

"Rhys, I know you got Essie's call. Call me tonight. I'm ready to talk."

CHAPTER 8

About forty-five minutes later, Raphael's phone rang, startling Essie and he out of the fitful slumber they'd fallen into while they awaited his return call. Raphael and Essie both jumped, and Raphael wiped the blur from his eyes before the realization of who might be on the line struck him. Patting Essie, he urged her to lift off his chest as he leaned forward and grabbed his cellphone before the ringing ended.

"Hello." His sleep filled greeting came out slightly garbled. "Rhys?"

Hearing Rhys's name put Essie on alert, and she sat up, all her focus and attention on Raphael and the conversation with Rhys. Nervousness overcame her as she wrung her hands and sat with her feet folded underneath her facing Raphael. Internally, she prayed that Rhys would help. It was no doubt that he could, but after she'd forced Raphael to turn his back on the man, she hoped that he wouldn't hold it against him. At this point, their safety depended on it.

She could have kicked her own self in the ass for asking Raphael to shun Rhys. She should've known the shitstorm was coming. However, life had been good. Too good. Normal. She didn't want to disrupt the normalcy to walk in the face of trouble. She should've taken more stock in the fact that trouble could still make its way to them. Everything had been copasetic so she didn't believe that anything would actually happen. Oh, how wrong she was. Now she may be the cause of them having to uproot and live a state of chaos for years to come, unless Rhys was willing to turn the other cheek and assist them in this situation, even if it came with debt repayment.

"Yeah, you and your wife rang?"

Raphael gritted his teeth at Rhys's blatant careless attitude. "You know if I'm calling it's an emergency. We wouldn't bother you for any other reason," Raphael bit out.

"Watch your tone with me," Rhys barked. "You're the one who wanted to dead all contact, remember? I was granting your wish."

Closing his eyes, Raphael stilled himself for a moment. He knew Rhys was being a dick, straight up. Even though it pissed him off, he couldn't blame him. He'd come to him, man to man and friend to friend, for assistance on his case, and he'd shut him down completely and arrogantly. He glanced over at Essie, and he could see her thoughts swirling through her mind. She blamed herself. He felt it. She shouldn't. To be honest, he didn't want to be involved in the crap himself, so it wasn't as if Essie had to do that much to convince him to turn it down. True, he'd initially agreed, but he honestly agreed out of guilt and to save face.

Rhys had been the sole person to help him escape Benin, him and Essie. On some level, he felt that he was forever indebted to him for that. If it weren't for Rhys, he wouldn't even be alive to have the family he has now. Hell, Essie may not have been either. So, it wasn't just because he wanted to be gung-ho and dive into that lifestyle. Simply put, he didn't want Rhys to have anything to hang over their heads. Like now.

"You're right," Raphael admitted. "Those were my wishes."

"It's late. You said you had an emergency. I'm just getting in the house, and all I want is a shower and my bed. What's the emergency?" Rhys asked, conceding to the conversation. He knew that was Raphael's way of apologizing.

"We had an incident, and we need your help." Raphael took a deep breath before he continued. "Some men invaded my house. Almost had the drop on me and Essie, but we handled business. But they came after Kaion, and you know I can't have that."

"Is Kaion hurt?"

"No. He called me, and I came and handled it. Thing is, his high school girlfriend with was him. Has her really shaken up. I came up with a story about old beef from the club, and she bought it. She's assured us she wouldn't say a word."

"Kaion's girlfriend, huh?" There was a pause, as if he was considering how much damage control he'd have to do. "How much did she see? How can you be sure she won't mention anything?"

Based on Rhys's question, his assumptions had been correct. Raphael reflected over the night's events and how Shantrice processed everything. She went from scared and intimidated to a rider effortlessly. Like she was somehow bred for the life without even realizing it. Raphael and Essie had been impressed, upset that she'd had to endure such danger, but impressed all the same.

"Trust me, she's handled. Even came up with her own plot so she didn't have to face her parents tonight. These kiddos are built different, her and Kai."

"Umph. Okay." Rhys took a beat before he probed further "So, this attack, what happened? I need all the details."

Raphael briefed Rhys on exactly what happened, and Rhys listened intently.

"Did they reveal who sent them?"

"No and the muthafucka who chased Kaion put a bullet to his own dome," Raphael explained. "But one of them in my house was a smartmouthed fucker. He didn't get the opportunity to say much, but I did notice one thing."

"What was that?"

"He had an African accent."

"Are you sure?"

"It's an accent I'll never forget." Raphael paused before asking the question that was burning in all of their minds. "Do you think it's who we think it is?"

Without skipping a beat, Rhys answered, "That's exactly who I believe it is. No, "I told you so's" needed."

Raphael went from a calm simmer to a burgeoning rage at that confirmation. He'd left all the mess with Dage and Jabal halfway across the world, and Abaku still wanted to come for him. If it was war he wanted, war he would get. One thing Raphael was not about to do was live in fear or have anyone attacking his family. Had he only come for him, he would have dealt with it. Essie and Kaion were off limits. There was nothing stopping him from coming at Abaku's neck. He'd already crossed the line in the sand, so now *all* lines would be crossed. Enemy lines included. He was trying to be Raph, the cool laidback dude. Now, he'd activated Raphael.

"Listen, why don't you, Essie, and Kaion stay at a hotel tonight? I'm on my way. I have to put a few calls in, but I'd feel better if you guys were away from the house."

"I'm not letting no muthafucka, especially Abaku, run me or my family from our home."

"It's not about running from your home. It's about your protecting your family. The house is just a structure. You can get that back. You won't ever get another Essie or Kaion. Go to a hotel, Raphael."

Raphael considered Rhys's words for second. He was right. He couldn't allow his anger to circumvent his common sense.

There was no telling how many people had been activated on this threat against him and his family. They may have been secure for the moment, but that could change at any moment. The next time Essie or Kaion might not be so lucky. He couldn't have that. Their blood would be on his hands. He'd never let that happen to them. He glanced over at Essie, who stared back at him with wide and fearful eyes.

"Fine. We'll do it."

"Good." Rhys breathed a sigh of relief. "In the meantime, I'm on my way to you. I'll call when I arrive. See you in a couple of hours."

"All right. Bet. See you then."

They disconnected the line, and Essie could barely contain her questions. She fired off at least ten in a back-to-back string as if Raphael was in an interrogation, and she was the detective. Raphael was patient with her. He knew she was coming from a place of love and protection, and even a bit of fear. He understood all that she was feeling because he felt the same way.

He reached for her hand and held them before answering. "Rhys does feel as though this has Abaku written on it. He's going to help. He's making phone calls, and he's on his way now. He wants us to stay at a hotel for tonight."

Essie stood, nodding her head. "Whatever he thinks is best. No arguments from me."

Easing up to Essie, Raphael wrapped his massive hands around her arms then peered into her deep-set brown eyes. His gaze was too much for Essie to endure, and she cast her eyes away from his line of vision. Though she'd looked away from him, Raphael didn't miss the pain and guilt that flickered in them. She was blaming herself for the events of the night. Using his forefinger, he touched her chin, gently bringing her face back so that they were eye to eye again.

"Hey, none of that. Don't do that."

"I'm not. It's just—"

Raphael raised his chin. A look of question graced his face. "And we're definitely not doing that. Straight up. Always. Remember?"

Essie's shoulders dropped as she fell into his warm embrace. There was literally nothing she could hide from this man. He knew her so well—too well. Better than she knew herself most times. He made it his mission to learn the inner workings of her. Hell, Kaion, too. Rarely anything they did—be it right, wrong, or indifferent—surprised him. That's how well he'd studied them.

Lifting out from his arms, she stood back, placing her hands in the back pockets of her fitted jeans. This time she did give him her undivided attention. "You already know that I blame myself. If I had just allowed you to deal with Rhys, this wouldn't have happened. If something would have happened to you or Kaion, I just don't..." Her words trailed off, laced with a tearful tremble. Her eyes watered, and she swiped at the droplets threatening to slide down her face.

Raphael brought her against him, encased in a bear hug. He cocooned her while allowing her to get her emotion out. She needed that release, and he would bear the brunt of it. She was his woman, and any pain that he could alleviate from her heart, he would. It wasn't his job; it was his solemn duty.

"First things first, you did not make that decision on your own. True, I agreed, at first, to help Rhys, but it wasn't because I wanted to, I feel indebted to him. Both of us decided I shouldn't get involved, so get that guilt trip out of your head. Next, we aren't going to blame each other for what Abaku set in motion. He could have let sleeping dogs lie, but he chose not to do that. He started this. Now, I'm going to finish it for all of us."

His lips crashed against hers as they both enjoyed the taste of each other. "Now, are you really good with going to a hotel?"

Nodding, Essie agreed without debate. "After everything that's happened, I'd rather be safe than sorry, and I need a minute to decompress from it all. A fresh atmosphere and a good night's rest will help." Grasping his face between the palms of her hands, she kissed him again. "As for the other stuff, you just stay safe and come back to us."

Bringing her hands to his lips, he kissed her knuckles before caressing her chin between his thumb and forefinger. "No matter what, I'm gonna always come back to y'all."

After booking a modernism suite at the Conrad, Raphael, Essie, and Kaion headed out to the hotel. Seeing the looks of relief and peace that settled over his family when they checked into their suite made Raphael smile. It costed a pretty penny for the high-end hotel, but he had to ensure their security and peace of mind. Kaion wasted no time dropping his bag in the smaller bedroom and diving straight for the remote for the flat-screen television mounted on the wall of the sitting area. While Raphael placed their luggage in the master bedroom, Essie headed to the butler's bar and made a drink. She reentered the bedroom, drink in hand, looking as if she'd erased years off her age in moments.

While they packed, Raphael had texted Rhys to tell him where they were staying. Rhys had said he'd meet him there at the hotel bar so they could discuss matters. It was late, but Raphael wouldn't be able to put his head down to rest without knowing Rhys's plan and putting efforts in motion to not only cover the debacle from earlier, but to avoid any further instances in the future.

As soon as Essie offered to make him a drink, his cellphone buzzed with a text from Rhys, alerting him of his presence.

"Can't. Rhys is here," he whispered.

She touched his arm with understanding. "It's okay. Go. I'll be in the soaker tub."

Raphael instructed Kaion to be the man and look out for Essie, then headed out. Once Raphael was downstairs, he called Rhys and then let him in with his key pass to the hotel. The two men greeted each other with a one-armed hug before walking in silence to the lounge to talk.

"I'm sorry for what you and your family have gone through. Abaku moved without our knowledge. We didn't have all the adequate intel we needed set up. He got past us with this." He pointed a finger at Raphael. "That won't happen again."

"So, what's the plan?" Raphael fanned his hands outward and hunched his shoulders.

"For one, our cleanup team has already intervened with the police investigation. We've taken over, so there are no worries about that coming back to you or your family. With this latest attempt on you all, I was able to get the agency to sign off on that intel. An alpha team is monitoring Abaku's moves as we speak. He won't be able to infiltrate like that again without our knowledge, I assure you."

"Do we know for sure it was him?"

"I'd bet every dollar I have. Everyone else has been quiet."

"Do we know how he got to me?"

"My contacts are working on that piece of information as we speak." Rhys took a sip of his whiskey and then sat it down. "Trust me, we're doing everything we can. I put my personal stamp on this. I got you. I know we exchanged words last time, but that was business." He pointed to him then up toward the elevators. "This…is family. You, Essie, and Kaion are like family to me."

Raphael eyed him for a moment before touching knuckles with Rhys. He knew that Rhys would have his back. They'd barely known each other, but the life-altering events that happened with him and Rhys in Benin had changed the both of them. Made them close. You don't almost lose your life with a man and not be close after that, especially with one that saved your life. Through all the bullshit, he knew Rhys had a special affection for them that no government bureaucratic bullshit could break. It was moments like this that reminded him of that.

Stretching his long legs out, Raphael sat back, somewhat relieved. Staring Rhys in the face as he brought a drink to his lips, he murmured, "I'm in."

Sitting forward, Rhys gave him a confused stare. "I thought you said—"

"Fuck what I said." He finished off the brown liquor as the ice cubes clinked together.

"Are you sure?"

"Muthafucka, are you sure? You were breathing down my neck not too long ago. Now you're acting all cautious and timid."

Rhys threw his hands up in surrender. "This is your family. I feel partially responsible for speaking ill on the situation that eventually happened." Hunching his shoulders, he gave Raphael a direct stare. "I just want to make sure you're good with this."

"Bringing down Abaku is my only focus right now. I won't be good until that happens. So, tell me what you need for me to do." Leaning forward, Raphael's jaw twitched as he spat, "I'm *in*."

A sly smile spread across Rhys's face as he lifted an envelope out of his pocket and handed it to Raphael. Raphael placed the empty glass he'd been holding on the table in front of them, retrieved the envelope from Rhys and opened it. Inside were training instructions, locations, and information on Abaku. Raphael nodded then folded the paperwork back into the envelope and placed it in his pocket. They stood, and Rhys pulled him into another manly embrace.

"Welcome to OMECA. Meet me down here in six hours, nine a.m. sharp. We've got work to do," Rhys whispered before they pulled away from each other.

"Nine a.m. it is."

"Oh, and Raph?" Rhys said, turning back around before he'd walked too far away. Raphael stopped in his tracks and turned back around to face Rhys. "I'd get some pussy tonight if I were you. It'll be a minute before you can again."

Raphael and Rhys grinned at the banter before walking in opposite directions. He didn't have to tell Raphael that it was already on his mind. Truth was, getting involved in this bullshit, he might not ever get any again.

CHAPTER 9

Bright and early the next morning, Rhys sat on the edge of the bed in his hotel room. His cell phone dinged with a message. His contact was in touch to let him know that everything was good to go. He smiled to himself before lifting from the bed with a good stretch to start his day. After hitting the shower and getting dressed, he made his way to his unmarked rental and drove across town to the diner.

From his vantage point in an inconspicuous street spot, he could see all the activity coming and going to the diner, exactly what he needed. He zeroed in with laser focus on the traffic flooding in and around the eatery. When he saw a late-model pearl white baby Benz pull up into a parking space, he leaned back out of the line of sight, connected his earpiece transmitter, and turned up the volume. When the woman opened the car door and stepped out, it was obvious that she was trying to remain inconspicuous herself. Instead, she made herself stick out like a sore thumb. Dressed in all black, she made her way toward the diner, pulling her baseball cap lower over her eyes to shield her face. Still, Rhys knew it was her, not solely because of her whip, but because the long, lemonade-style braids that cascaded down her back and extra-long stiletto nails were a dead giveaway. *Bird*. Rhys shook his head in disgust as she waltzed into the diner, obviously searching for someone.

He saw a man stand and stretch then return to his seat. Like a moth to a flame, the woman took the signal and walked hurriedly over to the man, taking the seat in the booth across from him. Rhys turned his transmitter so that he could have a good signal and hear every word that was exchanged between the two people.

"Listen, I don't want any trouble. That man getting shot at and killed? I had nothing to do with that." She waved her hands. "And I thought you said no one would get hurt?"

"Casualties happen," the man across from her said, lifting a toothpick and placing it in his mouth. "It's none of your concern anyway. You did your job. You marked Raphael so that our people could do their job. That's all you were hired to do."

Her shoulders fell a little bit. "But what about Raph? Is he hurt? His lady? What about his kid? I can't have no kid's blood on my hands—"

The man hurriedly leaned forward and spat. "Yo, shut the fuck up." His threatening verbal command halted any further words from escaping her mouth. "Why you worried about it anyway? You did what you had to do for the money, right?"

She shifted uncomfortably in her seat and pulled the cap lower on her head. "Yeah, but still. I may be mad that Raph moved on from me, but I never want to see him hurt. We've been through a lot and—"

"Spare me the sob story, Tatiana." He put his hand up. "I get it. You're still soft on the nigga. That's the problem with you girls. You always want the man who don't want you."

Fire danced in her eyes as she tossed a heated stare at him. Before she could respond with a smart comment, he interrupted with a finger point.

"Don't get mad with me about what I said. You did it for the money, remember?" A sinister laugh fell from his lips. "The other fifty stacks were wired to your account as we speak. Open your app and check."

Tatiana did as she was told, and the corners of her mouth turned up before she swiped it away with her hand.

"Nah, don't act like that money didn't just get you wet. I can smell you leaking behind those zeros."

"Fuck you."

"I would but I don't have that kinda time right now, baby." He lifted one of her braids and casually tossed it to the side of her face. "Maybe next time though."

She stood abruptly. "I wouldn't let you sniff my stuff."

Shrugging his shoulders, he scoffed. "Baby, you ain't even worth the trouble attached to that *stuff*." He pointed at her. "Exactly why Raphael got the fuck on."

Tatiana went to slap him, but he caught her hand. "Don't make a scene in here. You never know who is watching."

With that, Tatiana lowered her hand and quickly scanned around, praying she didn't see anyone she knew. Placing her cellphone back into her jacket pocket, she returned her gaze back to the man.

"Is that it? Are we done?"

"We were done the moment you checked the app."

"Good. Don't ever contact me again, Enu. Or whatever the fuck your name is."

Licking his lips clean of the sweet tea, he'd just sipped, he sucked his teeth. "Abaku sends his regards. Be easy."

Tatiana shook her head and charged out of the diner, never looking back. She damn near spun wheels exiting the parking lot and heading back in the direction she'd come from when she'd first arrived. Rhys cut off his transmitter and recording. He'd gotten just what he needed.

"Hello?" Rhys answered his cellphone.

"Tatiana is taken care of. She still believes it is some cat named Abaku who hired her to mark Raphael and Essie for him.

Payment was transferred as requested. Anything else you need from me, boss?"

"Nah, agent, you did well. You and the other agents wipe down the bar and turn it back over to the agent. I'm on my way to meet with Raphael."

"Copy that."

They disconnected the line, and Rhys pulled off just as inconspicuously as he'd driven up to the diner. Neither Tatiana nor his agent Emmanuel any the wiser. He'd been in this game long enough to know that even your right hand couldn't know all the moves your left hand made. He'd protect his operation at all costs. Even if that meant lying to the people who trusted him the most. He smiled to himself about his next step as he headed to the hotel to meet up with Raphael.

Raphael sat with his back pressed against the headboard in the hotel bed, shirtless, with one hand behind his head and the other wrapped lovingly around Essie. He only had ten minutes to go before the alarm would sound, alerting him that it was time for him to shit, shower, and shave before heading out to meet Rhys. He was sure there would be no time for formal and lasting goodbyes. Just these last few moments. Rather than sleep and get the rest he knew he should, he'd relished in soaking up the time with his wife. Besides, he couldn't rest if he wanted to. His mind was crowded with thoughts of the unknown and worries about the safety of his family while he was away. It pained him that he couldn't be in two places at one time or at the very least that they couldn't come along with him. Either option was far too great a danger, but it seemed far greater with him being removed from his family, on a suicide mission.

Essie shuffled beneath his arms, and a few seconds later, he felt her warm eyes on him. She was taking him in, he knew it. Bringing his eyes down to hers, they locked in on each other, and for the briefest of moments, all of the unsaid feelings passed between them. No verbal confirmations had to be said. Their hearts spoke to each other in a rhythm that only they understood.

"What are you doing up?"

Essie sat up in the bed and leaned in close to Raphael, wrapping her arms around his brick-hard stomach. "Same as you. I have been up all night. Can't sleep."

Bringing his lips to her forehead, he left a soft and succulent kiss to it. "You should. Let me worry about the rest."

"And you know that's never gonna happen. I know what you have to do. I just wish—"

"Shhh, I know." Raphael closed his eyes to shut out the same thoughts. "We'll all be all right. We have to believe that."

"I wish that I could," Essie said, her voice cracking with unshed emotion.

Raphael tilted her chin up to him, so they were eye-to-eye. "I'll come back to you," he croaked, unsuccessfully hiding his own emotion.

The quiver in his voice only caused the pooled tears in her eyes to flow like a faucet.

"You promise?" Essie choked out, her sobs causing her voice to quiver again.

"I promise," Raphael answered confidently this time, then kissed the top of her head.

Essie buried her face in his chest and he continued to rock her until sleep lulled her away.

A few minutes later , his alarm sounded, and Essie pecked his lips. Without another word, he sprang from the bed and headed to the restroom. Within fifteen minutes, Raphael returned freshly showered and ready to go meet up with Rhys. By the time he emerged, both Essie and Kaion were standing in the hotel room's living area waiting on him.

"This is not a farewell party," Raphael half-joked, trying to lighten the moment.

Kaion's lips turned up in an unexpected smile that he quickly forced away, and Essie folded her arms across her chest with her eyes rolling upward at his shenanigans. Raphael's way of downplaying serious issues that he didn't want them to worry about was either over reassurance or playfulness.

"We just wanted to tell you to be careful," Essie said with more confidence than that shone in her worry-laden eyes.

Raphael eased up on her and cupped her face in between his massive hands. The intensity of their love radiated like light beams pinging off the windowpane. "I'm going to be careful because I have to make my way back to you." He kissed her softly then raised his head, turning his attention to Kaion. "To both of you."

Kaion gave a half-smile, but he never took his eyes off Raphael. Eye to eye, man to man, just like he'd always taught him. Raphael reached out and placed a hand behind Kaion's neck.

"While I'm away, you're the man. Watch out for Essie, and Shantrice, too."

Raphael could see Kaion transform to a young man in that moment right before his eyes. His chest swelled with pride and an air of protection swooped over him. "I got you, Dad. I'ma hold it down."

Still holding him about the neck, Raphael guided Kaion to him, pulling him into an embrace. "I know you do. I trust you. And I got y'all too."

"I know you do, Dad," Kaion answered as they slapped hands.

With the flip of his wrist, he noticed the time on his Apple Watch and made his way to the door of the suite. When he opened the door, he heard Essie say, "Love." He stopped and turned to face her. He tilted his head and repeated the sentiment before walking out and closing the door.

Unbeknownst to Essie, Raphael relished the solace those fleeting moments brought to his heart. Indeed, she was the ying to his yang. The key to his heart. The Eve to his Adam. He was born and built just for her, and she for him. But the threat to their lives was real and imminent. It was that thought that allowed him to flip his emotions off. To be the man they needed, he had to revert to the man he used to be. And with that, Raph was reborn.

By the time he made it to the lobby, he saw Rhys sitting in a lounge chair, and when he spotted him, he stood up to greet him. Raphael reached him and the two slapped hands together before embracing in a one-armed hug.

"So, what's good?"

"I have to take you to the headquarters to get you in the system and meet the team that is going to have your back."

"What about my family?"

"We'll take care of them." When Raphael shot a doubtful look in his direction, he added, "By 'we,' I mean me. You know I got them. We'll outline the rest once we get you straightened out."

The ride to the secret headquarters for OMECA was quiet and somber. Raphael's mind was on his family heavily. Rhys knew this and respected it. He was venturing into unknown territory to confront an unknown enemy while leaving his family behind. It was a hard pill to swallow, and admittedly, these orders were tall shoes to fill. He'd never admit it but he wasn't exactly a hundred percent confident in Raphael's ability to complete the mission, either. He was basing his recommendation on the work that Raphael put in during the debacle in Benin. He had no clue if he was truly a thoroughbred or if it was dumb luck. However, seeing as though he'd handled the previous night's attack and come out on top, it provided some assurance that he'd chosen the right man for the job. He'd studied Abaku, Dage, and Jabal for years and never came as close as Raphael had gotten in mere days. He needed Raphael, honestly, way more than Raphael needed him. If it was one thing he knew for sure, Abaku had the full backing of his wealthy family, so even if Abaku hadn't been after Raphael at the moment, he was coming. All in all, the elimination of Abaku was a win-win for all parties involved.

Easing out of the Impala, Raphael looked up at the unassuming government building. It looked like some low-grade tech building, which was the perfect cover for an off-the-grid government agency. When Rhys walked around to his side of the car, he patted him on the arm.

"Let's get this started," Rhys said, leading the path into the facility.

Raphael and Rhys walked up to the door and walked inside. There was another door with a scan system and a card scanner. Rhys lifted some type of coded card and scanned it. Once it recognized him, he plugged in some information and the body scan system initiated on Raphael, scanning his body from head to toe. Once the scan was complete and clean, Rhys punched in a code and another set of doors opened, revealing an elevator.

"What the hell was that?" Raphael asked after the doors closed and they were lifted to another floor.

"Our security system. You can only access this building if you have a scan card. The building's security detected more than one person, so I had to input a visitor code. It automatically scans any visitors for threats to personnel, and once you came back clean, I had to give you temporary access to come inside," Rhys answered as Raphael gave him a bewildered gaze. "Like I told you, OMECA is something different."

As he finished his explanation, they stepped off the elevator and into a long corridor that led to another room with more computers, high tech gear, and security fail-safes. Waiting at the table was a group of people, two women and four men. They all halted what they were doing and stared up at Rhys and Raphael.

"Team!" Rhys yelled out, clapping his hands together. "This is the phenom, Raphael. Raphael, this is team OMECA." He went down the line introducing everyone. "This is Porter. She is over incoming intel and she's nifty with creating gadgets," he said of a mocha-brown woman with short, cropped hair before turning to a skinny, dark-complected young man. "Beside her is Benji, our systems and data analyst. Otherwise known as our hacker." Turning to his right, he introduced two men; one fair-skinned Black male with hazel eyes and a broad build and an Italian man with his hair slicked back into a short ponytail. He was also muscular, with a defined and chiseled jaw line. "These two are my field agents, Emmanuel and Tonio. Emmanuel hasn't seen a machine he couldn't operate, a vehicle he couldn't drive, or a shot he could miss. Tonio is—"

"The muscle," Tonio finished smugly.

Rhys shook his head with a smirk before gesturing to the last person. "And this is Beau."

She reached out and shook Raphael's hand. "Short for Beautiful." Her tone came off as sexy as she appeared. Her cinnamon skin was blemish free, and she had brown curly locks, sultry eyes, pouty lips, and a velvety voice.

"Raphael." He returned the sentiment. "And what is your role in this operation?"

Her tongue glided across her lips, moistening them before she said, "Diversion…among other things."

"Other things?" Raphael asked damn near entranced with her hypnotic eyes.

Her body moved fluidly in a sexy twist, holding Raphael's gaze with her eyes and her pouty lips opened ever so slightly as she quickly snatched something from her hip and flung it. Raphael's head moved swiftly and narrowly missed being grazed by a knife that speared past him and landed into the doorframe.

"Other things," Beau said sternly before turning away from Raphael.

A chuckle rumbled through Rhys as he patted Beau's arm. "Beautiful is her government name. We call her Beau around here. Out there she's known as Slice."

"Carving out beautiful masterpieces one person at a time," the entire team said in sing-song unison.

"You have a whole team, Rhys. Why did you need me? What's my role in all this?" Raphael questioned as he took in everyone around him.

"You're the only person who possesses qualities everyone has, and you are the only one who can lure Abaku out of hiding."

"I beg to differ." A deep and heavily accented voice intercepted the conversation between Rhys and Raphael, garnering everyone's attention. Their attention landed on Tonio, who stood sulking at Raphael. With a scowl on his face, he huffed. "There's only one muscle."

Fire ignited in Raphael. "Ain't nobody coming for your fake throne, so you can pipe all the way the fuck down."

Arrogant air inflated Tonio's chest as he stepped into the open space as if preparing for a duel. "Funny, orders coming from a nobody."

Raphael stepped around Rhys into the open space, unbothered by Tonio or his idle threats, his expression stoic, jaw clenched, and eyes unyielding. "Funny, only pussies get riled up when they feel threatened."

Tonio cracked his neck and with a couple of swift motions moved toward Raphael. Rhys barely made it between them as Emmanuel gripped Tonio from behind, restraining him about the neck.

"I'll fuck you up!" Tonio shouted as Rhys pressed with all his might to restrain Raphael.

"Easy, big fella. Easy," Emmanuel said sternly to Tonio.

The flicker in Tonio's eyes extinguished, and he raised his hands in surrender as he stepped back away from Raphael. "I'm good."

Raphael stood, never breaking the stare with Tonio, when Rhys finally turned and faced Tonio while standing guard in front of Raphael. "Don't break down now," Rhys said. "We all need each other."

"This is fucking bullshit, Rhys. We don't need him," Tonio yelled.

"If we didn't need him, Abaku would be in custody!" Rhys's heated words and the sharpness in his tone let everyone know he was over this fiasco. "We can't capture the bad guys if the good guys are too busy busting each other up. Everyone—and I do mean everyone—on this assignment is needed. Operatives and selected operatives."

His words were definitive as he stared down at everyone in the room, including Raphael. When both Raphael and Tonio seemed to put the lid on their boiling hotheads, Rhys walked over to Emmanuel, spoke privately for a few moments, then Emmanuel handed him a file.

"Benji, get Mr. Raphael Waters legal in our system," Rhys ordered. "Slice and Emmanuel, get the gear together that Raphael will need." He turned and faced Raphael. "Come with me, Raphael. We need to have a discussion."

Raphael followed behind Rhys as he carried a file into another room that appeared to be a conference area. Tonio stood beside Emmanuel, helping him with weapons, and when Raphael was within striking distance of Tonio, he snuck that dominant and forever lethal left hook right against Tonio's cheek. The hit was so solid a *thack* resounded throughout the room and blood curdled into his mouth as if someone had turned on a spigot. The noise was immediately followed by the sound of Tonio's groans and his knees hitting the linoleum.

Raphael leaned over Tonio as he was kneeled in prayer pose on the floor. "And that's the fuck why you need me, muthafucka. You a muscle. I'ma goon. Never forget that, bitch." Raphael's mouth was so close to Tonio that his spittle landed on his face.

Rhys doubled back and frantically pulled Raphael away while Emmanuel and Porter rushed to Tonio's aid.

Beau licked her sexy lips and a glint lit in her eyes. "Welcome to OMECA, Mr. Waters," she whispered to herself.

CHAPTER 10

After entering the conference room and shutting the door, Rhys paced the floor with the file folder under his arm and his arms crossed. "What the fuck was that?" he bellowed, slamming the folder onto the conference room table.

Sliding back in one of the leather highback chairs, Raphael slid down into a seat, folded his arms across his chest, and shrugged. "That was the reason you want me on this mission."

Rhys spun on him so fast, he almost lost his balance. "Fighting with that group is not beneficial to you. You'll need them." His finger pointing sternly toward the door where the other OMECA team members were.

"First of all—" Raphael held up his hand. "Y'all need me. Second, if you didn't notice, I wasn't the one who started that little ego trip with all that bitchassness on display. Disrespect in any form will not go unchecked from me. I don't give a fuck who you are."

Rhys pulled out the chair beside Raphael and sat down turning to face him. He cupped his scruffy stumble on his face. "Okay, you wanna address disrespect?"

"Any time and always."

Rhys opened the file and slid it toward Raphael. "Then address the real disrespect and stop worrying about a pissing contest with Tonio."

Raphael caught the photos before they slid out and stared down at them. Snapshot after snapshot revealed someone extremely familiar to him until he saw one that showed the face clearly, but he didn't know why. Holding the pictures in his hands, he looked at Rhys with a mixture of shock and confusion etched in his brow. Surely, this had zero to do with Abaku, so what did it have to do with him, and why was she on their radar?

"This is Tatiana. What is this about?"

Leaning forward with his hands clasped together, Rhys answered, "It's about me looking into the situation and having your family's back like I promised you that I would."

Raphael picked up the photos and examined them. She appeared to be hiding and shielding herself. It was as if she was trying to be inconspicuous. His eyebrow raised as he turned the photos to Rhys.

"What is going on in these photos, Rhys?"

"That"—he pointed to the photo—"is Tatiana Groves. You know her, correct?"

He shrugged. "Yeah, we go back. Had history. She was a little jealous of Essie, but nothing I can't handle or that was a big deal."

"Or so you thought." Rhys stood with his hands in his pocket. "My intel came in that there was a reason Abaku's people knew how to reach you, Essie, and Kaion. My intel states that the information was fed to them by Tatiana."

Shaking his head, Raphael threw the photos on the table. "Bullshit."

"Oh?" Rhys countered. "Did you attend a basketball game recently? Did you know that she recently received a huge cash wire transfer into her account?"

When Raphael didn't say a word, Rhys continued. "She was approached by someone on Abaku's team, offered money to mark you, accepted it, and this..." He pointed to the photos. "This is when she met up with her contact to complete the second half of her transfer. I even have her audio to prove it."

Without waiting for Raphael to give the green light, he pulled out the recording and pressed play. It played to the portion where she asked what happened to Raphael and he jumped up as he recognized her voice.

"Turn it off."

"So, what we—"

"I need to get my family into protective custody first, and I need Tatiana handled." Raphael wasted no time stating. He stood there brooding.

Old feelings of betrayal flooded Raphael. Granted, he'd never felt as deeply for Tatiana as she'd felt for him, nor had he been as loyal to her as he'd been to Rah and Alex, but there was still a mutual respect. An understanding. An understanding that he thought they shared. He tolerated her hood chick antics because they'd come up in the mud together. Tatiana had been the only person from his childhood he had left. Not that he needed any reminders of the hell he endured, but that familiarity endeared her to him. Though she didn't mean much to him, their shared history allowed him to hold onto her through their shared experience. Now, just like everyone else before her, she'd found a way to snatch that from him. She'd been the last piece of anything he held remotely good about his past, and with one payoff, she'd eliminated that.

His focus had to be about getting his family to safety, because he no longer trusted her being anywhere near them. Taking care of her, and then taking care of Abaku. Exactly in that order. Fuck Rhys and anybody else who thought otherwise. Cause just like Tonio, no one came for him with an army coming back for them. Even if it was the army of one…him.

Rhys nodded. "I got you, but I need you onboard fully. That means keeping your hot head at bay with the team. You're only doing Abaku a favor if you two kill each other. And don't worry, I got my time with Tonio, too."

"You help me with those two things, and I will sing Kumbaya with that muthafucka all day. But that *first*. Then Abaku."

———

Sienna sat at the dining table, her thoughts aimless as she stared out of the window, folding and refolding the gold cloth napkins. Memories of her and Essie running through their father's house as kids playing tag and giggling invaded her mind as she remembered the countless times they'd almost broken the expensive china dishes passed down through generations from their playful banter while setting the dinner table. Unlike usual sisterly or even sibling rivalries, they never blamed each other. No, they were true comrades. They refused to tell on each other, so they got in trouble together, received their punishments together, and dared to repeat their actions all over again together. Because what was the use of being obedient when you had someone to be disobedient with? They pushed the limits together because they knew nothing short of disgracing their family name would ever push their father over the edge with their behavior, and honestly, they had the most fun pushing the limits together.

Yes, that was a happier time. A time when she and her sister were two peas in a pod. Those times had remained and grown stronger over the years until Raphael. Yes, Raphael was the one factor that neither of them saw coming or knew that would be the one person who could ever separate the dynamic duo. Had she known that he'd be the reason that she was in hiding, lost her husband and her baby, and lost her dear sister, then she never would have agreed to Dage's plan. She would have asked him to bow out and think of another route to save his empire for their family. She didn't do that, though. Unlike her, Essie had been a free spirit. She wasn't the settle down and get married type. It wasn't mere assumption that she'd come up with that theory either. No, those words—those exact words—had spouted out of her sister's mouth and taken root in her memory. So, when Dage proposed the asinine idea, those roots grew and spread like a vine climbing the garden trellis. It seemed perfect at the time. She had no clue that those words would prove futile to the likes of Raphael Waters. He'd snuck in like a deadly weed and killed the entire free-spirited vibe that her sister once possessed. A boll weevil in a cotton patch, he was.

Indeed, Essie's love for Raphael had been the catalyst for the destruction of their relationship. Now with a clearer head, Sienna understood that either pregnant emotions or selfishness made her turn her back on her sister and deem Essie's love of Raphael a betrayal. It wasn't Essie's love. It was simply Raphael. After all, he was the reason behind the demise of her husband and the loss of her only child. Her sister had loved him, and she'd been blinded by that love the same as Sienna had been for Dage. In hindsight, Sienna felt she bore some blame for the debacle she'd put her sister in. In the end, they both did what they had to do for their men. Only Dage would have never hurt Essie, and Raphael would hurt Sienna. That is why he was the arch nemesis. He was the one who deserved the hand of wrath that Abaku and she were plotting. Not Essie. Not her sister. On days like today, it was never clearer. Either she'd have to convince Abaku to stop his treacherous plans against Essie, or she'd have to betray her husband's memory and confess to Essie what was happening so she could escape. It pained her to do that, because she knew Essie's love for Raphael ran deep, and saving her would ultimately mean possibly saving Raphael. However, it was a chance that she was now willing to take if it meant saving her sister. *I pray you can forgive me, Dage.*

Sienna was startled by a set of massive hands on her shoulders that slowly began to knead away the stressors of her day. Some of it. Not the parts that mattered, though. She leaned back in the chair she occupied and released a soft sigh.

"What thoughts are on your mind now, Sienna?" Abaku asked, continuing to massage her shoulders.

"Honestly?"

"Don't play games, Sienna," he scorned. "It's childish, and you are beyond that in age and in mentality. I asked so I want to know...*honestly*. I just hope you don't say your sister again."

"Then I shouldn't speak my truth."

She leaned forward, causing his hands to slip away from her, and stacked the remaining napkins together in a bundle. It was Abaku's time to release a weighted sigh. His patience was growing thin with Sienna's mood swings. It seemed as if the more she came to terms with Dage's and Da'Jenna's deaths, the more forgiving she became. He was not into the forgiveness business and damn sure not the forgetting business either. He was in the revenge business, which would lead him back to the money business.

His family was adamant that he got rid of the threats in order to entrust him with free-flowing funds and to rid the world of Raphael and Essie because of their loss of Dage. He had no problem with either. His problem lay with the woman who claimed to have unconditional love for his brother and love for him and his family. Her sister was an enemy to them, and if she loved Dage, truly loved Dage, then she was an enemy of hers as well.

Walking around her, he slid one of the heavy oak chairs away from the table, pulled his pant leg up, and slowly lowered himself into the seat with his eyes trained on Sienna. For a brief moment, he took her in. How he wished he met her before his brother then none of this tension would even be a factor. To be honest, Dage didn't know what to do with a woman like Sienna. She needed structure and guidance then she wouldn't be so damn combative. She'd be obedient and truly submissive. Dage had let western ways influence her. Her father was to blame as well. Instead of securing men to handle his business, he'd groomed his daughters. So unconventional. Too unconventional. If he'd had her, she'd simply nod her head and open her legs. Thanks to Dage and Sienna's father, he was left with a woman who opened her mouth instead, entirely too much at that.

Leaning with his elbows on his knees, Abaku interlaced his fingers. "What is on your mind about your sister?"

Sienna turned to face him with slow hesitation. It was obvious he was going to have this conversation. She only hoped that this time she could convince him to see her viewpoint. Gently, she placed her hands over his hands and caressed them.

"Abaku, I understand your position about Essie. She was wrong. She was." Her head fell forward as she considered her next words. "But she was a woman blinded by love. I was the same way. I did anything Dage asked of me without question, because he was my man. She and I…we are extremely loyal…even to a fault. I know that her choices in a way assisted to the demise of Dage and even Da'Jenna."

This time she paused and rubbed her flattened belly. To her surprise, Abaku did the same. His hand atop hers was a surprise and even slightly welcomed. Though she loathed his touch these days, at this moment, she needed some form of affection, and Abaku was familiar. He resembled Dage in looks, and he did care for her. So, she allowed it without rejecting him. Besides, she didn't want to do anything that would stop him from dismissing her altogether.

"But it was ultimately Raphael who did this. He killed Dage and Da'Jenna. Essie would have never wished or wanted any harm to come to any of us. So, I feel as though we can spare her. Once she sees that I am alive, she'll never choose Raphael over me."

Abaku's head tilted to one side as he watched her incredulously. "How do you think that will happen? She already chose him over you. She will do that again."

"Because she is just like me. The guilt of my presumed death is eating away at her. I'm sure of it. If she knows that she can have me back, in her life, without Raphael, she'll choose me. I've known her my entire life. She won't turn her back on me again."

He stood and pushed the chair back under the table and shook his head. "You are such a fool. If she is blinded by love as you say, what the hell makes you believe she will suddenly regain sight? You are holding on to the memory of what she used to be to you, Sienna. She chose her path and her allegiance when she sided with that American."

"You weren't there. You didn't see her face or hear her pleas—"

"Enough!" Abaku's voice boomed startling her. He pointed his finger in her face. "This is the last time I am going to tell you to let this notion go. If you say you love my brother then you prove it by helping me get rid of Raphael and Essie."

With that, Abaku turned to walk away. Sienna jumped from her seat with her eyes full of tears. She knew better than to test him, but she couldn't help it. She knew that Abaku was set up to begin his attack, and if she didn't stop him, he'd rain down his brand of hell on her sister.

"If Dage were in Essie's position, what would you do? Would you kill your brother?"

Abaku spun on her with a swiftness that made his steps wild. Flames burned in his eyes. "I wouldn't have to find out. My brother would have never done that. Your sister did."

"So, you're telling me that if I told Dage that I didn't want him to pursue this mission because my sister's feelings were involved, that he would have gone against my wishes?"

This question caused Abaku to pause. Sienna saw the contemplation in his eyes. He wasn't sure of that answer. He didn't have to say anything. It was written all over his demeanor.

"Answer me, Abaku. You know your brother so much. You tell me. Would he have let me and Da'Jenna go, killed us if we went against what he wanted?"

Abaku swallowed the lump that had formed in his throat. As much as he loved his brother, he knew that Sienna had a point there. He would have backed away. He would have spared Essie and Raphael for his wife and children regardless of the threats, prison time, or financial ruin. He was a man that was dedicated to the people he loved most. Those he loved most were his wife and unborn child.

He waved her off. "It's neither here nor there."

She invaded his space without regard to his reaction. Gripping his arm, she flung it, making him turn back to face her. "Don't give me that hogwash. You know he wouldn't have turned his back on me. He would have done exactly what Essie did."

Becoming aware of her hand on his arm, she moved it, and Abaku walked up on Sienna, slowly backing her up in the corner of the dining room. "It does not matter what he would have done. He's not here to test the theory. That's what's important."

"And you're right, it is. But it's important to kill the person who actually killed him!" she yelled, her voice reaching the pinnacle of frustration. They stared at each other for a few moments before tears sprang in Sienna's eyes. "Today is her birthday, Abaku. She's my sister."

Abaku's eyes softened as he witnessed her pain. When her tears finally fell, he swiped them away with his thumbs. "She's the only family I have left. Please."

Her lip trembled at the thought. Abaku examined her with concerned eyes then slid his thumb across her trembling lip, wiping away the lone tear that clung to the plumpness of her bottom lip.

"Shhh," he coaxed at her whimpers.

"Please, Abaku. I'll do anything."

His eyes lit up like a Christmas tree at her statement. Although Sienna knew what that meant, she was prepared to accept it. His tongue slid across his lips, and a sinister smile spread across his face.

"Anything?"

She nodded. "*Anything.*"

He cupped a hand behind her neck and brought her to him. Their foreheads touched. "You drive me fucking insane, Sienna." He huffed. "Fine," he bit out through gritted teeth.

Elation spread through Sienna, and she breathed out a teary yet grateful, "Thank you."

His once-closed eyes lifted to stare back into hers and his expression was void of any emotion except lust. "Don't thank me yet," he breathed out.

With one hand, he unzipped his pants then reached inside and freed his throbbing manhood through the open hole. Without a word, he gripped her neck and pushed her downward. Sienna's heart stopped as she moved to her knees, but she couldn't deny him. She'd never indulged him in that way out of respect for Dage's memory. He'd understood that. However, she knew now that all bets were off. He was cashing in his chips, and she was the banker. He'd agreed to spare her sister's life, and she'd do anything for her sister. And so she did.

CHAPTER 11

"What are you doing back here?" Essie asked, startled as Raphael and Rhys walked through the front door of their home.

"Dad?" Kaion said, surprised, as he rushed to the living room from upstairs after hearing Essie's voice.

Rhys waved a hand at them. "Hi, Essie and Kaion."

They waved back but never took their focus off Raphael. He walked up to them and hugged each one of them.

Patting Kaion on the shoulder, he turned to him. "Let me holler at Essie for a moment. Once we talk, I'll come and talk to you."

Without a question or any hesitation, he turned and headed back up the stairs. Raphael smiled at his change in attitude. He was a great kid, but ever since the attack, he'd noticed the instant growth and maturity in him. It made him proud.

Facing Essie, he motioned for her to follow him into the kitchen. They sat down, and Essie was all ears. Rhys handed Raphael an envelope, and he placed it down in front of Essie and opened it.

"Tatiana was the one who linked up with the accomplices of Abaku for a payout of one hundred grand," Raphael explained without further ado. "These are pictures of her meeting the accomplice for the second half of the payout."

Essie's confused expression matched Raphael's when he first heard the news. She scooped the photos up, scanning through each one frantically. "But how? Why?" Then she suddenly threw the photos on the table and her eyes shot up with fire in them. "The basketball game!" She jumped up. "I'll kill that bitch."

Raphael stood and gripped her arms. "Look at me." He caressed her chin and turned her to look at him. "Don't worry about that. Rhys has that handled. What I need for you all to do is pack a quick bag. Grab the important papers and the necessities. You're going under protective custody until it's clear."

"Raph—"

"Essie." He interrupted her with a tone of finality. "This here is nonnegotiable."

A serious and surreal moment passed between them before Essie conceded and went to gather her things. As she scurried away to take care of the things they needed, Raphael headed up the stairs to relay the message to Kaion.

When Raphael opened Kaion's bedroom door, Kaion turned with clothing in his hands. Raphael gave him a confused stare.

"We gotta leave, right?"

"How'd you know?"

"I'm the son of Alexandria Gatts and the product of your raising. I knew the moment I saw you that something was up and whatever it is, it wasn't good."

Raphael walked up to him and agreed. "You're right. You're going into protective custody. Rhys is going to see to it that you all are taken care of. It was someone in my past that helped facilitate that attack that night, so we gotta cover all bases. You and Essie's security is my number one priority. Everything else comes secondary."

Kaion zipped up his Gucci bag and turned to face Raphael. "What about Shantrice?"

"I'm gonna have details watching her and her family. I don't believe she'll be in danger, but we have the precautions set up. You might wanna call her and let her know you have to go for a while. Don't give no details." He reached in his back pocket and lifted a phone. "A burner. It's important that you keep in contact with her for her sanity and yours. She can't have the number. She needs to answer when you call."

Kaion took the phone from his hands and slid into his pocket. "Thank you. I appreciate that. I'll let her know."

"Aight. You got any questions for me?"

"Where are we headed?"

"California. I know it's far—"

Kaion put his hand up. "No need to explain. At least with you, I know it's for the best. When will we see you again?"

Raphael placed a hand on his shoulder and squeezed. "Soon, son. Soon."

With that, he left Kaion to finish his packing and met Rhys back down the stairs. Rhys and he discussed the particulars with Essie. Before long, a federal agent pulled up and, once he gained clearance with Rhys, he came in and loaded Essie and Kaion's belongings. They said their goodbyes to Raphael, and then they were escorted off to their new temporary location.

"Ensure they get there safely," Raphael ordered to Rhys as they left out.

"I will. It's a promise." Rhys glanced up at him. "You ready?"

"Been ready."

Tatiana giggled as she stumbled out of her BMW while on the phone. She could barely stand up straight in her stilettos as she made her way to her condo. The mixture of patron and other alcohol sloshed around in her belly as she attempted to flirt while she fumbled with her keys. Finally opening her front door, she trudged through with her cellphone pressed to her ear.

"So, when are you coming over, baby?" she giggled. "I'm in this hot dress, my skank heels, and I'm moist just for you."

Suddenly, her phone was removed from her hand, and she saw bits and pieces of it on the floor. When she turned around, she saw some Italian man standing behind her.

She landed a slap across the man's face. "My phone! What the fuck?" With a smirk, he rubbed his face. "Who the fuck are you? And how the fuck did you get into my place?"

Then a light turned on and she spun around to find Raphael sitting in the corner of the living room. He was wearing all black, just like the intruder. She smiled at first, happy to see him. Happy that he was alive. As fast as her smile came, so did her frown. He appeared menacing. She'd never seen the look in his eyes. Well, she had, but never toward her. Always toward some man in the streets. This caused her to pause, and she looked at him with dismay.

"What...what are you doing here, Raph? You could have called me."

"Oh, a phone call would have ruined the surprise."

Tatiana swallowed the lump in her throat and wrapped her arms around herself. "Why are you here, Raph? And who is this?" The words came out with a tremble.

Raphael gestured with his hand to the sofa to the right side of her. "Why don't you have a seat?"

Stepping back, she looked back and forth between the two men. Then shook her head. "No, why? What's going on?"

Tonio gripped her and pushed her toward the sofa. Tatiana tried to fight him, but between Tonio's brute strength and her drunkenness, she couldn't. She went to scream, and Tonio gripped his massive hand around her mouth, and the sounds came out as little more than muffled whimpers. Tonio shoved her down on the sofa. She attempted to jump off the sofa, and Tonio shoved her back down with one massive foot.

"Sit the fuck down," Raphael boomed.

Tatiana's head whipped toward him with a heated protest on her lips—until she saw the gun in his hand pointed directly at her. Her lips buttoned shut, and she eased back on her sofa.

Fear struck her and she rubbed her hands together to stop the shaking that had begun. "What are you doing?"

Tonio sat down on the sofa beside her with an envelope in his hands. Tatiana stared at him then back at Raphael. When she went to ask another question, Raphael interrupted her.

"We go far back, Tatiana. From the same hood. Went through the same struggles. Came up in the mud together."

"Yeah, Raph, we—"

He held up a finger, pausing whatever she was about to say. "And I know we ain't always been on the best terms and shit, but we had our time. We had an understanding. We had our own hustles and our own come up. We led our own lives. You were the only person I had in my past that I could look back on and feel a sense of nostalgia for. You were the only bright spot in my fucked-up past. For that, I remained loyal to you. Even when you pissed me off—and you had many ways and times that you pissed me all the way off, I never turned my back on you. I let you have your pettiness even to the detriment of my wife at times. Any other muthafucka, man or woman, who dared think about disrespecting my wife, would never be able to tell the story. But you, I gave the benefit of the doubt. It's fucked up, I know. But it's how I am built. Once I'm loyal to someone, I don't become disloyal until they prove they are no good to me. And you know I don't trust or care for a lot of muthafuckas, but you I let breathe no matter what you did because I cared about you and your wellbeing."

Nervousness caused her to whimper, and she nodded. "You're right, Raph. You are."

"Oh, I know." He scratched his head with the tip of the gun. "That's what has me baffled. For the life of me, I can't understand why of all people to betray, you'd choose me."

Her hands flew up. "I don't know what you mean, Raph—"

The slap of the envelope in her lap cut off the statement as her attention diverted to what Tonio had placed down on her. She picked it up, opened it, and slid the photos out of the envelope. After she flipped through the first few, her eyes widened, and she glanced back up at Raphael.

"I don't know…where did you…what—"

"You already betrayed me, Tatiana. Spare me the insult of my intelligence."

Tears sprang to her eyes and her chest heaved up and down as she wiped them, but the tears just kept flowing. "Raphael, I needed the money."

Raphael's bottom lip curled upward as he slightly nodded at her words. That's when he lifted the silencer in his other hand and began screwing it on the gun. "Money, huh?"

Pleading with her hands, she cried, "Please, Raphael. I'm sorry. It's me. Tatiana. I didn't know what was going to happen. You have to believe that."

"I believe what I see. I believe what I know. I know that's you in those photos. I know you received one hundred grand to identify me and my family, and I know that some man named Enu helped you that had something to do with another man named Abaku. Do you know who Abaku is?"

"No." She shook her head fiercely.

"He wants me dead, probably my wife, too."

Tatiana's head fell forward in dismay. The tears that had managed to stop began falling again. As they streaked down her face, she pleaded again with Raphael. "I had no clue. They said you wouldn't be hurt. I'm so sorry, Raphael. Please forgive me."

Raphael stood from the seat and walked toward her slowly. Once he was directly in front of her, he pulled her up to him and gripped her neck with one hand. "Oh, my Tatiana."

Tatiana recognized the dark stare in his eyes. Murder was the case that his eyes held in that mode. She'd known many a man who fell victim to death's fate when Raphael had the dark gloom filtered in his face.

"No, no," she pleaded, trying to back away from him.

It was of no use. He held her close and in place despite her protests. Removing his hand that held her neck, he brought his index finger to his lips. "Shhh. I promise it will be painless."

"Raphael, please." Fear danced in her eyes as tears dripped down her face.

"Shhh."

He closed his eyes, covering her lips with his hand and leaned his head against her forehead. With the gun gripped in his hand, he squeezed the trigger. *Pfff. Pfff.* Her widened eyes stared back at him as he held her neck. She gasped for breath, trying to scream or say something but was unable to with blood filling her lungs.

"Shhh, Tatiana." Raphael's eyes watered a bit as he stared at the light leaving her eyes. "You're almost there. It's almost over. You'll be there soon." As her eyes began to dilate, he whispered, "I forgive you."

The light extinguished, and staring at him were empty eyes. He let go, and her body slipped from him and slumped over on the sofa. Tonio picked up the photos and envelope and then stared back at Raphael.

"Good job. Didn't know if you had the balls to do it."

"I always have the balls. I just need a reason."

Tonio stuck out his fist, and Raphael bumped it. "Fair enough." He looked back at Tatiana's dead body on the sofa. "It's your call."

"Burn that bitch." Raphael ordered before Tonio placed the call and they walked out of the condo the same way they came in, undetected.

CHAPTER 12

Abaku stood at the door of his family's mansion, being led inside by armed guards. With the blessing of the Sabis, his mother's side of the family, they had granted him the funds, guards, arms, and intel, he needed to rejuvenate his business. Now, he was visiting his father, the Dages, so he could advise of his preparation to avenge Dage's death. His father had banished him for what he'd allowed to happen to Dage. It'd taken a while, but he knew once he proved that he was in a position to take down Raphael that he'd concede his ill feelings and greenlight him to do what needed to be done.

As he strode up to his father's office, he was excited yet nervous. His father, Bio Dage, had been no one to play around with. He'd always taken care of home, been the perfect husband to his wife Delilah, Dage's mother, and loved his sons immensely—though that allegiance sometimes proved more beneficial to Dage than to him. He knew his father loved him. However, he seriously doubted if the shoe were on the other foot that he would have barred his brother. They were so proud of him they never even referred to him by his first name, only his surname. Not that it made much difference. Dage was named after their father. He took the "junior" as Bio Dage, Jr. Abaku Dage was the oldest but was bypassed for that honor.

He used to be offended by it, but as he got older, and gained control of the business over his brother, he let the notion go.

Besides, he was the one in control, and Dage was his right-hand man. At least that honor was not stripped from him. Until Dage wound up dead. Now, he had to prove that he was worthy. And he would. He'd work hard to regain his father's confidence in him, by vindicating his brother's death.

Once Abaku entered, his father came into his private study from a private and secure entrance. When Bio saw Abaku, his face was stern, but Abaku caught the surprise in his eyes. "Ahh, the prodigal son returns," his father announced. "To what do I owe to this presence?"

Abaku bowed to him and then stood to state his case. "I wanted to report to you that I have had my business and funding reinstated. I am back in the position to take out the man who is responsible for Dage's death. I will avenge his death, father, and honor our family name."

"Do you have a plan in motion?" His baritone voice boomed.

"Yes, father. We are planning an attack on the American and his family in the next couple of days in Indiana. The son plays high school basketball, so it shouldn't be that difficult to locate them. I already have a play in motion on that part."

"Good. Good. The kid?"

Abaku understood the vague question as assurance that Raphael's son wouldn't be a problem. "He's about to graduate. He'll be good. Remember, he is only their adopted son. He's the biological son of that Alex woman who got offed in prison. I'm sure he has a trust to survive. He won't be a threat. He's not about this life and had nothing to do with all of this. My contacts confirmed that Raphael and Essie didn't get custody until after Alex's death, which was after Dage was killed."

Bio walked around his desk and sat on the front edge of it watching me closely. "And what of Essie? She's just as much to blame as Dage."

"I think Essie does not have to be disposed of. Raphael pulled the trigger. Essie was a lapdog caught in the middle of all this."

Bio stood, and his towering and unsympathetic presence smoldered Abaku. "Let's be clear, Abaku. Essie was an operative working with the Americans. She is just as much to blame. Even if Dage hadn't died, she was still a traitor to our people. It was that betrayal that laid the foundation for the death of Dage. She must go."

Abaku cleared his throat. Although he didn't want to spare Essie either, he'd made a promise to Sienna. He wanted to betray that promise, but over the months his heart had grown soft to her. He never allowed her to see that part because she'd take advantage, but he wanted to do something for her. She's the one that had lost the most in all this anyway.

Bio pointed his finger in Abaku's chest. "Were you not gung-ho to off Essie just as much as this Raphael?" Before Abaku could answer, a menacing smile graced Bio's face as he leaned forward in Abaku's face and wagged his forefinger in the air. "My daughter-in-law put you up to this, no?" Then he put his hand up to stop him from speaking. "You were to keep her in your back pocket and use her to complete the mission. I don't care if you are fucking your dead brother's widow. You can find more pussy. If her allegiance is no longer to the Dages then there is no use for her, either."

An air of surprise flashed in Abaku's face. He gave him an incredulous stare. "You would kill Dage's wife? He loved her. She carried his child."

"And what good did that do, Dage? His wife's family is responsible for his death and my grandchild. That reason alone should keep Sienna's allegiance to us," he boomed. "She is no use to us if she is not willing to sacrifice her sister. She's lucky she's even breathing now. She's indebted to the Dages. We funded her lush life, only to have her turn her back on us?" He banged his fist on his desk. "I will not allow it. Either Essie dies too, or I will kill them both with my bare hands." He gave him a stern glare. "And if I have to do it, don't you ever worry about gracing my front doorsteps again, or you will join them."

Abaku stood up straight, a clear understanding of his responsibilities. Although he understood the position that Sienna was in, he also understood his father's position. His father was the one person he could never cross, and his father had laid the ultimatum down. He'd have to do what he had to do. Sienna would have to understand. He'd take care of her, and she'd always be under the protection of the Dages. Once this was done, he'd not only have the keys to the kingdom from his mother's family but also from his father's. He'd be unstoppable. He'd rule with his business and schemes and be sure that he and Sienna were set for life. With Dage gone, his father had no choice but to make him heir to the Dage throne. No one was going to interfere with that, not Sienna and damn sure not Essie.

"Are we clear?" Bio asked sternly.

"Precisely."

Abaku and his security detail returned to their vehicle, and as they drove away, he sat in the backseat and scrubbed his hand down his face. His frustration was over the play that he'd have to make. He didn't necessarily disagree, but he didn't particularly agree, either. However, the ball was no longer in his court. Essie had decided her fate the moment she chose Raphael over Sienna. It wasn't his fault if she had to lie in the bed she'd made. He'd strong-armed Sienna thus far; he had no doubt he could continue to do so. When he considered all the factors of his power, influence, and money that he stood to gain from the completion of this mission, his conflicted feelings began to subside into personal joy. Settled on his decision, he picked up his burner cell and put the order in place.

"Is everything in place?" Abaku asked when his operative answered.

"We just need the word."

"Make the call, gain access to the location, and bring back my meal on a platter," Abaku directed.

"And the sides?"

"Only one side order, the woman."

"Consider it done." The man on the other end hung up. Dage turned off the cell and a sinister smile unfurled.

CHAPTER 13

Killing Tatiana fucked with Raphael in the worst way. She was the only person left with whom he'd established a long-term personal connection. He loved his wife, and she was his everything, but Tatiana and he had history. They'd always been there for each other in a crazy love-hate way, but he'd thought even in hate there was always an understanding. He clearly had her pegged wrong. Frustratingly, her betrayal had no effect on how he felt for her. He'd never had to lay down a person he was loyal to or loved, and that messed his head up.

He prayed he'd never have to do it again. There were only two people left that he had a deep connection to anyway, Kaion and Essie. He'd allow them to snuff him out before he would ever lay them down, no matter what they did.

The vibration of his cell phone brought his thoughts back to the current situation. Peeping at the line, he answered. "Hello?"

"Just checking in. You good?" Rhys's voice filtered through the mobile device.

"Yeah, I'm almost here." Raphael informed him. "I appreciate you allowing me to ensure that my family is settled and safe."

"No worries. You're doing me a solid. I figured I owed you one as well." Rhys took a deep breath. "The car will be there Sunday morning—"

"I'll be ready." Raphael interrupted him, letting him know his allegiance was still to OMECA and their mission.

"I trust you." Rhys stood up from his desk and peered out of the window. "They'll be fine, Raphael. We'll be sure of it."

Raphael took in his words. If Abaku could get to Tatiana, he had little faith in Rhys, the CIA, or OMECA to keep his family safe. Rather than agree or disagree, he finished up the call. "Let me handle this business and on Sunday, I'll be back on the other business."

When Raphael pulled up to the safe house that housed Essie and Kaion, he felt somewhat better. It was a neighborhood very similar to their own. Very unassuming. To their neighbors, it was simply a mother and son who moved from Florida because of a job transfer due to the pandemic. Their names were Janet Morris and Brian Morris. Two very common names, so they would be harder to locate.

As Ralph walked up to the ranch-styled home, he waved at the next-door neighbor out watering his lawn. The neighbor was an undercover agent with the CIA, a plant decoy who pretended to be the brother of the owner of the home, who came to visit when he was stateside from traveling overseas with his business. The neighbor waved back and bent down as if he were planting flowers, so he could inconspicuously radio in Raphael's arrival.

When Raphael got to the door, he did the assigned knock, telling Essie it was safe to answer. When she did, she gasped slightly, but played it coolly, stepping back to allow Raphael to come inside the house. As soon as the door was closed, and they entered the living room, she jumped into his arms. They embraced for what seemed like hours, until Raphael put her down and planted a longing kiss on her lips.

"What are you doing here?" she said in a hushed tone.

"I had to check out the situation for myself. I don't like the fact that you all had to pack up and leave without me. I can't have my head in the operation if I can't confirm the safety of my family."

He held her face between the palms of his hands taking in every feature of her face. "Where is Brian?"

"Right here," Kai answered from up the stairs.

Raphael spun around and motioned for him to come to him, and he did. Once they were face-to-face, they slapped hands together, and Raphael reeled him in for an embrace. "You've been taking care of Janet?"

"Of course." His voice brimmed with pride.

Essie wrapped her arm around Kaion's shoulder. "He is just as protective as you. You trained him very well. I'm proud of him."

Kaion smiled at her, and Raphael nodded his approval. "Aight, kiddo. Run upstairs for a bit. Let me holler at Janet."

Kaion nodded and obeyed. When he was back upstairs, Raphael walked around the home, inspecting every aspect of the house, even the fake pictures and figurines. "Good. So, everyone has been straight? Everything good?"

"We have not heard a peep. We've been watched well. Just missing you," Essie said, running her hand up down his back.

Raphael turned to face her and rubbed his forefinger down her face. "I miss y'all, too."

Essie shuttered at his touch. Their hands grazed each other as they interlocked fingers. She stepped into his space and whispered in his ear. "When do you leave?"

Raphael kissed her forehead and mumbled, "Sunday morning."

"Well, I guess we should use tonight to welcome you home properly." She twirled around slowly.

Rubbing his hands together, his lip bite came from watching her sexy ass in shorts and a tank top. Everything was hitting in all the right places. Raphael couldn't wait to peel those clothes off her and have a taste. He made up in his mind that Abaku's repentance would come from the barrel of gun, not so-called prison rehabilitation. His family would be running forever as long as Abaku was breathing. He couldn't have them in harm's way for the rest of their lives. Not on his watch.

He pulled Essie to him with an arm around her waist. Mesmerized by each other, they began to sway to the imaginary beat only they could hear. Stepping in time to the beat of each other's hearts, Raphael fell in love all over again—not that he'd ever fallen out. This situation was a stanch reminder of how precious life and love were. He felt it in his core.

Twirling her around, Raphael said, "I'd love to, but you gotta feed your man first. That was a long flight and ride over."

Essie giggled, placing her hands on her hips. "That's what I'm trying to do."

He burst into laughter, and Essie swatted him. They played around like school kids with crushes before she busied herself in the kitchen to prepare the two favorite men in her life their dinner. During that time, Raphael sat and enjoyed both Essie and Kaion. He didn't want to burden them with anything but rather show them joy. Put all of their weary souls at ease for just one night. Be normal again. That's exactly what they did. They talked, played board games, ate dinner, and watched a movie together, just like old times.

Afterward, Essie led Raphael upstairs to her bedroom. As soon the door was locked, they nearly attacked each other with wild passion. Tearing at each other's clothing, they didn't stop until they were both stripped bare as they stood kissing and exploring one another again. It felt as if they were rediscovering themselves. Easing her back onto the bed, Raphael took in her body in wonderment. How'd he get so blessed to have a woman as sexy as Essie? She glistened like a black diamond. Beauty, confidence, strength, and love radiated from her. It was the only time he regretted coming to check on them. Witnessing her in all her glory would only make it harder to leave them when the time came.

Kissing his way down the length of her, Essie's head fell back and she bit her lip to quell her moans. As Raphael reached the apex of her love, he captured her throbbing bud between his lips and softly suckled on her pearl.

"Raph," she moaned.

Her noises fueled him as he lapped up her flowing juices, determined not to miss a drop. He was feasting on that pearl as if it was his last meal. He was going to go away full and completely satisfied, and so was Essie. She gripped his head and pushed it further down, signaling she wanted him to plant his whole face there. She squeezed her legs, gripping his head in place, and released a rain shower of love into his mouth.

"Agh… agh…Raph. Oh my God."

Hearing her come undone brought out the beast in him. He eased up her body, tossed one of her legs over his shoulders and went to work. Slapping against her wetness, he pounded in and out of her. The smacking sound of their juices colliding, and the feel of her insides, made him brick up more.

"You feel so damn good," Raphael grunted.

He moved her leg from his shoulder to his waist, grinding deeply and filling her up to the hilt. She gripped his back and tightened her legs. All she could do was enjoy this ride and bask in the glow of their love.

"Raph, I'm cumming, baby. Ooh, it feels so…fucking…good," she bellowed, and her love came down, drenching him.

Gazing into her eyes, he reaffirmed his love. "God, I love you, Essie. I swear I love you so much." With that, he released with a low growl.

He collapsed beside her, pulling her into his arms. No words were exchanged. The only noise heard was the rise and fall of their ragged breathing. Soon, those breaths serenaded them into a peaceful sleep as they marinated in their love.

The next morning, Raphael dragged into the kitchen. The smell of coffee, bacon, eggs, and waffles greeted him. When he reached the kitchen, shirtless and in his joggers, Kaion and Essie both greeted him. They were almost done with their meals.

"Well, you look like crap," Kaion joked. "That West Coast time got you zapped out, huh?"

Tousling his hair, Raphael chuckled. "Something like that." He winked at Essie, and she stifled a giggle behind her coffee mug.

"Let me get up and grab you a cup and a plate," Essie said, moving to get out of her chair.

Raphael placed his hand up. "No, you're good, baby. Sit. Eat. I got it."

He made him a cup of coffee, black with two teaspoons of sugar, then made a plate of waffles and eggs. That bacon was calling his name, but he left it for Essie and Kaion. He was practicing cleaner eating, starting with the meats he chose to put in his body. This new mission needed his mind and body to be at its best. When he sat at the table, he prayed then shoveled a forkful into his mouth.

"Baby, as always, you do your thing." He leaned over and kissed her forehead.

"Thank you, baby."

Raphael then turned his focus on Kaion. "So, Kai, what do you have planned for today?" he asked.

"Nothing, same as most days. I typically play basketball in the back, read, or play on the PlayStation."

Nodding, Raphael said, "Okay, well, today, we'll head out back and do some exercising together. Keep our minds fresh and our bodies tight. What'd you say to that?"

Kaion agreed. "It's cool. I'm down with it." He placed the last bite of waffle in his mouth with a head nod.

"Aight. Bet. I got you, homie." Raphael held out his fist, and he and Kaion touched knuckles, sealing the deal.

When Kaion left to go upstairs to get dressed for their workout, Essie walked over to Raphael and sat in the chair beside him. She placed a loving hand on his arm and gently rubbed.

"Thank you for spending some one-on-one time with Kaion while you're here. He misses Indiana. He can't talk to his friends or his girlfriend. He has no one here besides me, and even though I know he loves me, I'm not the same as someone he can really enjoy. Also, he's a teen, and I have to go everywhere he goes until this calms down. It's a lot for him. He does not speak on it, but I know it is. He needs this time with you." She stood and kissed his cheek. "I love you, Raph."

Lifting her hand to his lips, he kissed the back of it tenderly. "I love you more. Both of you."

After an hour, Raphael and Kaion went in the backyard and completed a thirty-minute workout regimen specifically for strength and endurance. Both of them were a little winded once they finished, but for the most part, they were refreshed and running on all cylinders. Raphael was proud of his son for keeping up. He knew that it was all the basketball training that he'd had that helped him.

"Tell me. How are you feeling out here in Cali?"

Picking up his bottled water, he took a long swig then hunched his shoulders. "I mean, it's cool. I guess."

The side eye that Raphael cast at Kaion caused him to recoil.

"You know you can't bullshit me," Raphael said. "We straight up, always. Remember that." He pointed Kaion.

"I wanna like it, but it's hard. I miss my friends…my girl. Shantrice went through this with me, and I feel like I left her out in the cold. I don't even know how she truly feels because our goodbye was so quick. And my team. I abandoned them before the biggest game of our lives, and all I could say was that it was a family emergency," he said, his voice squeaking with a mixture of sadness and anger as he took a deep breath before continuing. "Now, I'm here, and I don't know anyone. I can't do anything. Then, when I can, it's always with Es—Janet." He paused, sighing in frustration at almost forgetting their aliases. "She's cool, but I don't want to be joined at her hip. Truthfully, she probably does not want to be joined at mine, either. Then there's the whole I-can't-be-me thing."

Raphael stood from the workout bench and eased over to Kaion, prompting him to stand up. He embraced him tightly. "Don't ever think I don't understand. I do. And I'm sorry. You've been through so much. I wanted to add positivity to your life, not more misery."

Kaion was so overwhelmed by the words Raphael spoke that he broke down in his arms. It was the apology he didn't even know he needed. No one, not even his mother and Aunt Shayne, had ever bothered to find out how he truly felt and how it affected him.

Raphael didn't release Kaion until his tears had subsided. He understood better than anyone the need for a young man to have a shoulder to cry on and the open space to do so without judgment or interference. He hadn't had that in anyone until he was grown, and by then, the damage had already been done. Had it not been for the love of Essie and Kaion, he'd be a ruthless, soulless, murderous bastard. And he would have been perfectly fine with that. Their love transformed him. He was still all that, but now with purpose, not with malice. It was a part of him that he could shut off for them and because of them. A part that he hoped that one day he could keep turned off. A part that he hoped that wasn't reignited by the upcoming mission.

"You good, baby boy?"

Kaion wiped the remaining tears and nodded. "I didn't mean to cry—"

Raphael put his hand up, and then gripped Kaion gently about the shoulder. "Don't you ever apologize for shedding tears. Real men cry too. If not, you'll be just as fucked up as I and the other string of men who don't know how to process emotions. Get that shit up off your chest. Tears are good for the soul. Understand?"

Kaion eyed him and answered, "I understand."

"Now, I'm gonna show you something else that will build your brain, muscles, and reaction time, and help reframe your thoughts," Raphael said as he dug into his bag and brought out boxing mitts for them both.

Confusion graced Kaion's face as he caught a set and look at the gloves. "How to box?" he questioned Raphael.

"How to fight and defend yourself. If it comes down to it, I need to know that you know how to get someone off you until help comes." He walked up close to him. "Also, some kill moves, but don't tell *Janet*."

Kaion and he laughed at him referring to Essie as Janet. Then Kaion got serious and gave him a worried gaze. "You really think it'll come down to that?"

"I'ma try my damnedest not to let it come to that, but in the event it does, I need you to be prepared. Preparedness is my responsibility. Yours is learning. So, pay attention."

For the next couple of hours, Raphael sparred with Kaion, showing him technique after technique. His final lesson was showing him quick moves on how to disable a gun and then how to kill a person with his hands. By the time they finished, Kaion was exhausted, so Raphael told him to wash up and rest the remainder of the day.

Raphael eased into the living room where Essie sat reading and kissed her cheek.

"Y'all done for today?" she asked.

"Yep," he answered, drinking a large gulp of water.

"And you took care of him?" Essie asked, flipping a page.

"Of course. He's straight now. The transition is still difficult, but he was able to relieve some pressure, so that's good."

"Great." Essie smiled up at him before he moved to ascend the stairs. "And Raph? The next time you want to teach Kaion how to do kill moves, inform me. You're his father, but I'm still the mama bear." She fanned her hands between them. "We clear?"

Raphael threw his hands up in surrender. "Perfectly."

CHAPTER 14

Abaku had been in an unusually good mood for the past couple of days. So good, in fact, that no matter what Sienna asked, he was game. She found his behavior strange, but she let it go and enjoyed the moments. He was treating her like a man who cared for his woman, and she preferred that versus the uptight, angry, and abusive man she'd known him to be.

Currently, she lay in front of the television with her feet sprawled across his lap. He rubbed her feet gently as they watched a movie on the tube. Near the ending of the movie, Abaku's phone buzzed, and he lifted it to see who was calling. Sienna could feel the energy shift immediately. When he tapped her feet, signaling for her to move them so he could get up, she mouthed the words, "What's wrong?"

Rather than answer, he threw up his forefinger, signaling her to give him a moment. Sienna knew better than to say a word, so she sat quietly. He didn't say a word but rather got up and walked away. Sienna watched the back of him as he stalked down the long hallway on the way to his office. Even though she had no clue what had happened, she felt a sinking feeling in her spirit. Easing off the sofa, she quietly tiptoed down the hall.

Shutting the door to his office, he could barely contain his anger as he spewed, "What the fuck do you mean they're not there?" Abaku pressed the cellphone to his face with a death grip on his device.

"Exactly what I meant," his contact reiterated. "He's not at the home. Neither is the woman. We've checked the school and areas that they normally frequent for the past two days. They are ghosts. All of them."

"Shit!" Abaku spat, slinging his phone across the room. Luckily, it didn't shatter. He paced for a few moments with his hands on his hips before he walked to the phone and retrieved it. "Hello?"

"I'm still here."

Abaku ran his fingers across his forehead. "I don't give a damn what you have to do. You put every available resource on this shit. You find his ass. Her, too. I'll call you in forty-eight hours, and when I do, I better have a pleasant report. I want his head on a fucking platter. Do you understand?"

"Understood."

———

Sienna's anxiety heightened. She'd heard Abaku say two words that she knew was meant for her sister: "her, too." He'd promised that Essie would be safe, but she knew that his intent for her was ill-fated. There was no way she could let her sister get caught up in the rapture with Raphael. She had to find a way to get a message to her. She could give a damn about her man, but she'd do whatever she could to save her sister. When she heard Abaku's footsteps, she hurriedly crept back to the living room and sprawled across the sofa, pretending to have dozed off.

When she felt Abaku sit underneath her again, she slowly lifted and stretched her arms outward as if she were just waking up.

"Everything all right?"

Abaku rubbed the back of his head and stood again. He walked in front of her and unbuckled his pants, allowing them to drop to his ankles. Grabbing her by the neck, he forcefully pulled her close to him.

"It will be," he practically growled out. Looking down at her with eyes that spoke his intent, he demanded, "Please me, Sienna."

Moving his hand up from her neck to her hair, he gripped a handful and pulled out his manhood with the other, tapping the tip against her lips. "Open up."

Sienna obeyed. She couldn't give him any reason to believe she'd heard his conversation, and his mood was one in which she knew she shouldn't argue. Taking a deep breath, she licked her lips and swallowed deeply before she parted her lips and inhaled him into her warm mouth.

"Ahhh, yes. Suck me just like that," he moaned with his head thrown backward.

She forced herself into it. She had to make the moment believable for him. Perhaps if he felt she were fully invested in him, he'd go easy on her sister. In fact, perhaps her feminine wiles were enough to get him to cancel his plans altogether. She hoped so. There was only one way to find out. She put on the performance of her life, and when Abaku released his seed into her mouth, she gobbled all of his essence down to the last creamy drop.

"Shit! Fuck! Sienna! Siennaaa!" He gripped her head in place as his frustrations oozed down the back of her throat. When she lifted her head and wiped the corners of her lips, he stared back at her with lustful eyes. "Take off your dress."

His command came out gruffly and seriously. Lifting slightly from her seated position, she pulled the soft material up and over her head, exposing her matching lace bra and panty set. Without a word, Abaku pulled her about the wrist to a standing position before spinning her around and pushing her on her knees on the sofa. He clawed at her lace panties, shredding them in the process. Before she could brace herself, he'd slid into her womanhood, filling her to the hilt.

"Shiitttt," he groaned, pausing to control his throbbing dick.

Gripping her about the waist, he began a slow grind in and out of her succulence. When she moistened against him, he began to pump wildly in and out of her. His rhythm was frenzied but not barbaric. He couldn't get enough of Sienna. He knew that his main reason for this impromptu sexual tryst was to clear his frustrations over the failed hit on Raphael. However, his need for her kept him planted there. The way her body's response to him turned him on was otherworldly. Watching her match him thrust for thrust, combined with her sweet soft moans, brought him over the edge. He tried to withhold his words, but his release was so powerful he couldn't hold back the words he belted out.

"Fuck, Siennaaa!" He dug his fingertips in her flesh and held her in place against him. "I fucking love you!"

He wanted to reel the words back in, but they were out there now. And yes, he meant them. Admittedly, it was the reason he didn't know if he could bring himself to take her out, despite the fact that she wanted him to spare her treacherous sister. He hadn't meant to fall for her, his brother's wife, but he had. Still, he would not address it. To address it meant he had to accept it for what it was.

Easing from inside of her, he lifted his pants and pulled them about his waist without saying another word. He felt Sienna's eyes on him, but never acknowledged her gaze.

Softly, she whispered to him, "What did you say?"

"Nothing."

Turning to sit at the edge of the sofa, Sienna rubbed her hands together and stared up at him. "Abaku—"

"Enough, Sienna!" His hand went up to halt the conversation and his tone held a finality that should have made her cease and desist.

Sienna knew that she had to make him discuss this. She was smart enough to understand that this moment was her holy grail—the only playing cards she had left in the deck. If she could play them right, she'd could come out victorious in this situation.

"Abaku, please. We should talk about this. We need to."

Burgeoning with anger born of embarrassment, he turned to face her and spewed, "Why? So I can listen to you declare your undying love for my dead brother?"

He knew the words were wrong. He felt the pang in his own heart when they flowed from his lips. The light gasp that escaped Sienna was confirmation of that. He loved his brother and had never wanted to disrespect him or his memory, but he couldn't help that he'd fallen for his widow. How could he not?

Abaku paced, rubbing his head. He was pissed about the situation with Raphael, pissed about the words he'd spoken, and pissed about the fact that Sienna had his heart and loins twisted so goddamn tight he couldn't see the forest for the trees.

She stood and slowly approached him in all her naked glory. She spoke gently, "All of this time, I thought you were only using me for your advantage. I had no idea you felt this way."

"Get dressed. We're not talking about this. I have business to attend to—"

Sienna stood in his space and captured his face between her hands. The sudden movement stopped his words as they stared into each other's eyes. She searched the depths of him, looking for any sign of deception and found none.

"Do you love me, Abaku?"

He pinched his lips together, refusing to give her the information she wanted to hear. He'd slipped once. He wouldn't do it again. He couldn't and wouldn't tolerate the rejection from her. Regardless of how she felt about his brother, he was deceased, and regardless of how she felt about him, she was his. He'd keep her no matter what. As long as she stayed in line, he'd protect her from the threat of the Dages and anyone else. He had no doubt that she would do that because she had no one else. Therefore, discussing his feelings was a moot point. She belonged to him by forced circumstance. That was enough for him.

When her lips touched his, he had to open his eyes to be sure the moment was real. Uncertainty and disbelief gripped him as he pulled back staring at her with doubtful eyes. Her gaze softened to him, and in return, she reflected love in hers. Confusion etched his brow as he was stuck between reading the moment correctly yet not believing it for what it was. Testing the waters, he wrapped one arm around her waist and pulled her against him. His hand slid down to her bare ass and palmed it as he used his other hand to lift her chin with his forefinger. He furrowed his brow when he searched her eyes again. This time she bit her lip with a sexy assurance that gave him the greenlight that he'd lowkey been hoped for. Taking the bait, he planted a deep kiss on her lips, and she deepened the kiss pulling his tongue into her mouth. He wrapped his other arm around her waist, committing fully to the moment, and she wrapped her arm around his neck, drawing him nearer.

Moans escaped them as he backed her back to the sofa, but she spun him so that his back faced the sofa. Unbuckling his pants again, they fell to his ankles and his man down below sprang forth, ready for action. Sienna pushed Abaku on the sofa, and he plopped down with a thud. A smile crept across his face as she straddled him.

"This is what you want?"

Understanding his reference, she nodded. "I didn't know how to tell you that I had fallen too." She lowered her eyes. "I thought you'd think me as a Jezebel of sorts."

He lifted her chin. "Never look down when speaking to me."

She held his gaze, and she could physically see him falling over the edge for her. She may have been his captive up to this point, but now, he was hers. He licked his lips. Happiness spread through his core; for once, he had what he wanted on his own terms.

"You are mine," he said possessively.

"That's exactly what I want to be," she whispered against his lips. "As long as I have you, there is nothing else I need, Abaku. Let me be yours, please?"

He closed his eyes. In order to have something real with her, he realized he had to be honest with her. Accepting that, he opened his eyes and stared at her. "My plan is the same. I will kill Raphael for my brother, but I cannot save your sister. The family wants her head. I do, too." He gripped her chin between the cuff of his hand. "But you are mine."

Gulping, Sienna nodded ever so slowly. "I understand. She chose Raphael over me. I wanted to save her, but I can't lose out on my second chance at love. You don't have to threaten me, Abaku. I accept your terms willingly." She removed his hand from her chin and kissed him all about his face. "I am yours."

With that, she sank down onto him, and he fell into the rapture of Sienna. Love swelled through him as she rode him into ecstasy. His allegiance was to his Sienna, above all, and he'd murder anyone who dared attempt to separate him from what was finally his.

"I love you, Sienna," he bellowed in the throes of their passion.

"And I, you, Abaku."

CHAPTER 15

In the days since declaring their love for each other, Abaku had opened up completely to Sienna about their plan for Raphael and Essie and what had usurped that plan. What he thought was an easy fix had not been. Abaku's team had been unable to locate Raphael or his family, which had sent him on a rampage. From all their research they had only deduced one fact: Raphael and his family were no longer in Indiana. While important, that information was not helpful in their ability to execute his plan, and Abaku had been on a vengeful path with his team, who were supposed to have been keeping tabs on him. He'd even gone so far as to poke out the eye of the main informant in front of his other men. He had to set an example, to prove a point to everyone around him.

In the past, Abaku had lived in the shadows. He'd crafted the schemes, but it was Dage who was the initiator. To most, it appeared that Dage was in charge, and Abaku was nothing more than his brotherly sidekick. Not only did Abaku have to prove that he could take down Raphael, but that he had been the mastermind all along. His team's incompetence made him fall short, and the only consolation he had was that he was man enough for Sienna.

"Fuck!" He slammed the phone down on the table after finding yet another dead end on his attempt to locate Raphael.

Sienna, who had been sitting there witnessing the entire exchange, stood from her seat and walked over to him in all of her regal glory. She placed a hand around his shoulder and gently massaged circles about his back.

"No worries, baby. We will find them."

"My father is looking for an update..." he began to fuss; however, Sienna sat in his lap and gripped his face in her hand.

"And you will provide one. Sometimes, you must allow the mouse to come to the trap instead of chasing it. You are overthinking this. Raphael will rear his head, and when he does, we will sever it and deliver it on a platter to Bio."

Abaku sat up straight and gazed up into Sienna's eyes with a smile. "Baby, that's it." Staring at him with confusion, she shook her head.

Abaku kissed her lips. "We let the mouse come to us," he repeated. Tapping her bottom, he asked, "Go and finish up dinner. I need to meet with my team. I have a plan."

Sienna stood as he scurried about. "What's the plan, baby?"

Abaku walked over to her and placed a soft peck on her lips. "Don't you worry about this stuff. Let me do that. You just go take care of dinner and let me take care of you tonight."

Dammit. She nodded with a grin. "I love it when you dirty talk to me."

Leaning over he nipped at her neck before popping her on the ass. "Then I'll get real nasty tonight." She giggled like a schoolgirl. "Go head, baby, and I'll be in there when dinner is ready."

Reaching up, she licked the tip of her tongue across his lips before eyeing him sexily and turning to walk off. He shivered at her sexual prowess before turning and heading to his office. Once his back was turned, Sienna stomped her foot. She'd given him a plan on accident, and she needed to know what it was. She hadn't had any luck locating her sister through her back channels, so she didn't know where she was, either. She needed to find out what Abaku had up his sleeve in order to track Essie and inform her of the happenings before he could reach them. If not, she'd have to bury her sister right next to Raphael. Of that, she was certain.

———

A few days had passed since Abaku decided to implement his plan, and Sienna was on pins and needles. She felt she was in a rush against time to find out exactly what Abaku knew and what he planned to do, so that she could warn Essie. Her gut today her that his plans were closer to execution than he let on, so she tried her best to keep her eyes and ears primed to any news she could use. So far, she was empty-handed. Still, she kept her nonchalant attitude on the forefront to quell any suspicions that Abaku may have had.

"You've barely touched your food," Abaku noted after swallowing the last bites of his chef salad.

Fanning her hand as he brought her out of her reverie, she sighed. "My stomach feels uneasy. That's all."

His eyebrows furrowed as he sat back and wiped his hands with the linen napkin. "When was the last time you had your visitor?"

"Oh no, it's not that. It came last month. I think it's the meal I had for breakfast earlier. The poached egg tasted a little off."

What she wouldn't tell him is that she'd gotten on birth control since he'd started having intercourse with her. Her doctor vowed to keep her secret, and she'd remained true to her promise. Unless it was Yeshua's will, she would not be birthing any more of the Dage clan's kids, especially not one with Abaku.

"Oh, okay." The words came with a tinge of disappointment.

Sensing he was about to jump on the subject of offspring, Sienna abruptly stood to her feet. "Excuse me while I head to the bathroom, please."

Abaku stood as she backed out of her seat and headed down the hallway. Inside the bathroom, she sat on the lid of the toilet, giving herself a few minutes. The possible death of her sister by her hands had her stomach to be in knots, and it was getting worse as each day passed. She couldn't confess that to Abaku, so she blamed it on her meal. He had the audacity to believe she'd get pregnant by him. She wouldn't carry his child if he were the last man on Earth to reproduce with. Any man who would force his deceased brother's wife into a sexual relationship is a man whose DNA you did not want to run through your bloodline's veins. His brother's keeper, he was not.

When she decided she'd hidden out long enough, she took some paper towels and wet them before dabbing her face and washing her hands. Quietly, she exited the bathroom, but on her way back to the dining room, she heard Abaku's hushed voice. Easing into the formal living room, she hid behind the wall so she could eavesdrop on his conversation.

"So, it worked?" Abaku said.

All she could hear afterward was a succession of unanswered questions. She was about to give up and leave out of the room when the information she'd been waiting on flooded her eardrums.

"Aye. Protective custody. I see," he said lowly. "Do we know where they are?" A sinister laugh escaped Abaku before he said, "If we can't find him, we'll smoke him out. I hear the weather is nice this time of year in LA."

Sienna eased out of the formal living room and back into the bathroom. She flushed the toilet then rewashed her hands, and when she exited, she saw Abaku easing up the hallway toward her direction.

"I was just about to check on you," he said, stepping into her space and cupping her face between his hands. "Are you all right, my love?"

"Yes, I just had to clear the contents, if you will."

"I'm so sorry, my love." He bent down and kissed her forehead. "You should maybe make an appointment with the obstetrician to be sure everything is good." He placed a hand onto her midsection. "Although, it'd be a wonderful thing if you were carrying my seed."

Sienna tasted bile in the back of her throat from that thought alone. She held it in long enough for him to peck her on the nose. When he pulled away this time, love reflected in his eyes as the possibilities of fatherhood danced in his mind.

"If it makes you feel better, I will make the appointment." Abaku smiled, shaking a victory fist. They shared an intimate giggle at the thought. "In the meantime, do you think you can put the food up for me? I'm going to lie down in the bed."

"Anything for you," he said before she turned and walked away.

Sienna didn't have to hear the entire conversation to deduce two things. Essie was in protective custody and living in Los Angeles. If she were in protective custody, there was only one person Essie would call for that kind of assistance. Rhys. She knew she'd have to make quick work tomorrow before Abaku's men found them.

CHAPTER 16

R hys walked into the headquarters for his OMECA team with new intel. Holding a stack of papers in his hand, he threw them down on the large conference table and took his seat at the head of the table. He was pleased to see Raphael back and immersed in his new role with OMECA. He was an asset they desperately needed with organized international criminal activity.

"Our number one target came up on the grid yesterday. Looks like he is making his way back into the wire fraud schemes," Rhys informed them as he passed out duplicated copies of paperwork. "Thanks to Porter for the details."

"No problems. He makes the shit look easy," Porter answered.

"A little too easy if you ask me," Raphael said to no one in particular as he read over the paperwork in hand.

Rhys spread his arms out. "How so? His money is probably drying up, and he needs a quick lick. Seems legit to me."

"And you think he'd go right back into the business that was the catalyst for the takedown of his entire operation?" Raphael shook his head. "It seems sloppy to me. That or he's intentionally baiting us. And by us, I mean *me*." He threw the paperwork back on the table.

"Why would he put it out there in the open, though? That's a little too sloppy, if you ask me," Beau said.

"Because he thinks I'm sloppy." Raphael shrugged.

"He does not know you're working with an operative program, though. It makes no sense," Emmanuel argued.

Tonio raised his hand. "Actually, it does. No, he does not know he's working with operatives, but he knows he has a relationship with US intelligence. Perhaps it's as if Raphael stated. The move is to get him to take the bait. He wants to smoke him out."

Rhys stood, considering all the information that had been placed on the table. "Okay, what do you all suppose we do?"

"I say don't bite and bring the fight to him," Raphael stated.

"Perhaps don't bite, but definitely let them bring the fight to us," Beau stated as everyone looked over in her direction. She shrugged. "We have strength in numbers and familiarity."

"True, but if we can catch Abaku off guard, we add the element of surprise," Tonio added as he and Raphael fist-bumped.

Rhys pointed between the two of them. "You two are bosom buddies now?"

"My sentiments exactly." Emmanuel shot a hard glare at Tonio.

Tonio cleared his throat. "You wanted us to become a real team, right?" He glanced back at Emmanuel, who lowered his eyes. "Raphael and I view issues eye to eye, more than I realized. I respect it."

A sly smile spread across Rhys's face. "Good deal." Walking to the middle of the room, Rhys placed his hands in his pockets. "We won't bite. However, I do feel as though home turf has the best advantage. Let's implement a plan to answer his call when he comes knocking."

Rhys sat in his office developing a strategy to lure Abaku and bring him to justice. His wheels were running a mile a minute and the intensity of being so close to nailing a case gave him a hard-on.

He lived for this. As he sat, outlining his plans for Abaku, his cell rang. Typically, when he was in a strategic mode, he didn't accept phone calls, but what showed on his phone was an exception.

Rhys answered the call but did not speak.

The person on the other end of the line began. "Call number Bravo Whiskey Igloo Lima Lima 78204."

Rhys moved to the encrypted laptop and typed as he spoke, and when his identity was confirmed, Rhys returned his own verification. "Alpha Romeo Igloo Charlie Hotel 19463."

Rhys heard the same style typing on the other end.

"Speak to me," Rhys said in a hushed tone.

"I have a telegram for you," the voice on the other end stated.

Swiping his hand down his face, he whispered, "From who?"

"I can only say that they will only speak to Janet."

That got Rhys's attention. No one was allowed to speak to anyone in their protective custody. The mere fact the agent had broken protocol to utter her name, even across a secured line, meant whoever was pressing him was someone of substance. Raphael knew exactly how to get in contact with her, and Kaion lived with her, so it could not be them. His internal system went on high alert at the thought of it possibly being Abaku causing a breach in their security.

"Who?"

He heard a commotion and a door close. "Is your office secured?"

"Of course."

"It's Sienna."

The shock of that name rocked Rhys to his core. It couldn't be. She'd died, or so he thought. He'd been in this career long enough to know that not everything was as it seemed. Anything was possible. He'd never laid eyes on her corpse, so that fact alone let him know that it was quite possible for her to be alive. He paused because he wondered what had taken her so long to reach out. Surely, she would have wanted to contact her sister.

"Patch her through."

"She only wants to speak to Janet."

"That won't happen unless she speaks to me first. She may be her sister, but she's under my custody. That takes precedence. Patch her through."

There was a brief pause and then all of a sudden, the line was filled with the voice of a resurrected woman. "Hello, Rhys."

Rhys fell back into his seat. "I'll be damned."

"I need to speak to *Janet*. It's imperative."

Now, she truly had his attention. He leaned forward. "How imperative?"

"Life or death."

CHAPTER 17

Essie had just walked inside the house from dropping Kaion off at school. She closed the front door, and the hairs on the back of her neck stood at attention. Before a word could be uttered, she spun around, pulling her handgun and cocking it before her eyes landed on Rhys sitting on her sofa with his hands up in the air.

"It's only me. No harm. No foul."

The air whooshed out of Essie's lungs as she placed one hand to her chest. "Don't do that shit, Rhys. I was scared out of my mind!"

"So I see." He smirked. "Excellent reaction time. I see Raph taught you well."

Popping one out of the chamber, she caught it and placed the gun back into its holster. "Why are you even here?" When she noticed Rhys go serious, panic coursed through her veins. "My husband?"

He stood, holding up his hand to stop her immediate assumptions. "He is fine." He stepped closer to her. "I am here because there is other pressing news I need to tell you about that he can't know at the moment."

When she scrunched her face in confusion, he stretched out his arm and gestured to the sofa. "Shall we have a seat?"

Slowly, Essie walked over to the sofa and sat down. She had no clue what Rhys was about to say to her, but she knew without knowing that it was serious—possibly catastrophic. She swallowed to quell the dryness that threatened to close her throat.

"What is it?" she asked, twiddling her fingers.

Rhys didn't fully know how to relay the information that he was about to relay, but he knew it had to be done. For the safety of everyone involved. However, he also knew that once this cat was out of the bag, Essie may not be able to withstand the blow. It was the only reason he regretted not informing Raphael of what was going on. Still, he had to take his chances this way instead of trying to tame hotheaded Raphael. That portion of him was a beast, and just like an animal in the wild, it could not be contained. Therefore, he had to ensure he kept Raph steady enough to reason with.

That position was one where Essie held the cards. No matter how untamed Raphael got, she was the only one who could reel him back in. After this news dropped, he'd need Essie to do just that.

"I received an interesting phone call yesterday." Turning to face her, he placed a hand on her shoulder. "I'm not sure how to tell you this, so I figure the only way is to come straight out with it." He eyed Essie, knowing he had her full attention. "Your sister, Sienna, is alive."

At first, Essie's mind couldn't process what he'd just spoken. Surely, she hadn't heard what she thought she heard. Faintly, she heard the word "What?" flow from her lips. On cue, Rhys repeated the same statement as before, and this time, Essie's entire body went into shock. Her hands flew to her mouth as tremors racked her body. Tears welled in her eyes and flowed down her cheeks as she made short gasping noises, trying to pull air into her lungs. Hyperventilation set in as she began to sweat and fan herself to alleviate the level of heat that coursed through her body. She stood feeling as though as she would pass out. Rhys jumped up and ran to the kitchen bringing back paper towels and a cold bottle of water.

He popped the top off the water bottle and handed it to her. "Here. Please drink this." She took the water and guzzled it as he used the paper towels to blot her damp forehead. "You have to calm down, Essie. Please. I can't tell Raphael that you're in the hospital and it's all my fault."

Essie fell back down on the sofa and leaned her head back. She closed her eyes, trying to control the rampant emotions she was experiencing. She had so many questions that they flickered through her mind like quick film. How was Sienna still alive? Where had she been? What had she been doing all this time? Why had she waited so long to reach out to her? Was she upset with her? Did she hate her? All those questions danced around as she began to come to grips with the news that Rhys had laid on her doorstep. Her sister was alive.

"Where is she? Can I talk to her?" Essie's only thoughts at the moment were to see her one and only sister and sibling. She loved Sienna with her entire heart and would give anything to see her and talk to her again, especially after having believed for all this time that she was dead.

Rhys nodded. "Yes, you can talk to her." Holding up his finger, he lifted his encrypted cell phone out of his pocket and dialed a number. After a few minutes and verification, the line was connected. "Yes, I have your sister right here. It'll be on speaker on my end, and you have five minutes."

He placed the phone on mute. Essie looked at him and asked, "What is it?"

"We have reason to believe that either she, you, or both of you are in imminent danger. Keep it brief and gather as much information as you can. Life or death, Essie. Remember that."

He handed the phone to her, and she took it from his hands, visibly shaken. She didn't know what to expect when she listened to the other end of the line, but she braced herself as best she could.

"Hello?"

"Essie!" Sienna's voice flowed through like the sweetest melody.

The tears that had dried up came back, and Essie forced herself to press through the phone call. "Sienna! Where are you? What happened to you? Why did you take so long to reach out to me?" The words shot out of her mouth like bullets.

"Listen, I do not have much time. I am with Abaku." Her words came out hushed but hurried.

"Abaku?" His name came out as a pained question. Had her sister really turned her back on her for the likes of Abaku Dage?

"I do not have time to explain. Just know that my trust in him was a huge mistake. I regret every bit of it. I'm contacting you because you, Raphael, and Kaion are in danger."

Rhys made a circle in the air with his index finger, prompting Essie to press Sienna for that information rather than continue down the path of personal emotion. It was clear that whatever reason had caused Sienna to reach out was far greater than rekindling their relationship right now.

"I'm listening," Essie said.

Sienna described in detail the plans laid forth by Abaku to avenge his brother's death, including the killing of both Raphael and Essie. She provided the date and how the attack was to come, and she pleaded with her leave.

"Why are you just now reaching out and giving me this information?" Essie asked, because she had to know.

"I am bitter about Dage, Essie. He was my husband. If it were not for your Raphael, I'd still have him and my daughter to this day. I won't lie. I don't care what happens to him. But you—you are my sister. I lost sight of that momentarily, but there is nothing greater than that. I may be angry with you about your choices, but that is my cross to carry. Your fate should not be left in the hands of the Dages. I won't allow it."

"The same way you feel about Dage is the exact same way I feel about Raphael, and more importantly, it's the same way he feels about me." Essie paused, giving Sienna time to soak in what she meant. "I will warn Raphael."

Sienna closed her eyes, nodding her agreement. "I expected nothing less."

"We will take heed, and I will save you, Sienna. Raphael will save you. For me."

"Take care of yourself—"

"You are a part of me. I won't let you down twice. I know and understand your reasons for hating Raphael because of what he did, but understand what his presence represents for both of us. Let me do this for you, sister. Let me save you."

Sienna gave it a brief thought as Rhys tapped his wrist indicating time was elapsing. Just before Rhys took the phone from Essie, Sienna blurted. "I will go along with your plan. My love for you is greater than my hate for Raphael."

"I love you," Essie whispered as Rhys took the phone.

"I love you more," Sienna said back.

"We'll be in touch, Sienna. My agent will assist you. Thank you." Without giving her a chance to respond, Rhys disconnected the line.

"What now?" Essie asked, eyeing him closely.

"Now, you get your husband on board with the plans to save Sienna, so that we can bring Abaku to justice."

"Ahh, so you need me to tame your loose cannon."

Rhys rubbed his forehead, sensing where the conversation was headed. "What do you need from me?"

"Assurance that you will save my sister. Abaku is dangerous. I want my sister safe, sound, and secured. Make it happen."

Rhys knew he needed Sienna and Essie to help with the intricate details, therefore he reluctantly agreed. He had to do whatever it took to close out this case. Operation OMECA allowed him to do just that.

CHAPTER 18

"What the fuck do you mean to *let him come to us?*" Raphael thundered, startling Rhys and Essie as he paced the office. "He could know where Essie and Kaion are housed. We don't know what all he truly knows," he fussed and turned to eye Essie when he spoke his next words. "And I'm not willing to bet Kaion or Essie's life on half-assed information from Sienna."

Essie cleared her throat. She knew that Raphael had her best interests at heart, but she loved her sister. She knew her sister well enough to know that whatever beef she had with her on account of Raphael, she'd squashed it in order to save her and escape Abaku. Before she could speak on it, Rhys spoke.

"Listen, Raphael. I know how you must feel, but we have to be strategic about this. The advantage we have is that Abaku does not know that we know he's gunning for us."

"Gunning for me and my family!" Raphael roared, cutting off anything else Rhys was about to say. "You seem to forget that your best link to him is through me."

Raphael stalked over to Rhys, his long legs taking determined strides. He stood in his space, glowering over him. He kept his hands astride him, but the thick vein in his neck and his bulging muscles visible through his black T-shirt showed his anguish. He was pissed.

"Besides, you know you're on a short leash with me after this stunt you pulled with my wife and her sister."

Rhys swallowed the nervousness. He knew Raphael would be upset with him for going to Essie first and involving her without notifying him about it. However, he knew that Sienna would only send Raphael off the deep end. He needed leverage. No matter how angry he was in the moment, Essie offered leverage and coverage over Rhys for his decision.

Before either man could utter another word, Essie popped up out of her seat. "Raph, that is enough." She shook her head as Rhys and Raphael turned wide eyes to her. "And you wonder why the man didn't come to you first." Her thick African accent shone through in her distress.

"Oh, I know exactly why this muthafucka didn't come to me," Raphael growled, glaring at Rhys, who held his white-hot gaze, albeit with a high degree of wariness.

Essie waltzed over to Raphael and pulled his arm, so they could go speak in private. She'd never disrespect him in front of any other man, but she would let her position be known. Sienna was her sister, and as much as she loved Raphael, she loved her sister, too. If she could choose both, she would. Every. Time.

She pulled him into the farthest corner of the office before she spoke again, quietly. "Baby, I know that Sienna is a sore spot for you. You don't trust her—" Raphael was about to speak but she raised her hand to stop what he was going to say. "But I do, Raph. I know my sister."

"You *knew* your sister, baby." He huffed. "*Come on*. Let's examine the cold, hard facts about all this, Essie. She's alive and waits this long to contact you, and she's living with the brother of the very man who wanted my head on a platter. You say you know your sister. I say you're too close to the situation to know the difference."

Essie's eyes narrowed to slits as she folded her arms across her chest. Her puffed-up chest warned him she was getting wound up. With an overarched eyebrow, she tilted her head forward to be sure he couched his next words clearly. "Know the difference between *what?*"

Not one to be deterred, Raphael manned up and with a straight face said sternly, "Know the difference between a sister's love and a setup."

The anger she'd bottled up came out full force through the slap of her hand across his cheek. He hadn't expected the response, so his face turned to the side from the force. Bringing his hand up to his face, he rubbed the side where she'd connected to get the sting out of her slap. It hurt like a son of a bitch, but he'd endure a thousand more licks to save her blind-ass life.

"Only because I know you love your sister and you want so badly to believe in her, will I accept the fact that you put your hands on me. You can slap me until you slap me to sleep. It won't change my mind on this. You can hate me now, so that I can save you later."

Her eyes lowered, because she knew she was wrong, and because he was being ever so humble about it. She knew it was probable that Raphael had killed anyone who laid a hand on him. Therefore, she knew that he loved her unconditionally.

"I apologize. I was wrong." Essie glanced upward, holding his attention so he could see the sincerity in her voice. "But you are wrong too. I know how you feel, but you didn't hear the desperation in her voice. I know my sister. She wants to help us." She placed her hand on Raphael's folded forearm. "Baby, please."

The scared and pleading expression in Essie's eyes penetrated his soul. He slipped his hand down his bearded face as he struggled not to let the David in her topple the Goliath in him. But it was of no use. Anyone could sling what they wanted his way, but it was her stones that leveled him every time. Still, his concern was for his family. He wouldn't be able to live with himself if something happened to her or Kaion, but before he took himself out, he'd take out any and every person responsible, including Rhys.

Raphael moved into Essie's space and cupped her face in between his massive hands. He had to make sure she knew and understood his position. "I'm going to do this for you. Only for you. Here are my terms. If Abaku shows up, fuck an arrest. I will kill him. If he or any of his crew gets close to you and Kai, I will kill them all. If your sister has set us up, I will kill her. And you will be okay with any of those outcomes because that is the only way I'm agreeing to them."

Slowly, Essie nodded her agreement. "If my sister is truthful, we save her."

"I agree."

With that, Raphael turned to walk away from Essie and back to Rhys. He pointed at him. "Me and you, outside. Now."

Rhys and Essie eyed each other, but there was no saving grace in this moment. Raphael opened the back door and walked out onto the patio, leaving Rhys still inside. A barked, "Now!" had him out of his chair and across the threshold.

"I want my family moved."

Rhys turned to him. "That takes too much coordination and time—"

Raphael spun on him so fast, he swallowed his thoughts. "Well, figure it the fuck out!" He walked up into Rhys's face, his hands steepled and pointed directly in Rhys's chest. "Let me be extremely, abundantly, and precisely clear. Abaku gets nowhere near my family, I will dead you and the entire CIA. I don't give a damn if I take my last breath doing so. So, either you come up with a solution, or I'm about to be a fucking problem."

"We can get you moved here quicker," Rhys volunteered. "If we make it a move as though you're doing it on your own, without government interference, it may lure Abaku out quicker. But we'll be waiting." Rhys thought for a moment as he clicked away on his cell while he watched Raphael stew over the situation. "There's a house down the street we can use."

"Let's do this. I'm not leaving my family in harm's way, and I'm not going to lure him directly to them."

"Agreed. I'll get it together by tomorrow."

Raphael walked back toward the door and stopped when he was next to Rhys. "If anything goes wrong, it's on your head." He pointed his finger in his face. "And I'm gonna be the muthafucka to cut your head off. Believe that."

Raphael stormed back inside the house, leaving Rhys with nothing but his threat and Rhys's thoughts. Although Rhys was nervous, he was pleased with the outcome. Despite Raphael's anger, his plan would work, which meant more money and more cases for OMECA. He felt somewhat disheartened to place Raphael and his family in the middle of his career case, especially since they were like family to him. However, it wasn't enough to miss this opportunity to blow his first solo case out of the water. He'd play his part to help ensure they were safe, and that fact made him feel much better for the situation that they were now facing.

CHAPTER 19

Raphael sat in the bed that night, pondering over the crazy turn of events with Sienna. She was alive. She contacted Essie. She had been living with Abaku for a year. She wanted to help. She wanted to help them both. She wanted to reconnect with her sister. She wanted to betray Abaku, and in turn, betray her husband's memory. She was alive. None of this made sense. The fact that she was willing to betray her sister for her husband, but now she suddenly had a change of heart about getting even with her sister about the loss of said husband, was way too out of reach for him to grasp. Everything about this said set up. Everything.

He wouldn't deny that she loved her sister. He'd seen that firsthand. That's the part that kept him twisted up about it. Since he'd known she loved her sister, it was possible that she was being completely honest. A year was a long time to grieve and reconsider things about your life. However, he wasn't a man that delved in possibilities. He worked solely in probability. It was more probable that this was a setup orchestrated by Sienna and Abaku rather than some sudden moral consciousness.

However, no one agreed with him. Rhys only wanted to solve his first case, so he'd stand behind any plan that got him closer to that goal. Essie was blinded by love, so she'd stand behind any plan that got her closer to her sister. He was the only one that saw that this had the potential to go left fast, but he loved his wife, and that was the chord that both Rhys and Essie had struck. He wasn't crazy. It was the reason why Rhys went to Essie to begin with. She was his Achilles heel, and he knew it.

That was exactly why he needed time away from Rhys to cool off, otherwise he'd be added to the same list that Abaku was on. It was why he told Rhys they could head out in the morning. He needed to be with his family and soak up more time with them. Their mere presence centered him and gave him clarity. He needed all the clarity he could get if he were moving forward on the word of Sienna Dage.

"You're going to be tired in the morning."

The words drifted from underneath him. When he looked down, he found the eyes of Essie staring back up at him. He could see those beautiful pools even in the darkness. Rather than respond, he placed his free arm behind his head and leaned back. She sat up, snuggling close to him. She ran her hand up and down his bare chest, feeling the cut muscle between his pectorals and abs.

"I'll be fine. What are you doing up?"

"We're connected. When you can't sleep, I can't sleep. I won't bother to ask what's eating at you. I already know."

Raphael glided a hand down his face to swipe away his uneasiness. Looking down at her, his facial expression softened. "I don't mean any disrespect, baby. I just need you to understand where I'm coming from with this."

Essie lifted up. Her attitude was rising, and Raphael could sense it. "I love my sister, Raphael."

"And I love *you!*" he barked. "And Kaion, and my own life, too." He released a deep breath as they both sat in the moment for a while. He lifted her chin, and that's when he noticed her lip was quivering. "Listen, baby, I get it. She's your sister. That's family, and you're loyal to your family. It's the way we are both built. That's the way it's supposed to be. As your man and as Kaion's father, I have an obligation to protect those closest to me, even if that means it's also against family who isn't loyal."

A steady stream of tears rolled down Essie's face. She knew what he meant, and because of Sienna's prior actions, she couldn't deny that he had a right to feel the way he felt. She would too, if it were anybody else in this situation. But it wasn't. It was her sister, and she couldn't deny that she loved her sister and would be loyal to her, even to her own detriment.

"I know that you only want to protect us, Raphael. I do get that. I don't want anything to happen to us, either, and yes, there is a possibility she is only doing this to set us up. The part I couldn't live with is not helping her and never knowing if she truly wanted my help. If something happened to her, and I didn't even try to save her, I couldn't live with myself. That's a version of me that you and Kaion couldn't live with either."

Her words punched Raphael right in his core, because if he were her he would do the same thing. His own father was a detriment to him, but that never stopped him from helping him. It never stopped him from loving the old man, either. He hated it because he was wired both ways. Rarely did they collide, and the one time they did, it was driving a wedge between him and his wife.

He decided right then and there that he'd have to tuck away his gangster, because he also heard what she didn't say. If he didn't help her try to save her sister, she couldn't live with him. She'd never forgive herself, and she'd never forgive him either. He'd just have to make sure that Essie and Kaion were overly protected and out of harm's way. He'd save her sister and reunite them. He prayed that what Sienna had spoken to Essie was the God's honest truth, because if she planned to deceive them for Abaku, he would kill her and deal with the consequences of his wife's feelings about it later.

He stared into her face and wiped the remaining tears. "I'll save your sister, Essie. I give you my word that I will extend to her the same protection as I do to you and Kai."

Essie released a breath that she didn't know she had been holding and flung herself into Raphael's arms. "Thank you. Thank you. Thank you." She hugged him tightly as he wrapped her in a warm embrace.

She raised up and kissed him all about his face. When she kissed his lips, he sucked them in and bit her bottom lip. Her eyes fluttered from the sensation, and she reinitiated the kiss again. This time they did not break their lip lock. The fervor in their kiss took over, and Raphael placed one hand underneath her thigh and moved her onto his lap. She jumped slightly when she felt his need for her beneath her. Wrapping her arms around his neck, she slowly grinded her womanhood on top of him, heightening their urge for one another.

Gliding his hands around her butt, he dipped his hands inside of her pajama shorts and slid them, along with her panties, down around the curve of her rear. She lifted, only giving him time to free one of her legs from the hold of the fabric. Bracing herself on her toes, she used Raphael's shoulders to balance herself as he lifted his body to remove his own sweatpants down and free himself. When she rested back on him, she froze, leaning her forehead against his. The heat from their attraction and the feel of him at her core almost sent her over the edge right then. Raphael understood the reason for her pause, because he was experiencing the same feeling. The moisture from his wife showcased her want and need of him, and it was almost too much for him to bear. He loved her so much that each time with her felt like a brand-new experience.

When they had found their bearings, he lifted her by her backside, and she eased down on his massive hard-on.

"Oh, Essie," Raphael murmured in a gravelly voice.

He held her waist, gripping her in place for a moment. The feel of her was too much. He had to pace himself or this ride wouldn't last long. When he was ready, he loosened his grip and nodded. It was his signal to let her know she was in control. He wanted her to be the captain of the ship tonight. He needed a release from the duties, and he wanted to show her he trusted her in all things, from the decisions in their lives to the lovemaking in the bedroom.

And take control she did.

Grinding slowly, she found a rhythm and ground her core into him, gliding back and forth ever so sexily against him. It was just the right amount of tenderness and roughness they both needed as he filled her to the hilt. Once in a groove, she picked up the pace, riding him like an untamed stallion, sending their bodies into frenzy.

"Ahhh, Raph!" she moaned out in ecstasy. "You feel so damn good. Oh, baby."

Raphael's face contorted as he bit out, "Damn, baby. You're about to take me there."

The combination of her sweet moans, her sensual tone, and her fluid movements were enough to rip the orgasm right out of him. She was in control of his body, and he didn't mind letting go for her and with her.

"Come with me, baby," Raphael pleaded, because he was past the point of no return. He would have to let it ride.

When he felt her muscles clench down on him, that was all he could take as her essence rained down on him. She panted his name over and over in throes of passion, delirious from the pleasure that sparked between them.

Gripping her waist, Raphael took three swift and deep plunges into her core and blew like a volcano into his wife.

"Essie! Shit—Essie!"

Her name rolled out of his mouth with his eyes clenched shut and his toes curled. He couldn't even breathe, it felt so good.

He wanted her to stay in place, but she moved off him and made her way downward, trailing kisses from his chest to his stomach. When she reached his manhood, she placed him in her warm mouth and slowly pulled, inhaling him deep inside her throat.

He gripped her by the hair, trying to force himself not to tug too tight. "Ooh Essie! Baby. What are you doing to me?"

He'd experienced mouthwork from her before, but this felt otherworldly, and he could barely hold on as the rollercoaster started back up the incline. He'd never had back-to-back completions this soon, but tonight, it was going to happen. The friction of her movement, combined with the moisture and light suction of her mouth, caused his seed to rush up into her awaiting mouth.

"Essie!" he belted out with a growl.

His entire body tensed as he gripped the sides of the bed so he wouldn't harm her from the power of the release. He rode the wave, and his lovely wife rode it right along with him. When he was finished, she lifted, and he pulled her against his chest. They were both so spent only the ragged sound of their breaths could be heard. It was so completely consuming that he dozed off to sleep before she did for the first time in their relationship.

CHAPTER 20

The plane ride and subsequent car ride back to OMECA headquarters was a lengthy and silent one for Rhys and Raphael. Rhys knew that Raphael was still stewing over how he'd handled the situation with Sienna. In his opinion, he'd stew on it until he could see that his plan was the most effective way to handle bringing Abaku down. Right now, Raphael couldn't fathom it because his emotions were in play. Rhys understood that, too. Raphael was a changed man. Essie and Kaion had changed him. Still, he needed the man Raphael was prior to becoming a family man to understand he'd done what was necessary. This had nothing to do with feelings, but rather finality. The finality of this Abaku drama for all of them.

As they rode in the back of the black SUV, Rhys rolled up the soundproof glass so that he could speak privately to Raphael. "Being upset with me is not going to change the fact that Abaku wants your head on a platter. I did what I needed to do. Don't let your emotions blind you from the reality of the situation."

"The only person blind is Essie." Turning his head from the window to Rhys, he glared at him. "But she won't be blind by herself if this does not pan out exactly how you planned it."

Turning completely to face Raphael, he folded his hands in his lap. "What exactly are you so upset about, Raphael? The way I see it, we're not only saving your life and freeing your family of this nightmare with Abaku, but we're saving Essie's sister while clearing up this matter faster than expected. All of that is a win for you."

Raphael frowned. His muscles bulged, and he didn't hesitate to spew his rage on Rhys. "Only if it plays out the way you've gassed Essie's head to believe. You and I both know this whole thing has the potential to backfire. There is no contingency plan. We are flying by the seat of our pants. It does not bother you because we ain't your family. Kai and Essie, they are mine! I don't give a damn about my head being on anybody's platter. I made my peace with death a long time ago. I ain't made my peace with theirs, and I won't. If anything happens to them before I take my last breath, I swear on my love for them that you and anybody else who gets in my way will take their last breath with us."

The rage in Raphael's eyes caused Rhys to see the seriousness of his threat. He'd unleashed the beast he was trying to contain. He could only pray that everything went according to plan, because he knew if anything went wrong, he'd have to lay Raphael down strictly out of self-preservation.

"Let's just focus on ensuring that the plan we do have in motion works."

"Now, that's the best piece of advice you've had since you stepped foot on my damn doorstep," Raphael stated with a finger point.

As they reached the headquarters of OMECA, both men stepped out with a renewed understanding that Plan A had to work. Now, they just had to prepare the team. As they entered the building, Rhys stuck his hand out to Raphael.

"Truce?"

Raphael shook it. "Truce…for now."

They headed down the corridor, and before they entered the main meeting room for OMECA, Raphael placed a hand on Rhys's arm to stop him from scanning his badge.

"What are you going to tell the team?"

"The truth. They won't like it, but they don't have a choice. Besides, I already have one person on my ass. I might as well make it a fucking party."

He scanned the badge, and they both entered as the team stopped what they were doing and focused their attention on the two men.

"Well, look what the cat drug in," Emmanuel quipped as he leaned back in his chair.

"Emmanuel, don't start," Rhys snapped.

He shrugged. "I'm just saying we're over here working hard and you're off having playdates with your new best friend."

"Oh, so you didn't learn that I didn't play the first time around, huh?" Raphael added, his temper rising.

Emmanuel stood. "I'm starting to think Tonio was right about you."

Rhys walked in front of Raphael. "Emmanuel! I said enough! Stand down."

Porter's eyes darted back and forth. "Sir, you can't blame him. He has a point. We were all left with instructions, and this operation can't run efficiently if we aren't all on one accord."

Beau turned around in her seat. "Let's just all relax. I'm sure their disappearing act was for good cause."

"You would think that," Benji muttered with a head shake as he continued to stare at his computer screen.

"What did you say? Your panties in a bunch?" Beau spat.

"Rather a bunch than loose," Porter said in Benji's defense.

"Oh, are you mad because you want a taste?" Beau mocked Porter, licking her tongue in a fluid motion. "Lady pond dippin' ass."

Tonio stood up. "Enough!" he bellowed, looking around. "I'm sure whatever it is has its reason. We're a team. Let's move as one."

Everyone turned to Tonio with shock. "Raphael is solid. I stand on that." He crossed his arms across his chest before taking a seat.

Unrelenting, Emmanuel opened his mouth to voice his concern again. "Well, I—"

"It's hard to have a voice in a group you're dismissed from," Rhys said, his calm tone a direct contrast to the burning in his eyes and his hand resting on his holster. "Sit down or be put down."

Emmanuel glared at Rhys, the muscle in his jaw ticking. Rhys didn't back down. He knew he couldn't. This wild band of outlaws was out of control, and if he couldn't prove that he could wrangle them, he'd lose command and put the current operation and any future ones at risk. That was the quickest way to get OMECA dismantled, and he'd rather make an example than make a mistake.

Emmanuel conceded with a grunt before ripping the chair out from underneath the conference table and taking a seat. The other members stared back and forth at each other before following suit one by one—although Beau didn't miss the opportunity to toss one last sneer to Porter before they sat. Last to sit was Raphael, with his eyes trained on Emmanuel.

"Thank you, Tonio," Rhys said as he re-snapped his holster. He remained standing and began pacing the floor. "I put this team together because you are the elite, the most efficient, the best, the brightest, and the craziest. Most of all, I put you together for your individual precision and attention to detail." He stopped pacing and turned to the large table and placed his hands on it. "So let me say that the one detail you all better get right is the one that says *I* am in charge. Whoever I bring on this team is a part of this team. If you have questions, ask, but gone are the days that your egos get to one-up anyone—that includes me. If you want out, speak now, because if this type of discord happens even once more, I'm sending your ashes back to your mamas with the American flag and a "thank you for your service" note. You're all excellent at what you do, but you're expendable. Don't forget it."

His eyes landed on Emmanuel, who stared at him with a scowl on his face. He'd given in once; he wouldn't dare concede again. Not first, anyway. Tonio took the pressure off him by agreeing first. Everyone else fell in line except Raphael.

"We didn't hear you agree to the terms," Emmanuel pointed out.

"You either, but I ain't complaining," Raphael shot back.

Beau, who was seated beside Raphael, placed a hand over his to calm him. They locked eyes before she mouthed, "Stay cool."

Emmanuel looked at the two of them and smirked.

"Careful, Beau. He's only here for himself. He does not give two damns about you or any of us."

"And unlike you, I don't have no dog tags hanging from my neck. You ready to mail 'em off? I can make a post office run on my way out."

It was Tonio's turn to put the warning out for Emmanuel. Rhys had made his position known, and in Emmanuel's new, heated exchange with Raphael, he hadn't noticed that Rhys had unholstered his weapon. Rhys was serious, and although Emmanuel's frustration was understood, Rhys's orders reigned supreme. Raphael was the golden child, and he was right about one thing: he was the only one not bound to a code beyond his own.

Emmanuel caught the clue from Tonio when he eyed Rhys's handgun resting on his thigh. He huffed and raised both hands. "Understood. Command. We're a team." The words felt bitter coming off his tongue, but he would not put a black dress on his mama because of a pissing contest with Raphael.

Rhys turned his attention to Raphael, whose eyes were still trained on Emmanuel. He grunted with a head nod, and Rhys accepted that as Raphael's intent to stand down. Rhys rubbed his temple before he got to the business at hand.

"We have new intel that has shifted the plan." Rhys glanced at Beau before continuing. "You are right about one thing—our disappearing act was for good cause."

Rhys walked to the widescreen monitor and switched it on. Using his phone, he typed in some information, and before them, a picture of Sienna appeared. He pointed to the screen.

"This is—"

"Sienna Dage," Benji whispered aloud.

"Bingo!" Rhys pointed at him. "Sienna Dage."

Porter held up her hand. "Wait. I'm confused. The background of this photo suggests that Sienna is alive. Those markets are new in that area. There's no way she was there unless she isn't dead."

"Exactly." Rhys turned to face all of them. "Sienna Dage is alive and well. She has been hiding under the confines of our target," he said and flipped the picture. "Abaku Dage." The picture of Abaku appeared on the screen and everyone gasped. Raphael's blood began to boil.

"Wait. How did you obtain this intel?" Beau asked, cutting to the chase.

"Our recon team have been investigating and placed a tail on them once they were found. This was all set in motion because my contacts received information from a reputable source," Rhys stated.

"Who?" Tonio asked.

"Sienna herself," Rhys stated, much to their surprise.

"Apparently, she wants to reconcile with her sister, Essie, who is Raphael's wife. Sienna has fed us information about a planned attack on Raphael," Rhys explained.

"So, what's the plan?" Emmanuel asked.

"The plan is we allow Abaku to believe we know nothing. He brings the fight to us. We capture him. End of story," Rhys explained.

Emmanuel scanned the room and raised his hand. "Am I the only one who sees a major issue with this plan? As in, it really ain't no plan."

"There's no contingency plan. When is the attack planned?" Porter asked.

"*Where* is it planned? We need details so we can get recon set up," Benji added.

Rhys held a hand up. "I understand your concern. However, we can only be as prepared as we can. Home-court advantage is the best. We have everyone and all the weapons we need to combat this threat. Our source says the attack happens in two days. It's short notice to plan, but we can and will do this."

Tonio sucked his teeth. "Come on, Rhys. We all pledged to this mission and OMECA, but this is suicide. What assurances do we have?"

"The same you as when you signed on, Tonio," Rhys spat. "It's a high risk, but who are we if we aren't risk takers?"

"Fucking fools," Emmanuel spat, disgusted. Leaning forward, he pierced Raphael. "This has your BS smell all over it."

Pointing to himself, Raphael laughed. "Mine? For once, I'm on your side, especially about this. My hands are tied as tightly as yours. I can guarantee you this, though. If Abaku wants a fight, he'll get one from me. My family is on the platter, and I won't risk them for anyone. Not even me. So, whether it's here or there, I'm ready."

Emmanuel took in Raphael's words, gauging him for a moment. A smirk crossed his face, and for the first time, he saw what Tonio had eventually seen in Raphael. Heart. And real recognized real. He sat back and nodded. "Aight then. What do we need to do?"

Pulling out a chair, Rhys sat down. "Now you're all speaking my language."

After they'd come up with a plan, everyone stood and Raphael prepared to go back to his protective location. He tied up loose ends with Rhys, Tonio, and Emmanuel, then headed toward the door. Beau was standing nearby, cleaning her weapons, as he was heading out.

"Do you really trust Sienna?" she asked, catching him off guard.

"What choice do I have?"

"Ah, the wife is putting the pressure on this," she said, recognizing the tension in his tone. You're trying to save her sister, aren't you?" Beau asked, tossing her rag on the table. "Why didn't you and Rhys tell the team that?"

"'Cause I'm not sure if I trust her sister."

"Well, I don't," Beau added. "I just want you to know that if this thing goes left, everyone is gonna be gunning for Sienna." She walked up close to him. "But are you ready for everyone to be gunning for your wife?"

She went to place her hands on his chest, and he gripped them. "I'm married." He threw her hands down. "Sounds like a threat on my wife."

Beau lifted her hands in surrender. "No threats. Just food for thought. It isn't me you need to worry about." She cast her eyes back toward the team. "You're the only one not wearing dog tags that invested in this mission. Remember that."

With that, she waltzed back over to her station and began reassembling her weapon. Raphael left, but her words hung heavy on his heart. He understood what she meant. For him, this was personal. For them, it wasn't. Anyone who appeared to be a threat would be eliminated. Essie included.

CHAPTER 21

Sienna sat at the long cherry oak dining table alone, eating her dinner. Her appetite was slim these days as she waited for news of what Abaku had planned for Raphael. The dim lighting gave off a somber ambiance while she picked over her leafy salad with flaked salmon. She'd prepared the light meal for her and Abaku, but he had been engrossed with his mission to kill the American and his traitor. She'd hardly seen him for the past three days. Each day he'd been away made her more nervous, because she knew he was closing in on his target. It was evident in the lack of communication.

He trusted her, but he also knew that deep down she loved her sister. How could she not? Just because he was in love with her didn't mean he didn't love his brother. He understood her without her having to say it, because he was in the same position. Therefore, she was left with her idle thoughts and prayers that Essie and even Raphael would survive whatever deadly plot was being hatched against them.

To Sienna's surprise, Abaku swaggered in the kitchen, sporting cream linen pants and a tan-colored, silk button-down shirt, a glass of bourbon in his hand. He looked as if the weight of the world had been lifted off his shoulders.

"You made it to dinner." Sienna's eyes sparkled with fake enthusiasm. "Would you like for me to make your plate?"

Abaku gave her a lazy smile that indicated he was buzzed off the liquor. Walking over to her, he bent down and kissed her forehead. "Sure, I'd love to eat with my lady."

She stood still, penned between the table and his closeness. "I'd begun to wonder, as you have been absent these last few days."

Abaku wrapped one arm around her waist, pulling her close to him. "Nothing of the sort, baby. I had to put this plan in action. The good news is that we've located Raphael. My people will be out there to set up recon, but I am personally taking care of Raphael with the full support and backing of my father. I want to look that bastard directly in the eyes as I pull the trigger." He released a sinister chortle before planting a kiss on Sienna's lips.

Sienna wrapped her arms around his neck. "Ah, so the time has come?"

"The time is now."

They shared another kiss before she headed to the kitchen to make his plate. The jiggle of her rear in the sundress caught his attention, and he tapped her on the behind. Giggling, she turned to face him with a wicked grin. Instead of sitting like he'd initially started to do, he followed her into the kitchen, and before she could make his plate, he picked her up and sat her on the kitchen island.

"What are you doing, crazy man?"

"Eating my dessert before my meal."

He pushed the hem of her dress up to her hips, and she obliged him by lifting up so he could shift the dress up to her waistline. Pulling her to the edge, he pushed her backward so her pussy and ass were placed like a plated meal before him. He faceplanted his mouth on her clit and went to work right there on the countertop. Leaning back, Sienna rolled her eyes, but allowed herself to sink into the pleasure so she could fake this moment with him. With her eyes closed, she had thoughts of Dage, and that made her body react to Abaku's touch.

"Oh shit, Sienna. You're so wet for me," he said between slurps. "You taste divine."

"Mmm, yes baby," she moaned to encourage him to speed up the process.

Her sexy grunts worked, as he forewent the oral intercourse they were engaged in, slipped down his pants, and removed her from the counter then slid her on his shaft and dove deep and hard into her core, slamming into her wet essence with vigor.

"Sienna!" he roared. "It's all mine. Fuck, babe."

Sienna wrapped her arms around his neck tightly and leaned into the crease of his neck then kissed it. "Baby, it feels so good," she murmured between their passionate throes. "Make me come, Abaku."

She threw her head back, and that was all she wrote for Abaku. He power-drilled into her core with a passionate furor he'd never felt before. Everything was coming into place for him. He was earning his father's respect, regaining his empire, avenging his brother's death, and getting the woman he never knew he needed or wanted. It was all at his fingertips. All he had to do was execute. For now, he'd celebrate the one mission he felt he'd finally won—becoming Sienna's man. With that thought coursing through him, he let out a roar as his climax peaked and he poured into her womb.

"Have my baby, Sienna," he cried out. "Have my baby!"

She released her sex onto him at the same time, and he held her in place into their ragged breaths returned to normal. Placing her down on her feet, her dress slipped back down her body, the hem touching her ankles. As he straightened his clothing, she went about the business of washing her hands and preparing his plate. Abaku eyed her cautiously while she whizzed around the kitchen. When she sat his plate down on the dining table, he pulled out her seat and she took it before he took his.

She took a sip of her wine and glanced up to see him focused on her. "What?" She released a giggle behind a small blush while pushing her hair behind her ear.

"How do you feel about my request?"

Sadness threatened to overcome her, but she powered through. Placing her glass down, she dabbed her mouth with the napkin and considered her words before she spoke.

"Losing a child is a hurt I have struggled with. I miss what could have been. I won't lie. It's not a full-out yes, but should we find ourselves with the possibility of a little one"—she looked into his eyes and placed her hand on his—"I won't deny us that opportunity. I'll love and cherish our little womb fruit the same as I would have baby Da'Jenna. I'm saying I'm open to the possibility."

Abaku smiled. He was impressed by Sienna. She'd lost and suffered so much that he didn't ever think that she'd rid herself of the ties to Dage. Yet, she was there offering her love to him. Her womb. He respected that she held some care from her losses without shutting him completely out. How could she love him if she couldn't offer herself? This proved to him that she was all in; she was trying, and that's all he could ask.

He gripped her hand with a look of sheer satisfaction. "I love you, Sienna."

Sienna smiled brightly. That admission solidified everything that she'd been working to accomplish. He'd withhold nothing from her now. She could safely infiltrate his plans to save her sister and escape his clutches before he understood fully what happened. It was treacherous and dangerous, but she had no problem bringing down Solomon when it came to the people she truly loved. She'd gladly be Delilah.

"The team is in place, and they will execute the plan tomorrow." Abaku and Sienna's eyes met as he clasped her hand within his. "Tomorrow, everyone associated with Raphael will be eliminated and then there will be only him for my taking."

Sienna squeezed his hand and nodded her approval. "I've waited so long for Raphael to get the fate that is coming to him. Will you be heading to Indiana to oversee it?"

The wine that Abaku had sipped slid down his throat and he let out a refreshing sigh before placing the glass back down on the table before him. A smirked crossed his face. "No, I won't, but that's all a part of my plan. My source has assured me of two things: he's not in Indiana, and he's expecting me. That's why I am sending my team first. If he does not know who's coming then he does not know who to avoid, and I stay off the radar until I can finish him off for myself. A bait and switch of sorts. They must be naive to believe I don't know their federal agents are waiting on me." He shook his head before eating a bite of his food. "Americans."

It was Sienna's turn to take a sip of her wine. She had bet on Abaku being in place. Now, she had to probe to find out more information, so that Essie and Raphael could be prepared. Otherwise, Raphael would believe she was a bad actor. She knew without even speaking to her sister that Raphael didn't trust her. Any mishap on her end would cause him to go over the edge, and she'd never be reunited with her sister.

"Source?" Sienna probed with squinched eyebrows.

"Oh, come now. You underestimate me? I understand that Dage was the frontman, but you have to know Dage's connections were because of me and my father. It took some time to rebuild and infiltrate, but with father's backing, our pipeline to international information is endless."

"No, I am just concerned about the source being correct about their information. We must succeed this time. It's the only way to come out of these shadows and live the way we want—the way we deserve."

Impressed, Abaku leaned over and kissed her cheek before caressing her chin with his index and middle finger. "Oh, we will succeed. My recon team confirmed the source's information this afternoon. It's a shame they'll bloody the streets of sunny California," he confirmed with a wink.

Sienna's throat dried up instantly, making it impossible to swallow. California? That wasn't Raphael's location. He was still stationed in Indiana with the special ops team. The persons in California were her sister and Kaion. She had to get the word to her sister so that Rhys could get them out of there immediately. Otherwise, she'd lose her sister, and if Raphael was true to his former self, her life and Abaku's wouldn't be far behind.

Casting a hardened gaze his way, she said, "The only shame is in the team failing to complete the task at hand."

Matching her expression, Abaku lifted an eyebrow and clenched his teeth. "And failure is not an option."

Lifting his glass to her, she reciprocated the same action, and they touched glasses.

CHAPTER 22

"Where the fuck are you?" Rhys bellowed into the phone. Raphael pulled the phone away from his ear. He had to stare at it for a minute to figure out who the fuck Rhys thought he was yelling at. "First off, pipe down," he barked back. "Second, I'm in California."

"What are you doing in California, Raphael? The plan was that you remained here so we could deal with this accordingly then move you out there."

"Nah, the plan was to lure Abaku to home turf. See, something Beau said made me think. If you were Abaku, or even if you were Sienna trying to make a play, would you come all the way to Indiana, where you knew federal agents would be ready for a takedown or at least on standby, or would you come to take out my family first, to lure me out?"

"Did she suggest that to you?"

"No, she made me remember that I couldn't trust Sienna's ass. I'm not leaving my family vulnerable with just your people. So, I left last night and came out here. I'm not in the house because I don't want to raise suspicions, but I'm not far from them. I can keep my eye out."

Rhys paced gripping his cell phone. "At least let me get some people out there."

"No, I don't want to draw attention. Keep what I've told you under wraps. I'll keep you updated, so you'll know what's happening."

166

"You'll need backup."

"Then you bring your ass out here and no one else." With that, he hung up the phone and moved back to the living room window to keep watch.

Rhys forgot Raphael was a street cat first and foremost. He'd made friendly with the neighbors across the street during his last visit with Essie and Kaion, and when he showed up this time, he used his street muscle to convince them to take an impromptu family vacation. Where his words failed him, his Glock did not. He'd paid good money to have the family scat so he could keep a watchful eye over the house with his wife and son, as well as the agents assigned to his family. In fact, he didn't even alert the agents, because he needed them to move freely as to not draw suspicions to their actions as well. He'd watched in silence all day and night. It was going on two a.m., and he was about to catch a few minutes of sleep when his phone buzzed again. He assumed it was Rhys again, but this time it was Essie.

"Hey, babe. Why are you—"

"Sienna just told me they are coming to California," she said in a rushed tone. Her voice was a mixture of panic and anger. "They are coming after us, Raph. Baby, please."

Before he could respond, he saw two black sedans pull in front of Essie's house. Four masked men with guns jumped out— two out of each vehicle. The one in charge pointed silently at the house next door, which was where the agents were housed. He signaled for the man who stepped out with him to move toward the house with Essie and Kaion. Each two-man team began moving stealthily toward each house.

"Essie, grab your gun." Raphael hung up and called Kaion, who answered on the second ring. "Kai?"

"Dad?"

"Get ready, *now*," he whispered and hung up.

Scanning the area, he made sure no one else was hanging in the background then darted across the street, locked and loaded. The men had split up. He would have to take the man in the front out with minimal noise so he didn't alert the other two assailants at the other house.

As soon as the man opened the front door, Raphael slipped in behind him. Essie was stretched out on the couch, seemingly asleep, and as soon as he raised his gun, Essie threw the blanket off her and pointed her handgun at his head. The man had just begun to curl his trigger finger when he felt the hard steel of a gun pressing into his skull.

"Drop it, muthafucka," Raphael ordered lowly, while Essie kept her gun trained on him.

He turned his gun upward and lifted his hands in the air. As he went to lower his weapon to the ground, Raphael hit him in the back of the head with the butt of his gun, and he crumpled to the floor in a heap. Essie still had her gun raised when Kaion's voice rang out.

"Essie! Watch out!"

Raphael dove to pull Essie toward him as a bullet screamed past, shattering the television and narrowly missing her. Essie fell into Raphael as they toppled over, bumping into the front door and causing it to slam shut. Raphael and Essie scrambled to get up, knowing that Kaion was in trouble.

"Keep your gun on him, Essie. If he moves, kill him!" Raphael ordered.

Kaion thundered down the steps and kicked the second masked man's arm, causing the gun to fly from his hands.

"You muthafuckas!" Kaion yelled.

The man used his now-free hand to swing at Kaion. The punch glanced off Kaion's face, but Kaion was swift with his return blow, which connected squarely with the man's chin, and he pushed him. The man fell over but was quick to hop to his feet, taking a combat stance.

"Come on! I'll kill you!" the masked assailant yelled, bobbing, prepared to battle with young Kaion.

Raphael charged full speed toward the masked man, catching him off guard, and tackled the man to the floor. The masked man delivered elbows to Raphael as they knocked over figurines and furniture. The bookshelf crashed on top of them, giving the masked man time to deliver a knee kick to Raphael's groin area.

"Urgh! Son of a bitch!" Raphael groaned out and curled over in pain.

Before the man could retaliate, Kaion ran up, delivering a kick to the side of the masked man's head, which gave Raphael time to get up and snatch the man's gun from the floor. Raphael swiped the gun and turned around just as the man pulled something from an ankle holster. Raphael let off two shots before he could aim his weapon. A pool of blood spread across the man's chest, and he slumped immediately. Raphael walked over to him and delivered one final bullet to his temple.

Kaion rushed over to Raphael as the back door opened, ducking behind him as Raphael raised the gun and delivered a kill shot to the dome of the third intruder. Kaion spotted the weapon in the first dead man's ankle holster and removed the weapon. It was a switchblade.

"Ugh!" The sound of despair came from Essie, followed by a loud thud.

Another masked assailant had run in, throwing open the front door and knocking Essie out cold. He took a shot at Raphael that missed as Raphael and Kaion scrambled to the kitchen, dodging the gunfire.

Raphael looked back, barking orders to Kaion as he exchanged gunfire with the fourth masked man. "Stay low!"

Raphael stood quickly, aiming at the man who ducked behind the sofa. When he clicked, he realized his clip was empty.

"Sounds like you're out!" the masked assailant laughed as he reloaded his clip and made his way slowly toward Raphael and Kaion.

"Fuck you!" Raphael yelled from behind the kitchen island. He turned to Kaion. "We don't have time, Kai. I'll be the diversion. Run out the back door to the house across the street. Call the police."

"No, Dad!" Kaion pleaded, fear trembling in his voice.

"No time! Go now!" Raphael said as he jumped up.

The masked man was about to shoot, but Essie plunged forward behind the man and jumped on his back. The movement knocked him off balance as he stumbled forward and flung Essie to the ground. Kaion jumped up, but instead of running out of the door, he flung the knife in his hand aimed at the man's chest. The knife landed at the base of his neck and blood spurted like a fountain. The assailant made a gurgling noise and gripped his neck, staggering forward. Raphael ran forward and jammed the knife deeper in his neck with a sharp blow from the heel of his hand. The man dropped his weapon, and Kaion rushed to retrieve it then scuttled over to Essie, who had slid over to sit with her back against the sofa. A huge knot was forming on her forehead.

"Make sure that first bastard at the door is still knocked out. I have his weapon." Essie held up both her gun and his. "Be careful," Essie warned.

Kaion directed her to stay there as he went to check on the situation with the first assailant.

Raphael was still wrestling with the bleeding man.

"Where the fuck is Abaku?" he growled.

Blood gurgled in the man's throat and spurted between his lips as he fought against death and Raphael.

"Tell me, you son of a bitch!"

Essie stood up and hobbled over to where Raphael was wrestling with the assailant to retrieve the information. She eased up on them and pointed the gun to the side of the man's head and pulled the trigger. The man's head fell to the side, his cold eyes staring back at Raphael as he went limp in his arms.

"Abaku is not here. He's still in Dubai. He sent a team," Essie offered. "Sienna told me that, too."

Kaion ran back into the kitchen. "The other man is gone. I saw a black sedan barreling down the street."

Raphael ran to the front door as Kaion went to tend to Essie. When he reached the front, he scanned the street and saw the second sedan was gone, just as Kaion had stated. Fury coursed through as he slammed the doorframe with his open palm.

"Fuck!"

Raphael ran back into the house, eyeing the carnage along the way. Three dead bodies and one escaped. He ran up to Essie and Kaion and hugged them before assessing them. He touched Kaion's face, where a bruise was developing on the bottom of his jaw. Then, he touched the knot on Essie's head, and she winced from the pain.

"Neither of you were hit, right?" Raphael asked, assessing their overall bodies.

"No," they said in unison.

"Listen, go to the house across the street. Enter with caution and blast the first thing you see moving," Raphael said to them.

They nodded and all headed out together. Once they were inside the other house, Raphael ran next door to the CIA safehouse. When he entered, he saw three of the CIA agents dead and knew that it was a professional hit. No one knew about Essie's location or the safehouse. There was a leak inside the CIA. That was the only way to explain how they knew about California and sent their team there. One thing he realized was Sienna couldn't have known who because she delivered that message at the last minute. However, it was also a good thing that she had. For one, he knew he would have lost his family that night, and equally important, it proved she was not involved in Abaku's plan to take them out. That decision to advise Essie of what was happening saved Sienna's life because he would have surely killed her himself.

Raphael ran across the street, alerting them of his presence before entering. He came into the house to find Essie and Kaion huddled together on the sofa. He hugged them.

"We have to leave now. The agents next door are all dead. I'm calling Rhys as soon as we get in the vehicle."

"How did Abaku know where to find us?" Essie asked as they got into the car.

"There's only one way," Raphael said as he eased down the street with his cell phone on speaker.

"Raphael! What's wrong?" Rhys asked.

"You've got a leak in your organization. Your agents at the safehouse are dead. Abaku sent four masked mercenaries to my family."

"Where are they now? Where are you now? Essie? Kaion?" Rhys's questions flew out like rapid fire.

"Three of the mercenaries are dead. One got away. Essie and Kaion are fine. We are going to an undisclosed location. I'm not telling you where we are until you get here."

"Anything else you can tell me?"

"I've got the plates from the other sedan. When you land, call me."

He disconnected the phone and made his way into the city. The safest place for them would be a hotel in a wealthier section of the city where a police presence was bound to be. He reached over and grabbed Essie's hand, and they intertwined fingers. He brought her hand to his lips for a kiss and Kaion sat forward, leaning his head on Essie's shoulder. She used her free hand to rub his cheek. All Raphael could think about was that he'd nearly lost his family tonight. Nothing less than God was on their side, with how everything went down. He was even more grateful he'd spent that time fine-tuning Kaion for moments like this, although he wished he had been wrong that it was necessary. He was a teenager, for Christ's sake. The feel of Essie's penetrating gaze brought his focus back to her. Both Essie and Raphael looked at each other knowingly. Tonight was too close for comfort. They had to end this before something happened to them, or worse, Kaion.

CHAPTER 23

Bright and early the next morning, Raphael's cell phone rang. The scattered sunlight peeking through the drapes hit Raphael's face as he squinted his eyes to adjust to the shrill sound of his phone and the light. Sitting up, he felt like a freight train had hit him. Both Essie and Kaion were piled into the king-sized bed with him. He lifted his phone from the nightstand to see the call was from Rhys and slipped out of the bed to speak to him in the bathroom.

"Speak to me," Raphael answered groggily.

"My plane just landed. I'm catching an Uber to wherever you are. I need the location," Rhys informed him.

"Bet."

Raphael gave Rhys the information to his hotel room then hung up and drained the weasel before washing his hands. His mind was churning. He'd just managed to doze off an hour before Rhys called. He was a mixture of anger and concern. Anger about his family and this apparent breach in the CIA, and concern for how all these attacks were affecting Kaion and Essie. When they arrived at the hotel, they didn't have any multi-bed rooms, so he'd opted for the king bed with a pullout sofa. Kaion was so shaken up he didn't even want to separate from them to sleep on the pullout. A teenager huddled up in the bed with his dad and stepmother was not normal.

Essie voluntarily stayed up a couple of hours to ice her forehead and ensure she was all right. Kaion took an extra hour after Essie finally settled to doze off himself. Raphael wouldn't close one eye until both of them were resting. He felt like such a burden on them, because these people were after him, but his family kept landing in the center of the controversy. That ended now. As soon as Rhys got there, he was going to demand his family be put into protective custody with people of his choice and an area of his choice, and come up with a plan to bring this war with the Dage family to an end.

"Stop blaming yourself." Raphael jumped at Essie's words as she entered the bathroom slowly.

He turned to face her. "You should be resting."

She walked to him, still shaken up from the night before. Placing her hands on his bare chest, she gently smoothed across it and kissed his pecs. "I can only rest so long, and stop avoiding what I said."

Raphael rubbed his hands down his face. "How can I not? It's because of me that you and Kai keep going through this. He's curled up in the bed, too afraid to sleep on the sofa bed let alone stay in his own room, because of the shit he keeps getting exposed to."

"Listen, I was already mixed up in that crazy ass family because of my sister, and Kai has had a wild life from the start, due to his mother. You can't take the blame for what we were already living through."

"But I'm not doing a good job of stopping what was started. I'ma man. Your man. His father. This isn't even supposed to be on your radar anymore." He turned around, leaning his elbows on the sink countertop and placing his face in his hands.

Essie wrapped her arms around his midsection and kissed his back. "Then end it."

Her words caught him off guard, and he raised up. She moved to the side of him as they stared at each other in the mirror. "I know part of the reason you have not handled this is because you've been trying to do this the right way. But fuck Rhys. Fuck OMECA. Fuck the CIA. But most of all, fuck Abaku and the entire Dage family. End it." She turned to face him, and he stared down at her. Her gaze was stern, her tone low and menacing. "Kill him and anyone else who's a threat. Just save Sienna. That is all I ask."

The old familiar glint flickered in Raphael's eyes, and his eyes glossed over into that distant and dark stare. Goon Raphael was back. Now that he had his wife's grace, he would save Sienna and finish the Dages. This time there would be no resurrections.

A knock on the door made them walk out of the bathroom. Essie moved back to the bed to sit, and Raphael checked the peephole before opening the door. It was Rhys. When he opened it, Rhys entered.

"Essie!" he said, side-stepping Raphael. "I'm so glad that you and Kaion are all right." He looked back and forth between them and the bleary-eyed Kaion.

"No thanks to your agents," Essie said tartly.

Raphael stood beside his family as they both stared at Rhys. "Yeah, how were your agents able to be picked off at an undisclosed and secure location?"

Rhys brought steepled hands to his face. "I do not know, but it is obvious someone is working against us. I will find out who it is. I promise you that." He looked back and forth between Raphael and Essie. "But first, we need to get you all to—"

Raphael put his hand up. "Lemme holler at you." Rhys and he stepped to the side, and Raph lowered his voice. "My family is my business. I'm gonna put them under protection with people I trust. I can't have their safety be an issue again. I don't know what your intentions are, but if they don't include me taking it to Abaku, then I'm out. Fuck your way. I deal with Abaku my way with your help, or my way without your help. That's the plan."

Rhys paused at his request. The tone of his voice and the look in his eyes told Rhys there was no negotiation with Raphael on this. Abaku had crossed the line, and there would be no absolution for his soul. Reluctantly, he agreed.

"We'll do it your way, Raphael, but we still need assistance."

"I'll handpick our assistance. You just make sure we have a way in, a way out, and access to whatever we need. This does not go out to anyone except the people I deem can be trusted. You got that?"

Rhys nodded. "Understood."

"Good." Raphael patted Rhys on the shoulder. "Give me a day to get my family settled. Get a room. I'll meet you back here."

CHAPTER 24

Abaku paced anxiously in his office, waiting to hear the results of the hit that he'd placed on Essie and Kaion. Initially, his plan was to go after Raphael directly, but after the intel he received that pinpointed the location of his family, he decided to smoke him out using that route. What better way than to catch Raphael at his most vulnerable moment than while he mourned for the loss of his wife and child? It was the perfect diversion. He wouldn't even have to have Raphael come to him or vice versa. He could pick him off during his grieving period. He'd counted on the fact that his grief would be so insurmountable that he would catch him slipping and that's when he'd put him out of his misery and help to join his family.

Now, all he needed was confirmation of their demise, and he could put the next steps in play to take out Raphael. He was one step closer to regaining his father's trust, the family money and access, and solidifying his relationship with Sienna. Soon, he'd have everything he wanted.

His royal blue silk shirt clung to his muscular chest, and the hem draped over tan linen pants. He exuded regality. He nursed the glass of bourbon in his hand with his arms folded across his chest, thoughts of his next course of action dancing in his mind. He barely heard the shrill sound of his cell phone, he was so engrossed in his inner thoughts.

"Tell me something good," Abaku breathed excitedly into the phone.

"The mission failed," his mercenary said tightly, his heavy breathing punctuating his words.

Abaku lifted his hand that held the glass and placed his index finger to his forehead. His eyes closed as he tried to process what he'd just heard. "What the hell do you mean it wasn't successful? It's a kid and a woman. How do you fuck that up?" His words came out peppery but it was obvious he was holding onto the fire behind them until he heard the story in its entirety.

"That's the thing. It wasn't. The agents are canceled, but the woman and child were ready for us. So was the initial target. He was there."

"What?" Abaku belted out, his anger spilling over. "The fuck you mean he was there!"

"Just what the fuck I said. My team is dead, and I narrowly made it out with my own life. I had to abort the mission, so I could relay the message to you."

"Where are you now?" Abaku demanded.

"In the black sedan, at our location. I'm waiting on my next orders from you." He took a deep breath. "We can still get them and him if you would like for us to make that move. You just need to find out how the fuck he knew when and where we were going to attack." A moment of silence passed between them, and the man got nervous. "Abaku?"

"Stay where you are at. Your instructions will come. I have a birdy I need to talk to about their song of choice."

They disconnected the line, and Abaku walked back to his desk and sat down. Lifting the screen of his laptop, he woke the machine up. After a few clicks, his map was trained on the coordinates. When he zoomed in, he saw his mercenary sitting in the car alone, banging his fist against his forehead with his cell phone in his hand. A sinister smile grew on his face when he reached into the pen cup on his desk and retrieved a set of keys. Using the keys, he unlocked the top drawer of his desk and removed an electric pad and stylus. Circling the stylus around the pad, when the red dot lit, he pressed the button as he continued to monitor the screen. The instant he pressed a button on the electric pad, the car exploded. Body parts and metal flew everywhere, and Abaku smirked before replacing everything and closing his laptop. *Incompetent fuck!* He stood and drank the remnants of his bourbon before slinging the glass across the room. It slammed into the bookcase and shattered into a million pieces onto the floor.

He was on a warpath, because he knew Raphael and his family were long gone. He couldn't tell his father what had happened, because he might suffer the same fate as his mercenary. He had to figure out who tipped Raphael and dead them. That was the only way his father would respect him and help him regroup.

Just then, it struck him. He picked up his phone and sent a text.

If you want your family to remain safe, you better call me immediately.

He slipped his cell phone on his desk, awaiting a phone call. If it didn't ring in the next fifteen minutes, he would put down another play. He was already in a murderous state of mind, so it was nothing for him to go on a killing spree. The way he felt, he still might. He didn't have to wait long; within two minutes his phone rang.

"The plan failed. They were waiting on us. You better tell me something, because if I sense one lie from you, I will end you and everybody you hold dear."

"Listen. You know I can't move the way I need to. I have a lens on my back from other people as well. I didn't know that Raphael would be there. No one has leaked anything on my end, especially not me."

Abaku's rage went soaring through the roof. "Well, how the fuck did he know? How the fuck did Essie know? No one was handled except the agents next door. Raphael and his family survived. All of them," he seethed, breathing through ragged breaths. "I will kill you—"

"Listen, this isn't on me. If you're mad with anyone, be mad at yourself. You didn't tie up loose ends on your part. Your leakage isn't with me or the team. Your leakage is on the person who advised Raphael and his family you were headed to his family instead of to him."

Abaku stopped pacing long enough to comprehend what was said. When he considered it, he sat on the edge of his desk, easing his sweaty palm down his pants leg. "What do you mean? You speak as though you have specifics. If you do, tell me."

"Look, I don't have much time. I gotta go. I'll be in touch when I can. But be careful where you lay your head."

The line disconnected, and Abaku stared at the phone in disbelief for a few seconds before he placed it on the desk beside him. He stood to go sit on the sofa as he pondered what was spoken to him, when it dawned on him the reference of the last statement. *Be careful where you lay your head.*

He leaped from the sofa like the springs had popped. "I know she didn't betray me. I *know* she didn't."

Rage spread from the core of his belly and rose through his veins. His breathing felt constricted as it heaved up and down, and he struggled to stop the racing inside. He couldn't accept that Sienna had betrayed him. It couldn't be. He refused to believe that. They'd confessed so much to each other. He'd confided in her. There's no way he could have misread her or their newfound love. She loved him. He loved her. They were a family.

She was in their conjoined bedroom, probably exercising. He stormed out of the office and up the stairs, down the massive hallway, and hooked a right, headed toward the room they now shared together. When he burst into the room, the door hit the wall so hard, the stopper snapped and the knob left a hole on the wall.

"Abaku!" She jumped, standing straight up from her prayer pose position and gripping the towel in her hand. "What's wrong, my love?"

Abaku said nothing, but rather gently closed the door. When it was shut, he leaned against it with his arms folded and his feet crossed at the ankles. He stood there glaring at her for what seemed like hours, unable to speak.

Sienna stood trembling. There's no way he could know. She was careful. The information only went to Rhys or Essie. He had no clue she'd been in contact with anyone else. She'd checked, rechecked, and double-checked her steps to ensure no trace of her treachery was left behind. Yet, he stood there glaring at her, causing fear to ripple through her body.

"Abaku," she said softly. "Is something wrong?"

"My mission failed," he said gruffly.

Feigning shock, Sienna threw down the towel. "What do you mean? Are you telling me you didn't kill them?"

"You seem shocked."

"That's because I am!" She paced in place, biting on her lip. "You need to get rid of that incompetent team. Reach out to your father for other men."

"Don't you want to know *how* we failed, first and foremost?"

Sienna stopped pacing and faced him. "Why does that matter? It matters that they did."

"No, why they failed is just as important as the mission."

Sienna placed her hands on her hips. "Okay, then, enlighten me on how they messed this up, so we can get down to the business of fixing this debacle."

Abaku lifted from the door and walked over to Sienna. She stood stiff as a board as he examined her from head to toe. He took in every feature. He noticed that her hair was black, with a brownish tint to the arch of her eyebrows, the deep pull her eyes held, the crease in the middle of her forehead, her velvety, chocolate skin, the swell of her plump breasts, the curve of her voluptuous figure, the dip in her back, the spread of her hips, the roundness of her booty, the thickness of her thighs, the definition of her calf muscles, even down to her beautiful feet with high arches and the second toe that was slightly longer than the big toe. She was sheer perfection.

Standing behind her, he slid his hand up her arm and pulled her into him. His grip tightened around her waist as he whispered in her ear. "They messed up because Raphael was not the target in this mission; Essie and his son were."

Sienna swallowed the lump in her throat. She hadn't considered that, but still it made no difference. "So? That does not explain how they missed."

He spun her around roughly. He gripped her sides staring her directly in the eyes. "They missed because Raphael was not supposed to be there. He helped them escape our attack."

She shrugged. "Well, I'm not surprised he was with them. He's Essie's husband. Where else was he supposed to be?"

"In Indiana," he said flatly. "See, my intel knew exactly where Raphael was and where he was supposed to be, until they lost sight of him. It's curious to me that he shows up at the precise time of the attack, and that your sister was aware of the attack."

"Wait. My sister?" Sienna asked. "How do you know my sister knew anything?"

"The only remaining agent told me so." He eyed her. "You seemed very defensive when I mentioned Essie. Why is that?"

Sienna shook her head. His inquiries were throwing her off. She was having to work double-time to say the right thing, think the right thing, and react the right way, and right now it was working against her.

"I only asked is all, Abaku."

Abaku tightened his grip to the point it was nearly pinching her sides. "How do you suppose Essie was prepared for our attack?"

Sienna winced from the pain. "How would I know, Abaku? It probably had to do with the fact that Raphael showed up. Anybody could have alerted her. Have you made sure your men were clean?"

"The only people who knew to go to California were the men who are now dead and *you*."

Sienna's blood ran cold. If they knew Raphael wasn't there, and their sole purpose was to kill Essie and Kaion, then it was obvious she had alerted Essie of his plan. Still, she had to try to place doubt in his mind.

"It wasn't me, Abaku. It could have been anyone. Those men? You don't know them."

Abaku placed his finger to her lips to silence her. "Shhh," he whispered. "Don't." When he looked at her, his expression was stern and unrelenting. "Those men had no personal ties to this matter. It was all business. All pay. The only person with personal ties was you. For months, you begged me to spare your sister then you began to change your tune after I opened myself up to you," he said, as if he started to have an epiphany.

Sienna began to tremble. There were no words she could say. They both knew that she'd done it. The words just hadn't been spoken aloud. Sweat formed on her forehead, and her eyes began to redden out of fear.

He gripped her face, squeezing her cheeks to the point her lips pouted out as if she had duck lips. "Don't you lie to me, Sienna. Did you warn your sister?"

Tears began to form in Sienna's eyes, but she refused to say anything. She wouldn't give him the satisfaction. Time elapsed as no words were shared between either of them. When it dawned on Abaku that she wasn't going to answer, his heart exploded with pain. Without a shadow of a doubt, he knew that she'd betrayed him. She'd betrayed his love for her. She'd betrayed his dreams for the future. For her treacherous-ass sister. Her sister, who was the reason his brother and her former husband was taking a dirt nap. Her sister. Dage was good enough for her to go against her own family, but not him. Where pain had once resided, anger replaced it on instant.

Sienna knew the moment anger had replaced the obvious pain and confusion that plagued Abaku. She felt him emotionally disconnect from her. When she dared look into his eyes, blackness had replaced them. The light of hope that he'd held in his eyes was gone. She didn't recognize the man that stood before her. Dage hadn't had a dark side, but Abaku obviously did. She knew better than to beg, so she continued to stand there in his clutches, waiting for what was next. Although she trembled inside, she stood stoic.

Abaku kissed her roughly and passionately. The move caught her off guard. Out of instinct, she wrapped her arms around his neck and fell into the passion of the kiss. When she touched him physically, it unleashed the madman within him.

He pushed her back away from him and then pushed her against the wall in the bedroom. He put his hand over her mouth to muffle her voice. From his waist he pulled out a switchblade. Sienna went to scream, but her sounds were swallowed when Abaku slammed his forehead into hers, dazing her.

"Since you can't keep your mouth closed, I'll close it for you."

Taking the switchblade, he pried her mouth open with his free hand. As she cried and squirmed underneath him, he reached into her mouth and forcefully pulled out her tongue. He placed the switchblade on her tongue and dragged the blade across. She screamed as best she could, arms flailing and body flopping, trying to get free. It didn't help. Just when she thought she would pass out from the pain, her tongue snapped out of her mouth and she fell back. He held the bloody lump of flesh in his hand as she shrieked, blood pouring from between her fingers. Her back hit the wall, and she fell to the floor.

Abaku kneeled before her, wagging her tongue in his hand. "All you had to do was play your position, Sienna. I would have given you the world. Now, all you're going to do is leave this world."

An avalanche of tears flooded her face as she put her hands up. Flinging the flesh to the floor, he gripped a chuck of her hair and forced her to stand. He leaned his head against her forehead as he turned his head back and forth.

"I loved you. With my whole heart." Abaku's eyes lifted, and he had the look of the devil himself.

Sienna's eyes widened as he jabbed the blade between her rib cage and twisted, shredding her pericardium sac. When he ripped it out, blood spewed over them. Blood filled her lungs as she gasped, trying to breathe. Abaku knew that she couldn't. He dropped her body to the ground and watched as she slowly drowned in her own blood. It was a slow and painful death, exactly what she deserved. Abaku watched as the light in her eyes dimmed then extinguished.

He turned to walk out so he could have the cleaners come and take care of everything. When he was headed to the door, something caught his attention, and he veered over to the dresser. He scanned the glossy piece of paper and the recent date printed at the corner of the image. His eyes bulged, and he let out a bloodcurdling cry. Running back over to Sienna, he shook her violently, but it was of no use.

"Why? Sienna! Why didn't you tell me?"

He fell beside her with the picture in his hand and his hands pressed again his forehead. Tears streamed down his face as he stared at the photo again. The only thing he could focus on were the words *Baby Dage*. His body went limp as the picture floated from his fingers, landing in a pool of Sienna's blood. He leaned back and wailed, realizing he'd lost everything he'd truly ever wanted.

CHAPTER 25

"Abaku!" Bio yelled as he entered the house. "Abaku!"
Bio's mind was running as fast as he was. When he received the phone call from his son, he couldn't make heads or tails of what he was saying. The only words that finally became audible enough for him to understand was that Sienna was dead. From the frantic sound and screaming, he didn't know what had happened or how she had died, but rather than continue to listen to Abaku fumble over an explanation, he did the next best thing: got into his car and hurried over to Abaku's house.

"Abaku!" he yelled once more before he opened their master bedroom door. "Holy Shit!" he shouted out the scene before him.

It looked like something out of a massacre scene in a horror movie. Blood was everywhere. Sienna's lifeless body was sprawled out on the floor, her empty eyes staring up toward the ceiling. In the torso area of her body, it was stained and soaked in red blood. Upon further inspection, Bio saw a bloody switchblade sitting beside Abaku. When he scanned his son, his clothes were smeared with heavy streaks of blood and his hands were covered with dried up blood as was his face. His head was leaned back against the wall, and he was staring out into space. Sure, his gaze was toward Bio, but it was as if he didn't see him, as if he was zoned completely out. He could tell by the dried streaks on his face that he had been crying. Bio ran up to his son.

"Abaku," he called out and snapped his fingers in front of his face. Abaku seemed to snap back into reality as he turned to look at his father. "Abaku, what happened?"

"I killed her." His answer was simplistic. No more. No less.

Bio fanned his arm outward. "I can see that, son. My question to you is why did you kill her? What happened?" he continued to press.

Abaku's blood boiled, thinking of Sienna's treachery. He'd trusted her, allowed himself to fall in love with her, spared her. His father had wanted her to be murdered right along with Raphael and Essie. Now, he understood why. He saw right through her facade. How could his father, who barely had interaction with the woman, see straight through her like mirrored glass, and he, who had spent over a year with the woman, could not? He knew why. He'd fallen for her feminine wiles instead of using his brain to see she was only using him. Plotting against him to save her sister. The same sister who was responsible for her husband and unborn child's demise.

She was stupid to think that Essie wouldn't betray her again. He'd placed his loyalty in the one person who couldn't even be loyal to the man who lost his life to make a better one for her. If she was stupid, then he was the ignoramus. She'd made her position known from the beginning. He should've trusted that tiger wouldn't change her stripes. She'd slithered into his veins and took up home in the chambers of his heart, making him think he was worth the change. What a joke. If she could discard her loyalty for her husband, what the hell did he think she would do for him?

"You were right, father," Abaku said, turning his head back forward and leaning back against the wall again. "She was a liar. She led me to believe she'd fallen in love with me. So, I placed my trust in her. And she lied. The entire time, she was pumping me for information only to feed it back to her sister, Essie."

Bio became infuriated at the news. He knew she was a disloyal bitch. He'd told Dage that from the beginning. He held his feelings back, because that's who Dage wanted. However, she smelled of nothing but a purebred gold digger to him. This woman had ruined both of his sons. If he could wake her up and kill her again, he would do it.

"I told you that she needed to be taken care of, Abaku. Why would you not listen to me?"

"Because I loved her father!" Abaku yelled.

"Oh, come now! The girl was a peasant when Dage wifed her up. You did not need his sloppy seconds in your life. You should've left that trash where she was from the beginning anyway, but since you decided to drag her along, you should have killed her earlier, like I'd instructed."

Abaku jumped to his feet with the agility of a panther. "I don't need to hear this shit right now, Father! I understand that, but I'm dealing with more regrets now than ever!"

Bio's eyebrows cinched together. "What are talking about, Abaku?"

Rather than speak, Abaku lifted the photo in his hand and handed it to his father. His father looked down at what he was presenting to him and accepted it. When he looked at the photo, Abaku spoke again. "She carried my child, Father. She had not told me before"—he paused and scanned the room—"this." He turned back to face his father.

"Where did you find this?" Bio asked, lifting the sonogram picture up to him.

"When I was leaving out of the room, it was on the dresser. Apparently, she found out two days ago," Abaku answered feeling dejected.

Bio threw a harsh gaze at Sienna. "Two days ago. That means she had no intention of telling you. Otherwise, she would have disclosed that information immediately."

Abaku ran his blood-covered hands over the top of his head. "But now, I've killed her, and she carried my child." His eyes welled with tears for the child he'd never come to know. "I've killed my baby, father."

For the life of him, Bio couldn't understand what it was about this woman—hell, these sisters, to be honest—that had his sons so damned foolish over them. He couldn't lie; he was glad she was dead. His only regret was that she hadn't been taken out with Dage and spared his remaining son this agony.

Bio walked over to his son and gripped him by the shoulder. "Listen to me." He jerked him so that Abaku was facing him. "Listen…to…me. That woman over there is nothing more than a parasite who has sucked the life out of my children. If she knew she was pregnant and still had not told you two days later, then that means she was never going to tell you. Given what you've already told me, she was probably trying to find a way to get rid of the baby underneath your nose, and then, you never would have known your child anyway." He placed the other hand on Abaku's other shoulder and looked him directly in the eyes. "Your child was never going to see the light of day, whether you killed that bitch or not. That's what you need to accept."

Abaku's face contorted as his father's words penetrated his ears, his mind, his heart, and then his soul. Given the circumstances surrounding the entire situation, he couldn't deny that his father was more than likely correct. Sienna probably would have had an abortion. On second thought, there was no probably about it. She would have had an abortion to keep from tying herself down to the Dage family, but more importantly, to keep from tying herself down to him. Abaku snatched the photo from his father's hand and stalked over to Sienna. Kneeling down, he opened her mouth and shoved the sonogram picture inside and shoved her mouth closed. She could take that picture to the same hell that he would place her in.

He stood and looked back at his father. "Her interference caused the entire family to escape. Raphael flew out to California and was there to protect his family. Three of my men died. I bodied the other for his incompetence. The federal agents are dead, too. There's no direct trace back to me other than the fact that Raphael knows the attack came from us."

Bio scratched his head. He was trying to be patient with his son, but he had royally fucked up. He did not know how he could be this snowballed over a woman who had already be used by his other son. Then it dawned on him how Dage and Abaku were forever in competition, even in death. Damned fools.

"I am so pissed with you right now I could scream. Not only do we not know where that bastard is, now we don't even have a play in place to tend to him." The look on his son's face showed that he did not need to hear any of this. "I'm sure you have already beaten yourself up about this situation, and I don't want to bludgeon you to death with the guilty speech. We do need to find a way to contend with this Raphael and his wife and son, but for now, we have to tend to this corpse lying in the middle of your master bedroom floor."

"My exact thoughts," Abaku offered.

"Let me call my people to have them come over. In the meantime, you change your clothes and—"

"I want to see to it myself that her body is disposed of properly. I am going with your crew," Abaku stated, interrupting his father.

Bio nodded. He did not argue with his son because he understood. "Keep those clothes on, then. There is no need messing up two sets of clothes. You will get rid of them afterward." He lifted his cell phone from his pocket. "Let me make this call."

As Bio discussed what he needed to be done, Abaku paced the floor. He listened as his father ordered up a cleanup crew and complete coverup from the head general himself. Again, he shunned his own incompetence. He was a grown man having to lean and depend on his father to take care of what he had not. It was embarrassing.

"They are on the way," Bio informed him. "Until we can devise a plan to locate and kill Raphael and his family, you will need a team of security men in place to watch over your home. I have a team that you can call. We will take care of that first thing in the morning. We do not need to take any chances with that rabid dog running around footloose and fancy free."

"Yes, sir." It was all that Abaku could muster.

When the cleaners arrived, Abaku led them to his master bedroom, where they made quick work of wrapping Sienna's body in cellophane wrap and then rewrapping her in large black plastic bags that they had to cut open to ensure that her body was properly secured. After they wrapped her body in duct tape to secure it, they carried her out to the unmarked van and tossed her body inside. Once she was taken care of, they came through and thoroughly cleaned all the blood with cleaning agents, then used a special cleaner to remove the evidence of blood and matter so that it would not be detected through UV black lights or any other DNA-identifying technology. Last, they swept the entire bedroom of fingerprints to eliminate any remnants of Abaku's involvement in any foul play.

To the world, it would appear as though she ran off and left Abaku. He didn't have to worry about nosy neighbors or anyone on the outside for that fact. She had not made friends. In fact, she had not adapted to living in Dubai at all. That should have been another signal to him that she was not invested to the long-haul dream of family with him, as she had been with Dage.

At this point, he even questioned her honesty with his brother. If she was so wicked to lead him astray, was she not leading Dage astray as well? Perhaps it was as his father had suspected, and she married Dage for the money. It was the only reason that she could be treacherous enough to involve her sister without remorse or regard for her feelings for the American, but then when there was no substantial financial benefit from the Dage family, that she would plead her sister's life. The nerve of that woman. Now, his regret was turning from the loss of his child to having impregnated her in the first place.

"Are you ready?" his father asked, bringing him out of his private thoughts.

Glancing around, he noticed the cleaners were gone, and the only people left were he and his father. He nodded. "Where are the men?"

"The cleaners left. The disposers are in the van waiting for you. I will stay here until you return. I cannot be caught up in this portion. I have to protect my wife—and your mother. Do you understand?"

Abaku understood exactly what he was saying. His father would help him, but he would not under any given circumstances suffer the consequences for Abaku's actions. He respected it, because he did have to look out for his wife, and Abaku's mother needed Bio's protection. He would have it no other way himself. He would never allow his father to suffer for his actions.

Nodding, he said, "I understand. I'll see you when I return."

Abaku strode out the door and hopped in the van with the disposers. They discussed with him the different locations to dispose of the body. When he chose the grinder, they called their contact, only known to them as The Butcher, to arrange for the disposal.

"Where are we headed?" Abaku asked one of the men.

The men looked at each other. "It's an old building formerly used by a meat-packing company. It still houses equipment that we use today for business…amongst other things," one of the men stated, garnering a few chuckles from the others.

"This will get the job done without a hiccup. Once we dismember the remains, it all goes in the grinder, and it's minced meat from there," the other man added.

"I see," Abaku stated, mesmerized by their thoroughness and efficiency.

"Why don't you sit back, sir, and allow us to handle this?" the first man said.

Abaku agreed and did as was requested. He wasn't stupid. Anybody who knew how to dispose of a body was not someone that he wanted to test the temperature with. He sat back and decided that he would only intervene again when it was time.

Once they arrived at the seemingly abandoned building, an armed guard tapped the van, clearing them to move the van inside an entryway within the building. As they passed through, Abaku could see the team of watchmen giving them the protection they needed to complete the task at hand. He hung back as the men exited the van to conduct business with The Butcher. He would not do business with Abaku present. He understood the need for ambiguity. He felt the same way. He had no interest in the man identifying his face, either.

Once the agreement was made, the men retrieved the bound body from the back of the van and gave Abaku the green light to exit. They entered a room, where Sienna's remains were placed on a cold slab and each man was given a bone saw. Abaku stood watch as they meticulously chopped the body down into parts. When they arrived at the head, Abaku was given a saw. He turned a quizzical eye to them, but their no-nonsense expressions told him it wasn't an ask. Abaku understood it to mean that if all hands were dirty, no mouths could snitch. Holding back his gag reflexes as best he could, he did his part to dismember Sienna's corpse.

Once he was done, the parts were packed in a pile and loaded on a cart.

"We'll take it from here, sir," the second man informed him.

"Sure, that is fine. I'd prefer to wait here, if that's all right?" Abaku said.

With a nod, the guards stood watch over Abaku as the other men made quick work of rolling the cart into the closed-off location in the back of the building. Soon, he heard the piercing sound of a contraption cranking and what sounded like metal shredding into pieces.

As The Butcher and the men did their work with Sienna's remains, Abaku took a moment to reflect over the rise and quick fall of their love. Despite the fact that he hated her, he also still loved her. That was an emotion he couldn't readily turn off. However, he couldn't do anything about his messed-up feelings for her. She was already gone. This was just a formality to ensure he did not get ensnared in the legal system himself. He hated that it ended this way, but a message had to be sent that when it came to the Dage family, only the ones loyal to them would survive to tell the story.

"Looks like you played your cards wrong, sweetheart. You should have bet on me instead. Now, look at you. What a waste," Abaku muttered to himself.

A putrid smell invaded Abaku nostrils, making him gag and cough, and the guard handed him a towel to cover his nose and mouth. When the towel was secured, Abaku turned to the guard.

"What the fuck is that smell?"

"Solvents used during disposal, sir," the guard responded through his toweled mask. "And the smell after that is for cleanup. I suggest you keep the towel to your nose and mouth and do less talking."

Following his advisement, Abaku stopped talking and protected his body from the awful smells emanating from the back of the warehouse. After a short time passed, the men who assisted with the disposal reappeared from the back of the building. "We can go now, sir," the first man said.

"Let's get the fuck outta here," Abaku agreed.

Abaku thought he would feel differently, but he did not. He knew then that killing Sienna and disposing of her corpse was the best course of action. They rode in the van then quickly stopped to exchange it for a sedan. He was quiet on the ride back to his house.

When he entered, his father stood up. "Is it done?"

"She is now food for the fishes," Abaku stated.

His father walked up to him and placed his hands on his shoulders. "Put her out of your mind. She is no longer your problem, but Raphael is still out there. That is your focus now. I need you to handle that, son. Please."

Abaku tilted his head to him and steeled himself. "Consider it done, Father."

"My boy," he said with a smile. "Now, take a shower and follow the directions the cleaners have provided. Bag the clothes, and I will get them from you in the morning for disposal." With that, Bio walked to the door to leave.

"I'm sorry that I disappointed you, Father."

Bio turned to face him with his hand on the doorknob. "Just make sure you put that bastard Raphael down. That's all I ask."

CHAPTER 26

Rhys walked back into the offices of OMECA on a mission. The only people who knew the whereabouts of Essie and Kaion, and the agents watching over them, were the agents' direct command, whom he ruled out because he had no reason to risk his men, and the OMECA crew, including Raphael. Of course, Raphael was ruled out, so that only left space for the leak to have come from Benji, Porter, Beau, Emmanuel, or Tonio. Today was grass-cutting time. He'd weed out the snake—or snakes—and handle them accordingly.

Rhys walked into the building, and everyone was already seated at the table. They'd been informed before he got on the plane about the incident at the safehouses. They were all sitting by, waiting on the next command. When Rhys saw them, he tamped down his anger so he would not give away his suspicions to the snake in their midst.

"We can confirm that three agents are dead. Raphael and his family are shaken up, but they are doing well. They are being relocated to a safe location. The agency is processing the relocation, so we don't have to concern ourselves with it."

"So, what do we do about Abaku?" Emmanuel asked.

"We do nothing right now. Abaku is on alert. This will give us time to devise a plan that helps us catch him when he's most vulnerable," Rhys lied smoothly.

"I hate to ask the obvious question lingering in the room, but how did he even learn the whereabouts of the Waters family?" Benji asked.

Rhys pointed his finger at him. "That is the million-dollar question. The entire incident is under investigation. Hopefully, we'll have answers sooner rather than later."

Everyone nodded as Rhys eyed each and every one of them before dismissing them to return to their respective duties. He was upset he couldn't pinpoint which of them was a traitor. The vetting process by the agency had been thorough, but there had to be something that they'd missed...that he'd missed...and he intended to find it. He'd placed a call to his trusted source to do a deeper history search on the team members of OMECA. At this point, they were leaving no stone unturned. It'd been two days already since he placed the call, and he was anxious. Anxious to know who was able to infiltrate his squad on his watch.

As he sat in his office, filling out paperwork about the three deceased agents, his phone rang. When he noticed who the call was from, he quickly answered it.

"What do you have for me?" Rhys asked.

"Something you will not believe!"

Rhys flung his office door open and stalked to the main conference room, calling an emergency meeting. He was furious at the blatant lack of research. The information was hidden in plain view. He couldn't believe it.

"What's going on, Rhys?" They all asked in unison.

Rhys stood quietly in front of them as they all huddled around in a circle. He didn't even want to take the time to address it. The information had been verified. In one swift motion, Rhys pulled his Glock, but before he could properly aim the gun, Beau flung a knife, which lodged in Rhys's shoulder. It happened so fast that everyone's attention went to Rhys, which gave Beau time to grab Benji in a submission hold while holding another knife to his throat. All the remaining team members pulled their guns and aimed them at Beau.

"Ah–ah–ah. Don't do nothing stupid. Y'all know I'm surgical with this shit."

"You bitch," Benji seethed. "Let me go."

"Aw, Benji. I'm disappointed in you," Beau said, her voice laden with seduction. "I thought you'd like this. You've been trying to scratch this pussy for a long time. Here's your chance." She took her tongue and licked his face. "Stay calm for me while I ease out, and this premium, Grade-A shit will be hot and ready for you."

"Unhand him, Beau," Rhys spewed between pants of pain. "This only ends one way, you lying bitch."

"That's your problem, Rhys. You always underestimate your opponent." She eased back toward the door as the others stepped closer to her. "Ever seen a live beheading? Keep moving!"

"Anybody wanna tell us what's going on here?" Emmanuel yelled with his gun trained on Beau.

"Meet the second cousin of Bio Dage," Rhys said to the team. "Her biological father wasn't listed on her birth certificate–only her stepfather. We still found the connection. Once we located the snake, it all made sense except one thing. Why did you warn Raphael?"

"My one miscalculation," she explained with an air of disgust in her tone. "I wasn't trying to warn him. I was trying to cast doubt in his mind about the rest of you. Make him think that one of you would be the leak. But that Raphael, he's a smart one. Too smart," she grumbled.

"You won't make it out of here alive, Beau," Rhys stated matter-of-factly.

"And I have no problem taking out his ass if I don't."

Porter yelled encouraging words to Benji as Beau continued to drag him backward and the rest of the team pressed forward. There was a quick exchange of glances between Porter and Benji, and just as Beau reached the threshold, Benji slid his hand down to his combat boot, releasing the automatic, spring-action boot dagger. Benji gripped the sides of the doorframe, jolting Beau to a stop, then lifted his boot and slammed it down, puncturing Beau's foot.

Beau shrieked in pain, instantly loosening her grip on Benji.

"Now!" Porter screamed.

Benji elbowed her in the stomach, causing her to lose her hold on him, and took advantage of her loose hold to throw himself away from her. Before Beau could recover, a series of bullets let off. Tonio, Emmanuel, and Rhys lit her up, her bullet-riddled body dancing back and forth as she fell back into the door then slid to the floor.

"And you forgot, we're generals with ours," Tonio stated with a smirk.

Porter ran over to Benji and hugged him, and he hugged her back. When Rhys dropped in the seat, wincing from the pain in his shoulder, Porter walked over to Rhys to check the wound. Emmanuel went about the business of ordering a cleanup for Beau. While Porter was working on Rhys, Tonio walked over to him to check on him.

"That's where that fly-by-the-seat shit gets you." They both laughed when Rhys held up his middle finger with his uninjured arm. "Are you good, though?"

Rhys nodded. "How did you know Beau was the traitor?"

Tonio stood back with his legs agape and arms folded. "From Raphael. He explained that her "advice" didn't sit well with him. He said he had a feeling that she would be our loose end. Looks like he was right."

Understanding passed between them before Rhys spoke again. "That's one major issue addressed. Now, I have to tend to the next one."

"What's that?" Porter asked after standing from gluing the puncture wound.

Rhys looked up at his remaining team members, who were all staring down at him inquisitively. He dropped his head. When he lifted it, sorrow danced in his eyes. "I have to tell Raphael that Sienna is dead."

CHAPTER 27

Raphael stood with the phone pressed to his ear long after Rhys had hung up. Beau had been taken care of, so she was no longer an issue, but the more troubling news that had come down the CIA wire was the part he struggled with. Sienna. Out of all the crap that he and Essie had been through together, this would undoubtedly be the worst. Abaku could storm in here right now, and the aftermath of it would not measure up to the pain he would have to place on Essie's heart. He wasn't anywhere near as attached to Sienna as Essie was, and the weight of the information nearly bowed him. His wife was a strong woman, but even strong people had their limits. This news would surely be Essie's. How could he tell her about her sister? How could he not?

When his arm got heavy holding the phone, he placed it down on the table. He dreaded walking into the kitchen, where his old security team from his former life with Alex watched over his family in a rental home in Indianapolis. He heard something he hadn't in a long time— laughter. They were playing a new card game about revoking people's Black cards and were having the best time. He relished it. It felt like what home should feel like. Not bullets and bloodshed. He'd longed to have this feeling back inside his home. The fact it was still only temporary housing made his heart soar; even in the midst of these circumstances he could still witness their joy. He could make them feel the one thing that they hadn't felt in months—safe.

Now he had to disrupt that sanctuary of safeness with the news of Sienna. It wasn't fair. He was a man, though. Essie's man. He had to step up and be there for her as her husband, her friend, her confidant, and right now, her comforter. Then he would be what he had to be for all of them. Their protector. He would kill Abaku for all the pain he'd inflicted on his family. His only decision now would be whether to kill him fast or slow.

Raphael made hasty steps toward the breakfast area where three armed men, Essie, and Kaion sat playing. Essie stopped mid-sentence and turned to in her seat to face him when she heard his footsteps. When she noticed the tormented expression on his face, she jumped to her feet, almost knocking over her glass of soda. She rushed to him meeting him halfway.

"Raph, what's wrong?" she asked, panicked.

Taking the cue, the three men stood, and Raphael could tell they were ready for whatever. Kaion stood, too. His concern was for Raphael. He walked over to Raphael and Essie, equally as concerned.

"Raphael, baby, what's wrong?" Essie pleaded again.

Looking down into her fear-stricken face, Raphael pulled Essie into a tight embrace, slowly rocking her back and forth. His chin rested on the top of her head, and he did something he hadn't done since his father's death. He cried. The tears fell like rain, and she felt the drops landing on her hair.

Without a word, Essie jerked back out of his embrace. She lifted fearful and sad eyes to him. "What happened, Raphael? It's my sister, isn't it? What happened to Sienna, Raph? What happened to my sister?"

She was hysterical with worry by the time the last question poured out. She could feel it in her bones. Something dire had happened. She didn't want to speculate, but she knew whatever it was, it was horrendous.

Raphael looked down into her eyes and inhaled sharply. "Sienna is gone, babe. She's—"

"Ughhhhhh!" She pushed him off her. "Don't you tell me that! Don't you speak that! It's not true. It's not true! My sister is not…it's not true!" she yelled.

Raphael took a step forward. "Baby, I know you don't want to accept it—"

"'Cause it's not true!" Essie yelled. "Who told you that? Rhys? Put him on the line. Right now! Do it now. Right now!" Her eyes darted around the room wildly, and the agents shrank back slightly, clearly alarmed at her manic response.

Raphael held up his hand, signaling for them to give him a moment, then walked back to grab his phone. When he returned, he dialed Rhys and placed him on speaker. "Rhys, Essie needs to confirm with you about what you told me."

Essie wasted no time waiting for a response. "Rhys, you lying piece of shit! You tell us the truth. What happened to my sister? Where is she?"

"Essie," Rhys breathed out. "My intelligence tells me that Abaku murdered Sienna in the home they shared in Dubai. It has been confirmed by special forces. The Dages are covering this up. Since we have no jurisdiction there, there is nothing we can do. I'm so sorry, Essie. Your sister is gone."

A bloodcurdling wail escaped Essie as Raphael dropped his phone to catch her from falling on the floor. All he could do was wrap his arms around her and rock as they sat on the floor with her tucked firmly between his legs. Kaion curled up on the floor next to them and wrapped his arms around her waist. One of the armed men stood watch over them as the other two protected the perimeter to give the family time to adjust to the heartbreaking news.

"Why?" Essie wailed out over and over again.

"He found out that she had assisted us," Raphael whispered as she continued to cry, sobs racking her body.

A full hour had passed with all three of them still in the same position before Essie's cries dissipated. When she finally looked up, she caressed Kaion's curly locks before asking him to go to his room. He gave her a kiss on the cheek and did exactly as she asked. Raphael stood and helped Essie to her feet, then asked the guard to give them a moment.

Raphael wiped the remaining tears from Essie's cheeks before pulling her into another hug. "I love you, Essie. I'm so sorry about Sienna."

"Don't be sorry. Get even," she said, and her voice was cold and harsh.

Raphael peered down at her. The most cold and callous eyes reflected at him. He'd never seen that look in her eyes before. Although he was familiar with the sight because he'd held that same merciless mien previous times himself.

"When you find Abaku, slaughter him, and make it deliberate and excruciating."

Raphael nodded. "For Sienna."

She met his eyes, her gaze burning. "For my sister."

CHAPTER 28

When Raphael got out of the back of the SUV with one of his armed guards, the sedan holding Rhys pulled up. Raphael nodded and the man pulled off, heading back to Indianapolis to tend after Raphael's family. Raphael opened the door to the backseat and got inside. Rhys was already back there, and at his command, they pulled off again, headed toward the airport. During the ride, Rhys explained the layout from the intel he'd received. He gave Raphael the fake documents, ID, and cash he'd need while in Dubai.

As they pulled up to the terminal, Rhys shook Raphael's hand. "This is where I get off. I'm sorry about the loss of Sienna. But you make sure he feels that shit."

"Indeed," Raphael said, opening the back door.

He stopped when Rhys put his hand on his arm and turned back. "I'm not giving Essie any more bad news, so you get in and get your ass out. Understand?"

Raphael tilted his head to him. "I don't give goodbye kisses to my wife, Rhys." With that, he opened the door and sauntered inside the terminal.

"Mr. Smith?" the greeter asked Raphael as he stepped outside the door of the terminal after arriving in Dubai.

Raphael smiled at the man. "Indeed," he stated as shook the man's hand.

"Our vehicle is over here." They walked the few paces to the truck. "Allow me to get the door for you."

The greeter and driver opened the door for Raphael, and he eased in the back with the only thing in his possession: a backpack. The man closed the door and walked around the vehicle to the driver's side and slipped behind the wheel. When he pulled off, he removed the hat with the fake hair and mustache.

"Nice look. You should keep it," Raphael teased.

"Fuck you," Tonio said and laughed as he steered into Dubai traffic.

Tonio had become one of Raphael's trusted associates after he helped him with Tatiana. He'd found out that he and Tonio had similar backgrounds growing up, and they connected over their shared miserable experiences. Tonio was the one who first hinted at the possibility of a leak in the department or the crew, due to the lack of information they could get to pinpoint Abaku. Even when they did, Rhys's hesitancy to attack further confirmed to them that he had his doubts on the loyalty of the people surrounding the case, both inside and outside of the bureau.

Tonio and Raphael had kept their newfound friendship under wraps due to the nature of the business. They had been correct in doing so. With the possibility of snakes such as Beau at every corner, they had to be careful who they aligned with and who they entrusted. Raphael had not been a member of the military or any federal agency, but he was a product of the hood. Hood knowledge beat any type of special forces training available. You just couldn't teach that kind of thought process. You had to live it. It had to be embedded. That's what it was for Raphael. Embedded. He used to dread his life, but everything he'd gone through prepared him for the crazy, twisted events he'd been living as of late. Therefore, he could do nothing but appreciate it for it was: survival skills.

"We have a base set up where we can map the layout of his home," Tonio said to Raphael, pulling him out of his quiet reverie.

"I ain't aiming for his home. I'm aiming for him and his daddy."

Tonio looked back at him in the mirror and shook his head. He didn't dare challenge Raphael on what he wanted to achieve in this mission. He understood why. If he killed the elder Dage's only other living child, he would bring the force of all Africa to rain down on Raphael's head—and the American government as well. Also, he needed the ultimate revenge for his wife's sister. Mostly, Raphael needed it to end. All those things Tonio could respect. While he admired Raphael's toughness and techniques, he didn't sign up for this life, unlike himself and the others. Albeit, he'd make a hell of a partner if he did. Still, he just needed both of them to make it out of Dubai alive.

"Since you're set on doing crazy shit, I got your back," Tonio teased as he pulled up to the safehouse location.

"And I've got yours. Let's get this done, so we can kiss Dubai goodbye."

For the next couple of days, they tracked every movement of Abaku, his men, and his family. Inside contacts were able to get them tapped into detailed conversations between Abaku and his father, and the planned attack on Raphael and his family. Apparently, he was the black sheep of the family who was hanging on to his legacy by a threat. The only reason his father hadn't put Abaku out of his misery to join his brother himself was that he'd killed Sienna. That granted him enough pardon to remain in Bio's good graces.

Raphael had something for both men. Since his father was the financial backer for Abaku, his compound was locked down tighter than Fort Knox. They would have to plan separate attacks, which was extremely risky. However, Raphael had thought of a plan that would work, but they would have to eliminate Abaku first. When he explained that portion of the plan to Tonio, he was all in.

Since Raphael and Tonio had been in Dubai, they had to spend a little bit longer doing recon, because Abaku had hired security for his home. They figured he sensed that Raphael may retaliate, and he'd hired them in anticipation. It only ensured that Raphael and Tonio were far more strategic than they initially planned to be. And at last, they finally found their way in.

The white cable van that Raphael and Tonio had been sitting in could finally move, since they'd received the confirmation that Abaku was at his house. When the van began to move through the neighborhood, it appeared as if they were leaving a neighbor's house after a job.

"Get ready," the driver, another undercover agent from the bureau, said as he drove. "10 paces…nine, eight, seven, six, five, four, three, two, one."

As soon as he said one, Raphael slid the van doors open, and he and Tonio took fire at the security guards in the front. The semi-automatic assault rifles chopped down man after man, as the few remaining took cover and began to fire back.

Cries from the security guards echoed in between the gunfire. "We're under attack! Get Abaku to safety!"

Raphael and Tonio jumped out of the van, exchanging gunfire with the three security guards who'd come from their posts to assist.

"I'll cover you with the two to the left while you make for the door," Tonio said. "Eyes up."

"Eyes open." Raphael nodded.

"Go!" Tonio yelled as he stood and let his chopper bang at the two security guards.

Raphael aimed, shooting at the third and grazing his arm. That was enough time for him to rush him. The man struggled against Raphael as he was held in a gripping bear hug. Raphael reared his head back and slammed his forehead into the man's forehead. His forehead split and blood rushed out flowing into his eyes.

"Ugh! My eyes! You muthafucka!" he screamed, clutching his forehead.

Raphael let go and gripped the man behind his neck, forcing him inside the house. As soon as they entered, two more security guards let loose a volley of bullets, hitting the man. Raphael grabbed the security guard's gun out of his holster and popped one security guard in the neck. He fell back, his gun still letting off rounds as he gripped his neck to stop the blood flow.

Raphael threw the dead man down. He exchanged gunfire with the other security guard as he made his way into the house. He dove behind a loveseat as the guard sat crouched behind the wall partition between the kitchen and living room.

"Abaku! I know you're here!" Raphael screamed. "The Grim Reaper is here to collect your soul, you muthafucka!"

"I'm right here, you bastard!" Abaku yelled as another round of gunfire let off from the opposite direction of the guard.

Thinking fast, Raphael flipped the sofa over on top of him and pushed forward, sliding along the marble flooring toward the security guard. The sofa penned the security as Raphael leaned forward and shot toward Abaku, causing him to retreat. He lifted the gun to shoot up at the security guard when his gun jammed. The guard had gotten his balance back and was just about to unload his clip on Raphael when the back of his head exploded like a watermelon being smashed on concrete.

Raphael heard more gunfire being exchanged between Tonio and Abaku as he struggled to get up so he could get a better view. Wiping the brain matter that had spattered on his face, he crouched down, scuttling toward Tonio.

"Hallway to the left," Tonio said lowly to Raphael.

They both nodded, and Raphael took off to the left and Tonio to the right, both shooting toward Abaku. Raphael heard Tonio scream, and he knew he'd been hit. Raphael stood back as he and Abaku exchanged missed rounds at each other.

"You think you can come to me? In my house! In my land! And kill me?"

"That's the plan, and I always execute!"

Raphael went to let off another shot in Abaku's direction when his gun clicked. He was out of ammunition.

"Fuck!" he hissed.

Abaku laughed and stepped into the living room. "Not this time."

He let off a bullet, and at the same time Raphael hurled the gun at Abaku. The gun hit Abaku dead center in the head, and Raphael rushed him, knocking Abaku backward and causing him to drop his gun. Raphael didn't let up. He headbutted Abaku, dazing him as reared back and hit him with a two-piece hand combination to the face. Using all of his strength, Abaku fell forward and kneed Raphael in the groin. The move caught Raphael off guard and he left his neck exposed. Abaku spun Raphael around, gripping his neck into the crook of his muscular arm.

"Now, you die!" Abaku yelled as he choked Raphael.

Raphael fought against Abaku and fought for air. He hit his arm, trying to pry it loose, but to no avail. Abaku had a death grip on him. He knew he had only seconds left when he pulled his booted foot up and stomped down as hard as he could. He felt it when he made contact and heard at least one toe snap. Abaku loosened his grip and stumbled backward with a shriek. Raphael turned around, heaving for air. Before Abaku could regroup, Raphael charged at him, knocking him back into the hallway against the wall.

"Ahhhhh!" Raphael roared as he went to work tenderizing Abaku's abs and face. "This is for my family!" he said before he punched him in the face again.

Abaku slid down the wall in a bloody heap, gasping for air. He saw blood on Raphael's side and gripped it, pushing his fingers into the wounded area where he'd shot him. The pain caused Raphael to buckle.

"Fuck!" he wailed out as Abaku continued to twist his fingers in the wound.

Abaku kneed Raphael in the face, and when he fell forward, Abaku used all his might to wrap the torn sleeve of his shirt around Raphael's neck to strangle him.

"Die, you son of a bitch, just die!" Abaku yelled out as they wrestled for control.

Fearing for his life, Raphael managed to reach his side pocket but grew too weak to reach inside. He kicked and screamed as he fought to keep his consciousness. An image of Essie and Kaion came to his mind.

"Fuck you and your little family, Raphael," Abaku seethed. "After I kill you, I'm going to kill them. I'll have fun playing with your wife before I throw her naked body into a meat grinder. Just like I did her bitch of a sister."

Those were the words that gave Raphael the strength he needed to push his hand in his side pocket. The small blade whipped out, and he brought his arm around, stabbing Abaku in the side several times in quick, fluid motions. Abaku released him, twisting away and screaming in agony as he held his side. He staggered a few feet away, struggling to breathe and catch his bearings. Raphael sat there staring at him menacingly, gripping his own side from the pain, but his adrenaline was pumping, and his eyes were laser-focused on Abaku. He watched as Abaku finally made it to an upright position and began sliding against the wall, leaving a bloody trail in his wake.

Raphael's aggression crept up his spine and gave him new strength. He walked over to him and punched him once. He watched him fall over, barely catching himself, then punched him again. He fell to one knee, and Raphael punched him again. Blood spurted out of Abaku's mouth, and he spit teeth and blood out.

"Come here," Raphael growled as he made confident steps over to him.

Gripping him by the front of his neck, Raphael lifted Abaku up and slammed him against the wall repeatedly. Each slam was more forceful than the next. He slammed him so hard he tore a hole in the sheetrock. Holding him firmly against the wall, he squeezed.

"I'm gonna pop your cork," Raphael promised, determined to end this once and for all.

He felt Abaku's windpipe crush beneath his hands and still he kept squeezing. He squeezed until he stopped breathing. He squeezed until his eyes bulged. He squeezed until his neck snapped. Only then did he let his lifeless body fall to the floor. He stood back, heaving, relishing in the fact that Abaku Dage was dead. Realization set in as the pain and burning in his side took root. He hobbled into the kitchen to check on Tonio, who was shot in the belly and chest and bleeding profusely.

"Stay with me, Tonio. I got you," Raphael said and ripped part of his shirt then applied pressure to his wounds.

He realized time was of the essence. They had to get out of there before Abaku's family showed up, and so he and Tonio could get the medical help they needed. Raphael hobbled over to the kitchen, pulling out drawer after drawer until he found duct tape. Moving back to Tonio, he ripped more shreds of the shirt and duct-taped them across both wounds. He then did the same to his. Pulling out his phone, he pressed the code for the driver to come back and then grabbed a butcher knife and headed back to the hallway.

Staring at the deceased body of Abaku, he smirked. Sinisterly, he took out his phone and took a photo of him, then he took the knife and began chopping at his neck until he severed his head off his body. Lifting the head by the hair, he walked through the house to the garage, where he found a black trash bag. He placed the head in the bag, tied it up, and carried it back into the kitchen. Soon, the driver came and ran in the house.

"It's a bloody massacre out there," he said, eyes wide.

"In here, too."

"Get Tonio to the van. He's gonna need medical help, stat," Raphael said, stumbling.

"You too, it seems."

Another agent came in and helped Raphael hobble out of Abaku's house with the trash bag in hand. Once they were all inside, the van sped off, headed to their facility for medical care.

"What's in the bag?" one of the men asked.

"My consolation prize."

As they rode, Raphael sat back, thinking of how it was finally over with Abaku, but that he still had one more mission to complete before he could go home to his family. He was determined not to leave a single stone unturned.

CHAPTER 29

It'd been a long week for Raphael and Tonio. After being rushed to the temporary medical facility, they were rushed out of the country for their safety and held at another medical facility for emergency surgery. Neither of them would have made it if they'd tried to go back to the United States. Although Raphael's wound was not as severe, he still had to undergo surgery to remove the bullet, clean the path, and seal the wound. Tonio's wounds, however, were severe. While the wound to his chest was not life-threatening, the wound to his stomach was damn near fatal. He'd suffered severe internal bleeding, and for a moment it was touch and go. However, Tonio made it, and was recovered enough for them to move to the bureau's secured medical facility.

"Brother," Tonio said as he sat in the hospital bed.

Raphael slapped hands with him as he took a seat beside him. "So we're brothers now?" Raphael joked.

Tonio looked over his body. "After these fucking war wounds, we better be." He laughed then winced at the pain it brought on.

Turning serious, Raphael asked, "Can I ask you something, Tonio?"

He shrugged. "It's not like I'm going anywhere." He eyed Raphael for a moment and could tell that something was eating at him. "Shoot."

Raphael exhaled a weighted breath. "You don't get tired of this lifestyle? All these missions and killings?"

Swiping a hand down his face, Tonio considered his words for a moment. "At first I didn't. Lately..." His voice trailed off for a time, and they both let it linger. "Do you want to know the real reason Rhys chose the members of OMECA?"

Raphael folded his arms across his chest and leaned back in the seat that he occupied. "This ought to be very interesting."

"When he refers to us as the wild ones, he isn't lying. We go against the grain. Buck the system. We're the reject agents. The ones who cause too much trouble, because we ask too many questions. We were so good they couldn't let us go. However, we always got the shit assignments. The grunt work that nobody wanted or couldn't accomplish. Then came Rhys with OMECA. Most of us joined just to be a part of something that felt real again, for once. So, when you ask if I'm tired? Fuck, yeah. I put my life on the line every day for an organization and country that don't give two damns. I thought OMECA was gonna be different."

Raphael's eyebrows raised. "Thought?"

Tonio eyed him for a moment and waved it off. "Yeah, just same ol' agency bullshit, if you ask me. That's all I meant."

Raphael felt there was more Tonio hadn't told him, but he let it go. Besides, he was only there himself in a temporary capacity. He didn't need to get caught up in any more OMECA crap or have Tonio excommunicated because they felt he wasn't trustworthy.

"I feel you," Raphael said as both men sat in their thoughts for a while.

"So, how are you holding up? Humpty Dumpy back together again?"

Raphael offered a real laugh before nodding. "Yeah, Essie ain't gotta rip y'all a new asshole over her man, if that's what you're asking." Raphael sat back, getting serious. "Real talk though. I'm ready to blow this place, so I'ma need you to get ready to get outta here."

"Doctor says if I'm good today, we can blow this popsicle stand tomorrow," Tonio informed him. They slapped hands again, and Tonio turned serious. "And the other matter?"

"It is being taken care of today," Raphael informed him. "Word has it that Bio Dage has a bounty on our heads. Abaku's mother has taken to her bed due to the loss of her child."

Tonio shook his head. "Damn. No one should suffer misery that great, even if her child asked for it."

Raphael considered his sins. He'd hate for Kaion to ever pay the price for the life he led. God knows he hoped Kaion never had to be involved in this lifestyle again, because he couldn't live with himself if he did and something were to happen to him as a result.

"I agree." Raphael stood and patted Tonio on the shoulder. "Rest, brother. I'm confident you'll receive your walking papers. We've got a long day ahead of us tomorrow."

They slapped hands once more before bidding each other good night.

***

Raphael left the facility, headed to the safehouse where the agents who'd assisted them in Dubai were waiting for him. Entering the back, he walked over to the table and watched carefully as the men worked on the device.

"Will we be ready today?" Raphael asked.

"Yes, sir," one of the young techs answered. "The last test was successful. We'll be implanting the device shortly."

Raphael thanked him as he moved to another section with Agent Green, who had been the driver of the van for him and Tonio.

"Remember, the delivery will be carried out at six p.m. sharp. Once we get the green light, we have no time. Your window is ten minutes, tops. After that, you and Tonio will board so we can be sure to get you back as quickly and as safely as possible. Rhys and the team will be waiting for you all upon arrival. Are you good on the instructions?" Agent Green asked, ensuring the details were completely clear.

"I'm perfect."

They bumped fists, and Raphael thanked him for his help. As he saw the package being sealed, a smirk crossed his face. Yes, indeed. No one should have to suffer such misery. It was the reason he was glad to be the one to bring the misery to an end.

CHAPTER 30

People milled about, conversing on the somber occasion. Bio Dage sat in his massive gathering room in his compound, too far out of it to fully engage. Still, he tried to be a gracious host in the absence of his wife and Naji, Abaku's mother. His wife, Delilah, had found herself tending to Naji, because like her, she'd lost her only child and son to the hands of Raphael. Naji had attended Abaku's funeral, but she couldn't stand for the so-called celebration of life afterward. In that regard, Bio could barely stand it himself. All he could think about was the fact that he'd lost not one but both of his children to the American. Yet, as the man of the house and the father to his sons, he had to forge forward.

Abaku would be shocked at the amount of mourning carrying on for him, especially from his father. His father loved him just as much as Bio, Jr., affectionately known as simply Dage. Though Abaku thought he favored his namesake over him, that was never the case. Sure, he encouraged and even implemented a tad bit of sibling rivalry, but to him, it was needed at times to keep their competitive edge. It was only when they were trying to one-up each other that his boys put their best efforts forward. The other reason Abaku felt like he was the black sheep of the family was because of the positions their father put them in. True enough, Bio kept Abaku in the background running the business and the business schemes, but that was because Abaku had a brilliant mind—and because he was a bit of a hothead. There was no way to conduct business with your son consistently threatening people, even if they deserved it.

Dage, on the other hand, was suave and charming. He was the face of the operation. That was Abaku's problem. He pretended to be well with being in the background, but he longed to be the face. He felt the face received more respect. The face was able to move in and around circles that no one else could ever dream of being connected with. Both options were a moot point now. He'd lost them both in this war over a money scam that never saw fruition.

He was determined to locate the American and lay him down like the dog he was. His family had suffered too much hurt and loss over him. His family had to be avenged. There was just no other way. His back-channel contacts were fast at work to help locate everyone involved, even if it was American intelligence. He had his old military friends on the case to work with anyone from their government to Interpol to find, capture, and bring Raphael to him. He wanted him alive and unharmed, because the harm would be issued by him. He was the judge, jury, and executioner, and when he rained down his judgment on Raphael's head, he'd make sure that it was done with his brand of justice.

"I'm so sorry for your loss, Mr. Dage," a mourner who approached him said.

He stood and hugged him. "Thank you for your love and concern. Your kindness is greatly appreciated."

The brief interaction was his call to immerse himself back into the fold with the multitude of mourners there to celebrate the life of Abaku. He went around the room hugging and speaking with all manner of people, from employees to friends, associates, and family members. He made sure everyone felt welcomed and enjoyed the lavish buffet that was spread about the room. He wanted everyone to eat and partake in life. He would live today up for his son, and tomorrow he'd bring death.

When the general and his men walked in, Bio noticed them and excused himself. Following his cue, they followed Bio out of the meeting room where the celebration was being held, down the hallway, and into the back of the house, where his office was located. Bio understood that if they were at his home, it was surely not a conversation that they could have in public.

"Gentlemen, may I ask the nature of this visit on the day of my son's mourning?" Bio asked, his tone laden with both irritation and curiosity.

The head of the men bowed his head in respect. "Our apologies, Mr. Dage. We do understand the nature of the time and mean no disrespect to you, your family, or the memory of Abaku."

Bio only nodded. He wasn't upset with them, but he preferred to deal with the devil in the details on any other day than this day.

"You're fine. What is it?"

"We've heard news that the Americans have left," the head general explained. "They did not tarry in Dubai after the hit on your son."

Bio hit his desk with a balled-up fist. "What do you mean *gone*? He had to have help from the American government. There's no way."

The general nodded. "Your assumption is correct. It won't ever be publicly affirmed or denied, but we know what we know."

"Where is he now?" Bio fired off. His temper was escalating by the moment, and he needed to know that some parts of his potential plan were still intact.

The general shook his head. "I'm so sorry, Mr. Dage. We don't have that information either, but we are working on it."

Upon hearing that news, Bio gritted his teeth. He couldn't fathom the lack of incompetency. "You mean to tell me that this man comes to the country, kills *my* son, and leaves without a trace?" He snapped his fingers. "Just poof. Gone. Just like that?"

The general and the two men with him said nothing. What was there to say? The obvious answer was yes, that's exactly what happened, but what would confirming that prove? Bio knew the answer. He paced the floor in silence for a length before walking up to the general.

"You listen to me." He poked at the man's chest. "I refuse to give his mother—" His voice had risen higher with each word, and he paused to take a deep breath before continuing. "I'm not giving his mother any more bad news. So, you find him or find out something beneficial that I can use to track his rabid ass down. Do I make myself abundantly clear?"

The general simply nodded. "Abundantly, sir."

The men turned to file out, and Bio plopped down in the chair in his office. He had to regroup after that disappointing conversation. He didn't want to feel how he was feeling, especially today, because now he was almost beside himself with anger. Instead of heading back to his guests, he went to the one place that provided him solace, his bedroom and his wife.

When he entered, he found Naji lying on the bed with her face to the ceiling. When he came in, he saw her eyes move toward the door to see who had entered, then she refocused on the ceiling. He stood there for a moment, just staring after her.

"What is it, Bio?" Her tone was even, not hostile, but not necessarily warm and inviting either.

Bio gingerly swaggered over to the bed and sat down beside the mother of his son. He placed a hand on her thigh as she moved to prop herself up on the pillows. "How are you feeling, Naji?"

She let out a snide chortle. "I've lost my only child. Forgive me if I don't feel at all."

Bio understood that feeling exactly. "I know, Naji. I feel the same. So does Delilah. You know I won't let this slide. I will avenge them for you—"

"Enough!" Her voice was strong and definitive. "Junior ran off trying to even a score and lost his life. Abaku tried to avenge his death, but more importantly, tried to get back into your good graces, and he lost his life. I don't want to hear any more about avenging a damn thing."

Bio wasn't upset. He understood her grief. Rather than push the issue, he patted her knee and apologized. "You're right. I'm sorry to disturb you. Is Delilah around?"

Naji fell back against the pillows. "She's in the guest bedroom down the hall. We were in here talking, and she told me to stay and lie down while she changed in the other room."

"Okay. Rest up. I'll check in on you later on," Bio said as he left the room and trudged down the hall to where his wife was.

When he opened the door, he found her partially clothed. She was a vision. Right now, he needed a sight for sore eyes. It was partial comfort for the hole that was left in his heart. He approached, and she gasped from the feel of his arms around her.

"Bio!" she squealed as he squeezed her in a hug.

She leaned into his embrace. She needed it, too. Though Abaku wasn't her biological son, he was still her son, nonetheless. Naji had been there for her during her loss, and she was reliving the pain again with Naji and Bio through the loss of Abaku.

She turned to face him, cupping his face in her hands. "Are you okay, my love?"

That simple question leveled Bio. He placed his head on her shoulder and wept the tears that hadn't fallen. He'd been so consumed with rage that hurt took a backseat. In the comfort of his wife's arms, he felt at peace enough to release the emotion that took precedence over all of his feelings. Loss. She held him and rocked him until he could speak.

"It's my fault," Bio said.

"It's not your fault, Bio."

"It is!" His words came out harsher than he intended. "I never should've left them in charge with the business. I never should've allowed Abaku to complete this. I should've taken care of it."

"What if you were the one that I had to bury?"

"Better me than my sons."

She used her fingers to swipe the tears from his face. Eyeing him lovingly, she said, "Oh honey. I'm not saying that. I'm only saying if it had been you, then inevitably it would have been the boys, too. Do you think that either one of them wouldn't have tried to avenge your death? No matter what, they would have. We've lost too much. Let's not blame each other, and let's not continue down this path."

"You sound like Naji right now."

"Then you should listen to the both of us. No more, Bio. No more."

He fell into her embrace, and they stood there like that for a long while. When he finally felt better, he released her and kissed her lips.

"You center me," he said softly to her.

"You are my peace as well, Bio." She kissed his forehead. "Allow me to finish dressing. I will check in on Naji and come downstairs with you to mingle with her guests and take in the gifts and flowers."

"Sounds good." He walked to the door to leave, but before turning the knob, he said, "I love you."

She blew a kiss back at him. "I love you."

Bio eased out of the room and headed back down the stairs, where there were still a good number of people standing about and conversing. He used that time to mingle with them and listen to funny stories about Abaku and even Dage. When he looked up, he saw his beautiful wife approaching. Together, they worked the crowds of people who'd come out by the droves to celebrate his son. Although it was a sad occasion, he was made better by the overwhelming outpouring of love and support for his son and his family.

For the next hour, they mingled and talked to guest after guest and was happy when the last few of them finally trickled out. It had been an exhausting day, and having to entertain while grieving was not for the faint at heart.

"Finally, everyone is gone," Bio stated, making himself a stiff drink. "Is Naji okay?"

"Yes, I made her a plate thirty minutes ago and took it to her. She's resting now," Delilah said as she walked into the living room and took a seat.

Just then, the doorbell rang, and Dage placed his glass tumbler down to go answer it. He prayed it was not someone coming over to converse. They were officially done for the evening. When he opened the door, it was the delivery service with the flowers and gifts.

"Deliveries for the Dage family," the young man stated.

"Yes, come and place them all in the living room," Bio directed.

Rather than wait for the young delivery driver to gather them all, he helped him bring them inside and then tipped him for his service.

"Thank you very much, sir and I am sorry to hear of your loss." With that, the young man left, and Bio closed and locked the door, happy to have peace.

Just then, Naji appeared and walked into the living room with Bio. "Are all these for us for Abaku?"

"Yes, they are," Delilah answered, sniffing the different assortment of floral arrangements.

Naji walked over to a big box and read the tag aloud. "To the Dage family. We hope your misery ends soon. Please accept this token of our love and support."

Bio's interest was piqued. He walked over to the box and picked it up. He took it to his favorite seat, and Naji and Delilah followed him.

"That's an interesting sentiment," Delilah stated.

"It certainly is," Bio agreed as he unraveled the box and began opening it.

When he flipped open the lid, the two women screamed and stumbled back, reaching for each other. "Son of a bitch!" Bio seethed.

Naji passed out and Delilah vomited as they stared back at the severed head of their son, Abaku.

Bio pulled out his phone to call the general, but before he could dial the number, the head exploded, killing Bio, Naji, and Delilah instantly. All that could be heard was the house alarm and sirens from their cars as the house and their bodies burned to ash.

Raphael eyed the screen playing the video of the Dage house lighting up the sky before closing the device, dismantling it, and dropping pieces of it into the water as he walked. When he arrived at the Humvee to escort them to the military airport, Tonio turned his head, giving him the look. Raphael nodded as they entered and pulled away.

"Ashes to ashes. Dust to dust," Raphael whispered, relieved to finally close the chapters of his life that had plagued him for years.

EPILOGUE

I t had been three months since the entire fiasco. The nations of Benin and Dubai mourned the deaths of the Dages in native fashion. However, no ties were found or linked back to America, and more importantly, not back to Raphael. His family was free and clear from the life that brought them together but had tried to continue to rip them apart.

Carmel had been a neutral ground for all of them. It was away from the life they used to live, but close enough for Kaion to still keep in contact with his friends, especially Shantrice. She'd grounded him in a way a young girl shouldn't have to, and for that, Kaion would forever be grateful and loyal to her. No one knew what the future would hold for them, but they were connected by the twisted bond that they shared.

Essie had made peace with the fact that she would truly never see her sister again. Though she didn't have any remains, they still decided to have a funeral for her between the three of them. It was held at a graveside. Though no body rested there, it gave Essie a sense of closure. She knew her sister's spirit was in a better place, and that was of the utmost importance to her. In fact, her headstone read, "For the peace you didn't obtain on this side of heaven." It was a beautiful tribute, and her resting place was in Indianapolis, so Essie didn't have to go far to visit and chat with her. It brought Essie comfort, and her happiness was all Raphael wanted.

As a family, they'd enrolled in counseling. Though they could never disclose the nature of several of the incidents they went through, learning how to talk, address their feelings, and process their grief was a major mental relief. It made them better with interactions with each other, and they could slowly see their little family healing and thriving in a way that it never had before.

A Frisbee hit Raphael in the back, and he turned around as Essie ran to up to him. He looked down and laughed, retrieving the Frisbee and handing it to Essie.

"Oh, so this is how y'all do me?"

"Sorry, Mr. Waters!" Shantrice shouted out with an embarrassed look on her face.

Cupping his hands around his mouth, Raphael shouted back. "Nah, you meant that," he said with a chuckle as she hid her face, and Kaion tickled her to get her to loosen up.

"Don't be bothering my girl, Dad!" Kaion faked a mean mug then laughed.

Raphael cocked his head to the side, impressed. "All right now, son. That's right. Defend your woman at all costs." He pointed to him with a wink, and Kaion pointed back.

Essie playfully slapped Raphael on the arm. "Don't encourage him."

Raphael wrapped his arms around Essie and spun her around. "Oh yeah, why not?" he asked as she giggled and squealed in delight. "He's gotta learn sometime, baby."

He placed her down on her feet as she sighed. "I know. I know. I just don't want to see him grow into a man just yet."

"Nah, you just don't want him doing the nasty," Raphael joked.

She burst out laughing and hit him again. "You ass." She nodded. "But you're right though. I just want him to enjoy being a kid, young and in love."

Raphael shrugged. "We can't stop it, baby. We can only prepare him. That's the most important thing to do."

"So, what are you over here preparing for?" she asked, looking up at Raphael.

Raphael hugged her close and then kissed her on the top of the head. He panned around at Kaion and Shantrice laughing and throwing the Frisbee back and forth. He took in all the surroundings. He noticed the people playing with their dogs and the children running up and down the grass. He noticed life. What life looked and felt like when you could just simply...live. His eyes turned back to the little children playing and rolling around in the grass.

"Considering one of those?" Essie asked, tipping her head in the direction of the children.

"I have not thought of it because of our past and, well, our current life." Raphael gazed into her eyes. "Do you want some little ones?"

"With you, I want whatever you want. I'm happy with you, and if we add to that, I wouldn't be mad at it. It'd be an honor to carry your seed."

Raphael smiled at her. "No, baby, the honor would be all mine." He bit his lip looking at her with a sexy glint. "In fact, we might have to work on that addition tonight."

"I like the sound of that!"

Raphael's watch alerted him of a text, and he patted Essie on her rear. "Go on over there with those two lovebirds. I ain't mad at him for loving on his woman, but he's still living under my roof, too. Ain't no playing house," he said jokingly, but they both knew he was serious. "I'm going to take a quick walk, and I'll be back before it's time to eat."

Essie kissed him and then trotted off back to Kaion and Shantrice. Raphael stared after her for a minute before he turned and began to walk. When he got in the secluded area by the gardens, he saw Rhys walking up to him.

"Way to keep a man waiting," Rhys said with a bit of irritation in his tone.

"Well, I told you it wasn't a good time. So, I came when I wanted. Damn, Rhys. No how are you doing or nothing? Just straight to the cuss out, huh?"

"My bad." He rubbed his forehead. "How are you doing?"

Raphael laughed. "Get outta here. I'm good."

Rhys placed his hands in his pockets, rocking back and forth on from heel to toe. "So have you given any consideration as to what I asked?"

Raphael placed his hands in his pockets and held his head down. Rhys had approached him about becoming an official member of the OMECA team. He made promises of great pay and protection for the family...anything he could think of to bend him toward coming aboard on a permanent basis. The life thrilled him when he was nothing more than a get-money kid. Life had a way of maturing you that couldn't be ignored. Ignoring those inklings were instances that led to destruction. He had too much to live for to ignore the inkling that had tugged at him. The sign of an excellent fighter was knowing when to hang up your boxing gloves. It was time to hang his.

"Yes, I've given a lot of thought to what you asked," Raphael said lifting his head up to stare Rhys directly in the eyes. With a stern expression, he said, "And the answer is no."

Rhys extended his arm, placing his hand on Raphael's forearm. "Come on, Raph. This is a sweet deal, and you know it."

Raphael wagged his finger at him. "What I know is that's my final answer, Rhys. I'm a family man."

Rhys grimaced. He released a huff to control his anger. His bosses were so impressed they'd promised all kind of personal and professional incentives if he could get Raphael to agree to come on as an official mercenary. He was perfect. The man was a machine, and he operated with the highest level of skill and sensibility. If he couldn't bag him for the position, he'd have to search high and low for someone else. After all that he'd done for him, quite frankly, it pissed him off.

Rhys cupped his chin. "I must say after everything we've been through and all I've done for you, I'm highly disappointed."

Raphael looked at his watch then cocked his head to the side. "Really? You were there when I married my wife. I'm surprised you don't understand." He peered out past Rhys for a brief second and then returned his attention back to him. "Then again, I'm not."

"But you want to know what I don't understand? Something that just never quite added up for me."

It was Rhys's turn to look at Raphael quizzically. "What's that?"

"If Abaku was after me, as you stated when you first came to visit me, if he wanted my head on a platter so badly, why would he switch gears to track my family in California? I mean, he knew exactly where I was when he issued that first attack on us in South Bend. Why change it up and not keeping coming?"

Rhys shrugged. "Hell, I don't know, Raph."

Raphael turned and walked a few paces and Rhys followed him. "It just seems strange that he'd pay Tatiana money to identify who I was, come after me once, and then wait until I separated from my family and go after them."

Rhys stopped walking. "Maybe he figured he had to come at you from a different angle."

Raphael snapped his fingers and turned to face Rhys. "You know, I think that is exactly the answer. If a person does not fall into your strategy, then you approach it from a different angle. It's the perfect tactic."

"Exactly." Rhys said, throwing his hands in the air and continuing forward.

Raphael allowed Rhys to move a few paces away then said. "But you know there's one flaw in that tactic. At least from Abaku's perspective."

"And what's that?" Rhys asked stopping to turn back to Raphael.

When he turned, Raphael had his gun pulled and trained on Rhys. "Neither Abaku nor Sienna knew anything about my prior involvement with Tatiana."

Rhys held his hands up. "What are you doing, Raph? I've been there for you every step of the way."

"Wrong. You've been there for me when you needed me to be there for you. You set up that fake hit on me and my family in the beginning. You didn't like that I didn't fall into your strategy, so you used another angle. You knew if my family truly felt threatened that I would do whatever I had to in order to protect them. Admit it."

Rhys stood there for a minute contemplating what to say. Then he opted for the truth. He nodded his head. "Yes, so what? No one got hurt. No one was going to get hurt. In the end, we got what we both wanted."

"You sent me on the trail, kicking up attention on myself and my family, because I wouldn't willingly come on the team. You put my family at risk."

Rhys swallowed the lump in his throat, realizing that Raphael was nearly vibrating with anger. It became painfully obvious that Raphael had no plans to let him off the hook for what he'd done to force his hand. The only thing he could do at this point was beg for his life.

"Listen, I'm sorry, Raphael. I was wrong. Dead wrong. You don't have to do this, Raphael. I swear. I promise I won't bother you or your family again. Just don't do this."

"Yeah, you're right. You won't bother me or my family again."

Just then, Tonio and Emmanuel stepped behind Rhys from the shadows. Tonio trained his gun to the back of Rhys's head while Emmanuel relieved him of his weapons. It was then and only then that Raphael put his gun down and re-holstered it.

"Brother," Raphael acknowledged Tonio.

"Brother," Tonio returned the sentiment.

"What the fuck are you all doing?" Rhys asked, his tone indignant.

Raphael smirked. "Well, Rhys. It's as you said, acceptance is your downfall. Your non-willingness to accept when people do not want to be a part of your plan is why we are at this crossroads today. You forgot the most important thing about me. It's always family over everything. Now, you won't be able to bother my family again. That goes for anybody I consider family. There was one good thing that came out of this. I was able to find some extended family in this entire ordeal. So, your disloyal ass won't be able to fuck with anyone else again."

With that, Tonio and Emmanuel grabbed Rhys. He tried to fight against them, but Tonio stuck him with a syringe that quickly subdued him. As they prepared to carry him to their unmarked van, Tonio mouthed a thank you to Raphael, and Emmanuel nodded and then saluted Raphael. Raphael saluted them both back as they dragged Rhys to the awaiting van. He didn't have to kill Rhys to know that he'd never be heard from again. That thought finally gave him a true sense of peace. With that knowledge, Raphael turned and went back to show his family how to throw a Frisbee properly.

ACKNOWLEDGMENTS

Author Eddy Clark:

I would like to take this moment to thank my co-author D. Andrea Whitfield. I am looking forward to the next installment and future works. I would also like to thank Black Odyssey Media. Thank God, my family, and friends. Last, but not least, I would like to give thanks to everyone who has supported and purchased it, and those who will continue to grow with this franchise in the future.

Author D. Andrea Whitfield:

As always, my forever thanks goes to God first and foremost. Without Him, none of this would be possible. Many thanks to Shawanda and Black Odyssey Media for her guidance and support. Last, but never least, to Eddy, thank you for entrusting me with your literary visions. It has been an honor and pleasure to work with you. To the readers, I know you will continue to enjoy Raphael's story of survival and redemption.

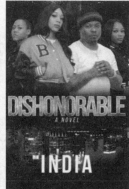

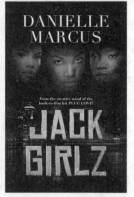

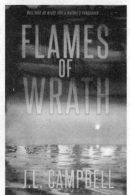